THE GIRL FROM FELONY BAY

J. E. Thompson

WALDEN POND PRESS
An Imprint of HarperCollinsPublishers

Walden Pond Press is an imprint of HarperCollins Publishers.
Walden Pond Press and the skipping stone logo are trademarks
and registered trademarks of Walden Media, LLC.

The Girl from Felony Bay

Library of Congress Cataloging-in-Publication Data
Thompson, John.
The girl from Felony Bay / John Thompson. — First edition.
    pages cm
Summary: "When Abbey's father falls into a coma and is accused of a crime
he didn't commit, Abbey sets out to prove his innocence—and repay a
century-old debt"— Provided by publisher.
    ISBN 978-0-06-210446-5 (hardcover bdg.)
    [1. Mystery and detective stories. 2. Families—Fiction. 3. Fathers—Fiction.
4. Coma—Fiction. 5. Charleston (S.C.)—Fiction.] I. Title.
PZ7.T3715957Gi 2013   2012025338
[Fic]—dc23   CIP
                                                                          AC

Typography by Alicia Mikles
13 14 15 16 17   CG/RRDH   10 9 8 7 6 5 4 3 2 1
❖
First Edition

For Amanda and Liza

One

My name is Abbey Force, and my story starts about a year ago, on the last day of school when we were getting out for summer break. It was a time when I was feeling meaner than a stepped-on rattlesnake, because in the previous nine months I had lost everything that mattered to me: my pony, my home, and my dad.

But before we get too far into things, here's a bit of backstory for you. I come from a family of what are called French Huguenots. In the early seventeen hundreds, at a time when South Carolina was part of the colony known as the Carolinas, my ancestors fled religious persecution in France and carved a plantation out of the wilderness in a place called Leadenwah Island. Those early people were tough. They were big-time risk takers; they had fast tempers and didn't pull any punches.

Before the accident that put him in a coma, my dad liked to say that acorns don't fall far from the trees that grew them. I think it was his way of telling me that I was headstrong and stubborn as a mule, had a big mouth, and didn't shy away from fights. He also used to joke that I was a Force to be reckoned with. Ha, ha.

It was a Friday afternoon, and I was slouched in the back of a school bus full of lower-school kids as it trundled down the length of Leadenwah Island. It was my very last time on this bus, because next year I was going to be in seventh grade, and I would be riding the middle-school bus. Just like he always did, the driver, Mr. Jancowski, stopped every couple hundred yards and dropped off another group of students.

All around me kids were shouting and giggling, delighted at the prospect of three months without classes, tests, or homework. I was trying to ignore them. I was dreading summer, every bloody day of it, because this summer wasn't going to be like any other summer of my life.

Before this year I had always looked forward to summer vacation, just like any other kid. June, July, and August had seemed like an endless merry-go-round of pony riding, swimming, crabbing, spending time with my friends and my dad, and exploring the nearly one thousand acres of Reward, the plantation that had been in my family for more than three hundred years. Back in those days, I was pretty darn certain I had to be one of the luckiest people on earth.

But there is an old saying that luck is fickle. In the past nine months, I had found out just how true that saying was. Everything in my life had changed, every single part of it, and all for the worse. A year earlier my father had been healthy and happy and highly respected. Now he lay in a hospital in a coma, unable to defend himself against the charge that he had committed a terrible theft. I knew he was innocent in spite of what the facts seemed to say, and while I was determined to prove what I believed, I sure hadn't had much success so far. In the meantime Reward Plantation had been put up for sale to pay Daddy's debts and was now owned by strangers. Even my Welsh pony, Timmy, had been sold to the same people who bought Reward. And to make matters worse, I was stuck living with Uncle Charlie and Ruth. More on them later.

Anyway, I was stewing over all those things on the bus ride, feeling the anger rise up in me the way it seemed to do so often when I thought about how unfair life had been. That was when we came to another stop, and Jimmy Simmons made his move. He used the confusion of other kids standing up to get off the bus to climb out of his own seat, move forward several rows to where the smaller kids sat, and drop down next to little Skoogie Middleton.

I saw trouble coming right away.

Jimmy Simmons was going into seventh grade next year just like me; only he should have been in ninth or tenth grade. I wasn't sure why the school had decided to move him up this particular year. It's not like his grades had improved; he'd gotten Fs on almost every test. Maybe they had a law in South Carolina that a school couldn't hold somebody back more than three times. Or maybe you couldn't be in sixth grade anymore once you started to shave. Maybe Jimmy's teacher felt sorry for him, which was fairly unlikely for a kid who should have had WARNING: IDIOT BULLY tattooed on his forehead. Or maybe the principal had needed a few speeding tickets fixed, and Jimmy's father, Deputy Bubba Simmons, had agreed to do it if they moved his kid up.

Either way, all Jimmy ever did was sit in the back

of the class and glare at everyone in the room. All of the kids, and I think even some of the teachers, were a little afraid of him. He had big, meaty shoulders, a buzz cut, ugly red zits, and an angry lower lip that he liked to stick out over his top lip. All of us in the sixth grade had our fingers crossed he was going to be held back again and become the next class's problem, but now he was all ours.

Needless to say, Jimmy Simmons wasn't dropping into the seat next to Skoogie Middleton to wish him a happy summer. Skoogie was a small kid, a fifth grader who lived with his dirt-poor and mostly crippled grandmother in a tiny trailer down the road from Reward, and Jimmy had sat beside Skoogie because it was his last chance to pick on someone before school was finally out.

The last of the exiting kids finally stumbled out, and the bus doors closed. I watched Mr. Jancowski, the three-hundred-pound bus driver, look in his rearview mirror, notice where Jimmy was now sitting, then call out, "Back in your seat, Simmons."

Jimmy totally ignored him.

"Back in your seat, Simmons. Don't make me come back there."

Jimmy kept ignoring him just like everyone on the

bus knew he would. No way Mr. Jancowski was ever going to haul his two-ton lard butt out of the driver's seat and waddle back down the aisle, because he hadn't done it one time that whole year.

As Mr. Jancowski finally sighed and took his foot off the brake, I saw Jimmy put his arm around Skoogie, who had moved over as close to the window as he could. Jimmy said, "Raggedy Andy, Raggedy Andy." That was his way of making fun of a kid who didn't have any money and wore crummy clothes.

Jimmy dragged Skoogie into a headlock, then started to give him a noogie. Noogies hurt anytime, but when it's a hundred and forty pounds against eighty-five pounds, they really hurt. I could see Skoogie fighting to push Jimmy away but having no success.

Unfortunately for Jimmy Simmons, I'd spent the whole bus ride getting madder and madder, thinking how lousy life had been for me and my dad and how I couldn't seem to do a thing about it. When the bus stopped again and a couple more kids got up and walked toward the front, I got up, too, even though it wasn't my stop. My eyes were fixed on the back of Jimmy Simmons's head.

At that moment, I wasn't thinking about how much bigger Jimmy Simmons was or how much he weighed or how one of his hands could probably wrap around my neck and choke me. I was thinking about "Raggedy Andy, Raggedy Andy," about some jerk giving noogies to a little kid who didn't deserve them and who couldn't defend himself. I was so angry about how my own life was bullying me and how I couldn't do anything about it, but I thought that I could do something about Jimmy Simmons.

I walked up the aisle to right behind where Skoogie and Jimmy were sitting. Other kids were moving in front of me heading toward the exit, so Mr. Jancowski couldn't see me. "Leave him alone," I said.

Jimmy swung his head around and smirked. "Go away."

"I said leave him alone."

Jimmy craned his head farther, trying to look at me as if he really didn't understand why I would try to stop him. "Why do you care?" He gave Skoogie's head another hard rub. "Raggedy Andy likes it, don't you, Raggedy Andy?"

"Stop saying that."

Jimmy turned again. "Get off it, Force. He wears rags. He's like a peon."

"Just because a person doesn't have money is no reason to pick on them," I said, wondering why I was trying to argue logic with a moron.

Jimmy guffawed. "Sure it is."

"You know, Jimmy, when Skoogie grows up, he won't be poor anymore. But you'll still be stupid."

Jimmy swung all the way around. "Sit down, Force, or I'll pound you."

The only weapon I had was an empty book bag. I had brought it with me and had unzipped it on my way down the aisle. Now I turned it over and pulled the open end down over Jimmy's head. While he was blinded, I whacked him around the ears a couple times.

It took Jimmy all of two seconds to rip the book bag off his head. He hurled it away, stood, and spun around, stepping into the aisle. His ugly face was bloated with anger.

"Force," he said, shaking his head, "y'all got a death wish."

"Pick on somebody your own size," I said. Not the most original thing I'd ever said, but I wasn't going for clever.

He laughed. "Like you?"

"If you want."

I was five feet tall and weighed ninety-five pounds. Jimmy was six inches taller than me and outweighed me by at least fifty pounds. No wonder he laughed.

The kids who were getting off at that stop had mostly cleared the aisle. Mr. Jancowski was looking in his mirror. "If you're not getting off, sit down. Simmons, that means you. Don't make me come back there."

I don't think Mr. Jancowski could see me behind Jimmy Simmons's mass, so he wasn't yelling at me. For the record, I may be small, but I'm as fast as a scalded lizard. I also know how to hit. My father taught me to box because he said girls should be able to protect themselves just the same as boys. He also said that if I was ever going to start a fight, I needed to try and finish it before the other guy got in a good punch.

I saw Jimmy's big hands coming at me, right for my throat like he was planning to give me a good choking. So I used my boxing and hit him with a three-punch combination, all of them on his big, zitty nose.

Jimmy's hands stopped, and his eyes went wide. He seemed amazed that I had hit him so fast. He seemed even more amazed when he wiped his hand under his nostrils and saw that there was blood pouring out.

"Simmons," Mr. Jancowski shouted again, "I told you to sit down. Don't make me come back there.

Jimmy's nose was bleeding bad enough that he had to try and stop it with his T-shirt. One of the other kids on the bus called out, "Simmons just got his butt whipped by a girl." Laughter followed. I guess everybody loves to see a bully get what he deserves.

Jimmy's eyes were cutting from me to the kids who were laughing, then back to me. He seemed enraged, confused, and embarrassed all at the same time. I used the opportunity to scoot into the seat beside Skoogie.

"Simmons!" Mr. Jancowski was nearly apoplectic now. "Y'all sit down 'fore I come back there and make you sit."

Jimmy looked at me and growled, "I'm gonna kill you, Force," but he walked toward the rear of the bus and took a seat.

I almost laughed. It was the last day of school, and Skoogie's and my stop was just ahead. Jimmy Simmons was as mad as a hornet, but I didn't think he was smart enough to remember anything into next week. With any luck I wouldn't see him again for at least three months.

The bus started moving again, but I sat at an angle so I could keep an eye on Jimmy, in case of a last-minute surprise attack. "You okay, Skoogie?" I whispered.

He nodded and gave me a smile. "Thanks, Abbey."

I just winked and gave him a gentle poke with my elbow. "Us Felony Bay kids gotta stick together."

Felony Bay Road was the name of the little dirt

road we both lived on and also the name of a small, hidden bay just off the Leadenwah River that had a lot of history. As we got closer to our stop, I stayed on my guard. Even though he seemed busy with his bloody nose, I figured Jimmy Simmons would never let us off the bus without trying a punch or kick or some other last-minute stunt to get even.

I heard the brakes squeal and felt the bus begin to slow. We came to a halt, and the doors opened. I stood and moved into the aisle to let Skoogie get ahead of me; then we walked to the front of the bus and got off. I was holding my breath the entire time, expecting at any second to hear Jimmy's enraged cry and see him charging down the aisle. To my amazement nothing happened. When I looked back, he was still dabbing his blood-soaked T-shirt to his nose.

When our feet hit the pavement, we turned and waved back at Mr. Jancowski. "Have a great summer," he said. The doors swung closed, and the bus started to move. Skoogie and I smiled at each other.

Unfortunately, like I said before, luck is fickle. This time it lasted only about five seconds. To my horror, the bus's flashers went back on, and it pulled over to the side of the road.

A moment later the doors opened, and Jimmy

Simmons stepped onto the soft shoulder. He waved good-bye to Mr. Jancowski, but as soon as the doors closed and the bus started to drive away, he took his bloody T-shirt away from his nose and gave me a wolfish smile.

"Like I said, Force, I'm gonna kill you," Jimmy shouted. He sounded like somebody with a bad head cold, but it made the blood freeze in my veins.

I shot a glance at Skoogie. "Run," I whispered.

"No," he said, his voice trembling with fright.

"Go. Tell your grandmother what's happening." I knew even as I said it that it wouldn't do any good. What was an old lady who wasn't exactly mobile going to do? Still, it sounded better than nothing.

Jimmy Simmons was coming toward us, taking his time and enjoying himself.

"Run," I said again.

Skoogie looked at Jimmy, then nodded. "Okay." He took off.

"Ain't y'all gonna try and run away, too, Force?" Jimmy asked. "You ain't got Jancowski to protect you now."

I was scared, but I certainly wasn't going to turn and run, not from an idiot like Jimmy Simmons. My father always told me that running away from problems only made them worse. Of course, Daddy was in the hospital, in a coma, but I had to assume if he had been on his feet, he would have told me that fights and problems were in the same category.

"I don't need anybody to protect me from you," I said, desperately hoping it was true.

Jimmy came to a stop just out of range of my fists. "Y'all're quite the little lucky puncher," he said, giving me a mocking smile.

"Not lucky. You're just easy to hit."

That made his lower lip stick out, and his nose wrinkled until his whole face was bunched up like a pig's. "Let's see how y'all like to wrestle."

He took a step toward me, and I snapped a jab at his nose. He ducked back, just out of range, my fist missing by a fraction of an inch; then he charged, managing to grab a handful of my hair and hold on. I tried to spin and get loose, but he had too good a grip.

He pulled me closer and tried to get me in a hammerlock. I threw a few punches, but Jimmy was too close, wrapping me up with his arms so I couldn't hit. His armpit was in my face, and I could smell his stink, a combination of bacon grease and old sweat. I fought and kicked and tried to jerk free, but he got an arm around my neck and started to squeeze.

"Like this, Force? Feel good?" he grunted.

I said nothing. I clawed at his hands and arms, but my fingernails were too short to do much damage. I cursed myself for not growing them long like some of the other girls did.

"Beg for mercy, Force," he said, squeezing harder.

I tried to elbow him, but I was in the wrong position. My elbow just bounced off his belt. I still said nothing, but I felt his arm tighten around my windpipe. My vision started to go dark at the corners, and I felt my knees buckle.

He squeezed even harder. My lungs were burning, and I was running out of air. I was starting to realize that if Jimmy didn't let go, I might actually die right here on the side of the road, in the choke hold of an idiot. In that same instant, I thought about Daddy. If I died, I wouldn't be able to go to the hospital and talk to him and read to him. And I certainly wouldn't be able to finally prove that he was innocent.

"Mercy," I said, using up the last of my air, the word no more than a choking gasp.

Jimmy didn't let up. "Too late," he said.

I was too far gone to feel panic. I was about to pass out when I heard a sound like a dull *bong*. In the next instant, I felt Jimmy's arm relax and cool air rush into my lungs.

When my vision returned, I was down on my hands and knees in the gravel. Jimmy Simmons was several feet away. He was bent over, holding his head, saying, "Ow, ow, ow."

I looked around and saw Skoogie and beside him his grandmother, Mrs. Middleton. She was an old African American lady who looked like she could be a hundred but was probably in her sixties or seventies. She was as skinny as a stick and kind of hunched over. Her legs were bad, and she had to use a walker to get around.

In spite of that, she had managed to drag herself all the way here from the trailer where she and Skoogie lived. She had also brought her garden spade, and she had used it to whack Jimmy over the head. I guessed that her shovel blade connecting with Jimmy's skull had been the *bong* I'd heard.

"You all right, child?" Mrs. Middleton asked.

I nodded, even though I really wasn't sure.

"That boy like to have choked the life outta you."

"Y'all tried to kill me," Jimmy whined. "I'm gonna tell my dad, and he's gonna arrest y'all. Then you'll be sorry."

"Tell him whatever you want," Mrs. Middleton said. "I tell him the truth."

"You hurt my head. You need to drive me home."

Mrs. Middleton coughed out a bitter laugh. "Y'all got off the bus at the wrong stop. You get your own self home."

I looked at Jimmy. His head wasn't bleeding, but he probably had a big goose egg. It served him right. "We're not done," I managed to say, even though my throat felt like I'd been gargling with sandpaper.

Mrs. Middleton let out another laugh, this one warm and full from deep in her belly. "Girl, you a spitfire."

Jimmy turned his eyes to me, and I could see the storm clouds gathered there. "Next time I'll finish this," he said.

"Next time you won't even get to lay a hand on me," I said.

Two

Dinner that night with Uncle Charlie and Ruth
started out like most nights. Ruth was in the
kitchen either thawing dinner or opening a can
of dinner and getting ready to heat it up in the micro-
wave. Along with the premade stuff, there was a bag of
chopped lettuce and a bottle of dressing. That was basically how we ate every night, unless we had leftovers.

Uncle Charlie was sitting on the porch drinking a
big glass of bourbon. He drank two of them out there
every night unless it was too hot, too cold, or too rainy,
in which case he would drink his bourbon in front of
the TV in the living room. Sometimes the bourbon

made him goofy; those were his good nights. Other nights it just made him mean. It made him double mean on the days when he'd been playing cards in town and had lost money.

Uncle Charlie was Daddy's brother, but he wasn't anything like Daddy. Daddy was smart and funny and kind and hardworking, and Uncle Charlie was, well . . . the opposite. Daddy always said you didn't get to choose your family, and Uncle Charlie sure proved it. Choosing him for a brother would be like asking for a broken arm for Christmas, maybe worse. Ruth was Uncle Charlie's wife. She was technically my aunt, but she didn't seem like an aunt. So I just called her Ruth.

As a rule I tried to avoid Uncle Charlie when he was drinking or getting ready to start drinking. That meant I pretty much avoided him all the time. I stayed in my room reading or doing homework until it was time to do chores, and then I snuck downstairs to the kitchen, did them as fast as I could, and snuck back upstairs. Most nights Uncle Charlie just sucked on his bourbon and didn't think about me, but that wasn't the case on this night.

"Hey, Squib," he shouted from the porch. Squib was a nickname he had given me. I had looked it up in the dictionary and knew that a squib was either a sarcastic saying or a little firecracker that burned with a hissing noise and then made a small pop. I was pretty sure Uncle Charlie had no idea what the word actually meant, but from the way he said it, his own meaning wasn't anything very nice. He knew I didn't like the name, and that made him use it even more.

"Squib," he shouted a second later. "I'm talking to you. Get out here."

I tried to read his tone to figure out how bad his mood was. I just knew if he was in a good mood, there was no way he'd be calling me outside, and if he was in a really bad mood there was no way I wanted him to come up to my room and corner me where there was no escape. I closed my book and hurried downstairs and out onto the porch, where I was careful to keep some distance. Sometimes when he'd been drinking Uncle Charlie liked to hit.

"What?" I asked.

He sipped on his drink and squinted at me with the same face he'd use if he'd just discovered the meat in his lunch sandwich had gone bad. Uncle Charlie is about six feet two, nearly as tall as Daddy, but no longer thin. He's not exactly fat, either, at least not yet. He reminds me of a candle that's been sitting in the sun too long and is starting to bulge in the wrong places. Also, he has the beginning of three chins, red broken veins on his cheeks, and wispy hair that can't seem to make a decision whether to lie down or stand up. Kind of like Uncle Charlie, now that I think about it.

"Deputy Simmons called. Told me you sucker punched his son. Told me you and some other kids ganged up on the boy."

I laughed. "That's a lie."

Uncle Charlie brought his hand down hard on the arm of the chair. "Bubba Simmons don't lie. Not to his friends."

"His son, Jimmy, lies like a rug."

"You sayin' you didn't punch his kid?"

"I punched him, but I didn't sucker punch him. We were face-to-face. He went for me first."

"Young ladies aren't supposed to hit boys."

"Boys aren't supposed to try and choke young ladies."

I knew I should let it go, but I couldn't. Uncle Charlie's cheeks had already gotten redder. He hated what he called "guff," which is what other people call "logic." He got angriest of all when he was dead wrong and I called him on it, or when he didn't have a clue what he was talking about. Like now.

He took a slug of bourbon, then pointed a finger

at me. "Stop sassin' me, girl. Y'all keep away from Bubba's son, and if you see him y'all apologize. You're just lucky Bubba's not pressing charges."

"Pressing charges? Against who? Me, a girl? Skoogie Middleton, a skinny little fifth grader? Skoogie's grandmother, who can barely walk?" I shook my head. "Jimmy Simmons was trying to choke me to death, and Mrs. Middleton stopped him. I hope Bubba does press charges."

"That's Deputy Simmons to you, Squib."

"Yeah, well, the judge'll have a good laugh before he throws Deputy Simmons and his stupid son in jail."

I knew even as I said the last part that I'd pushed it too far. Uncle Charlie's face was now the color of a swollen zit. He came out of his chair, but I was ready. I jumped off the porch steps and raced out into the yard. Uncle Charlie came to the edge of the steps, stopped, and looked down. We both knew he was way too slow to catch me. His face was muddled with evening heat and confusion, and his second bourbon was kicking in right on schedule, making him forget about what it was that had made him angry in the first place but not making him a bit uncertain about the fact that he was angry.

He pointed his finger at me. "One'a these days, Squib, y'all're gonna be too slow."

The problem was, I knew he was probably right, but it wasn't going to stop me from putting him in his place. Daddy and Uncle Charlie's father had left them both what Daddy said was "a fair pile of money." In Daddy's language, a fair pile meant we weren't rich, but we were a long way from being poor. That money had been passed down generation to generation from when my family mined phosphate in the late 1800s. Daddy had needed to spend a big part of his pile on doctor bills when my mother got cancer. I don't really remember it, because it happened when I was three, but I know that Daddy did everything he could to save her. In the end, Mom died, and a lot of the money was gone.

Where Uncle Charlie was concerned, it was no secret around Charleston, South Carolina, that he had a powerful love of gambling and an equally powerful dislike of work. Over the years, Uncle Charlie had dribbled his inheritance into the hands of luckier gamblers.

When he hadn't been gambling, Uncle Charlie had fancied himself a treasure hunter and bought some old pirate maps that Daddy said were probably fakes. Uncle Charlie had funded some "expeditions" to try and find his buried gold in the Bahamas and South America. He had always believed that his luck would eventually turn and he would either start winning at cards or dice or find some long-lost gold hoard. Like Daddy always said, luck is fickle. But there's unlucky and there's just plain dumb, and Uncle Charlie was more often in the second category.

In the end, my grandfather had needed to make a choice about whether to split Reward between his two sons or keep it whole. Figuring Uncle Charlie couldn't even afford the taxes and that he would just lose his half in a poker game anyway, he'd given it all to Daddy. Right away Daddy had fixed up a tenant house real nice and offered it to Uncle Charlie and Ruth to live in rent-free. Uncle Charlie was a lousy real-estate salesman when he actually worked, which wasn't very often, so there was no way they could have kept a roof over their heads any other way. But it didn't matter. Uncle Charlie and Ruth had never forgiven Daddy for inheriting Reward.

This past year, when Reward had been put up for sale to settle Daddy's debts, Uncle Charlie had been the listing real estate agent and had insisted that he had a twenty-five-year rent-free agreement with my father that would remain in effect no matter who bought the property. The new owner apparently hadn't cared, because Uncle Charlie and Ruth were still living in the tenant house.

In order to keep my distance from Uncle Charlie, I walked around the outside of the house and went into the kitchen through the back door. I set the table for dinner and fed Rufus, our black Lab. For the past nine months, I'd been taking Rufus for all his walks and making sure he got fed, and as a result he'd come to like me about twice as well as Uncle Charlie and Ruth.

By the time I finished, Ruth had spooned the canned stuff she had heated up into some bowls and put them on the table. The food was brown and smelled like it could have been stew. Uncle Charlie came in off the porch, shaking the ice in his empty bourbon glass and still giving me a mean squint.

Dinner with Uncle Charlie and Ruth never involved a whole lot of talking. It involved mostly silence and chewing, with maybe one or both of them occasionally looking up from the business of eating to ask me whether I'd done this chore or that chore or to criticize something I had or hadn't done. Unlike the dinners Daddy and I used to have, the ones with Uncle Charlie and Ruth didn't include talk about how their days had gone or what they had done or interesting questions. They just ate, and when they were finished, dinner was over.

So imagine my surprise when, on this particular

night, Ruth went to the cupboard and brought out two wineglasses, took a jug of white wine out of the refrigerator, and poured some for herself and Uncle Charlie. When she did, the cloud over Uncle Charlie's head seemed to go away. They both looked at each other and smiled and raised their glasses. Ruth said, "Here's to better times ahead."

Uncle Charlie gave her a sly grin and a wink. "'Bout darn time," he said. Then he swallowed half his wine in one big gulp.

I looked back and forth between them and tried to pick up a clue. What did Ruth mean about better times ahead? Had Uncle Charlie gotten a real job? I sure didn't think that was likely. I knew I should keep my mouth shut because neither one of them would tell me anything if I asked, but I couldn't help it. "What's going on?" I blurted.

Uncle Charlie gave me a sideways glance. I could see something flash in his eyes almost like slyness. He gave me a smug little grin. "Never you mind, Squib. Y'all'll find out when it's time."

I felt Ruth's eyes on me, and when I turned to look at her, she sat up suddenly.

"Oh, yeah," she said, lifting off the chair a little and reaching into the back pocket of her blue jeans.

"Almost forgot." She handed me an envelope that was badly wrinkled from being sat on.

I looked at the envelope and saw that it was from Miss Walker's School for Girls, where I had gone before Daddy's accident. After everything that had happened, there hadn't been any money for tuition, so this past school year I'd had to attend the public school.

Truth be told, I didn't really mind going to a new school where I didn't know anyone, because I thought it was what I deserved. Just before Daddy's accident, I'd had one of my dreams. One that told me something really bad was about to happen. It was the second time in my life that I'd had one. The first had come before my mother died, but I had been very young, and there was nothing I could have done even if I had understood what the dream meant. However, it was different with Daddy's dream. I should have warned him, and it was my fault that I hadn't.

Actually I did try once, but he just smiled and patted my head and said he was touched that I worried about him. It was obvious that I hadn't tried hard enough. I should have yelled and screamed, convinced him that something bad was going to happen. Maybe that way I could have kept him off that ladder.

Both of those dreams stuck hard in my memory

because they were scary and horrible and seemed to last all night long. Both times when I finally woke up, my sheets were drenched with sweat, and I was totally exhausted. Also, while I usually never remember the colors in my dreams, both of these had been in Technicolor. The dream about my mother had been deep burgundy, the color of a funeral. The dream had come just days before the doctors told her that she had cancer. The dream about my father had been deep purple, but the sense of the dream had been exactly the same as my mother's, full of impending doom and sadness.

The envelope from Miss Walker's sent a nervous buzz through my stomach. Why were they writing to me? I had gone to Miss Walker's ever since we moved to Charleston, from my last year of preschool through fifth grade, and I had loved it as much as a kid can love school. Miss Walker's was a wonderful place, and I missed my old friends and teachers and coaches and pretty much everything else.

I sensed Uncle Charlie and Ruth watching me. Part of me wanted to take my envelope up to my room and open it in private, but the other part didn't want to wait.

"You gonna open it?" Uncle Charlie asked. "Maybe they changed your grades from your last year there to Fs," he added with a smirk.

"Funny." I looked up at him. "Why would they do that? So my report card could match yours?"

He snapped his fingers and nodded toward the envelope. "Open it, Squib."

I turned the envelope over. Right away I saw that the glue on the flap was barely holding, coming open the moment I started to put my finger under it. I felt a rush of anger at the realization that Ruth had steamed the letter open, read it, and tried to reseal it. Anger turned my cheeks bright red and made my hands tremble. Uncle Charlie and Ruth already knew what the letter said, but of course they would deny it if I accused them.

I removed a sheet of Miss Walker's stationery and unfolded it. In one corner I could see a dried smudge that looked like some of the canned stew we had eaten for dinner. I ignored it and read the letter and felt a bright shot of excitement that made me forget everything else.

"Miss Walker's is offering me a scholarship," I said, unable to keep the excitement from my voice as I looked up at Uncle Charlie and Ruth. "A hundred percent. You don't have to pay for anything."

Uncle Charlie and Ruth were both gazing back at me with flat expressions. There was no surprise, no joy, not even a sense of relief that I would be farther away from them for most of the day. Just deadpan. I felt the bright star that had just seemed to explode inside my heart shrink back to a cold, dry husk.

"It says it's a merit scholarship," I said, trying again, my voice soft. I had a desperate hope that they simply had not understood the first time, but a voice inside told me I was wrong. Ruth had opened the letter. They already knew.

Uncle Charlie raised his eyebrows. "It's charity."

"Huh?"

"You heard me. It's charity."

"No," I said, hearing my volume rise. I couldn't believe I had heard him correctly. "It's a scholarship."

"Like Shakespeare says, 'A pig by any other name is still a pig.' It's charity. Our family doesn't take charity."

"Look in the dictionary," I said. I wasn't even going to point out that the Shakespeare quote was about a rose. "A scholarship is not charity."

"It is if I say it is."

"And our family doesn't take charity," I said. I could hear the mockery in my tone, but I couldn't stop. I knew the real reason they didn't want me to go to Miss Walker's was that the school didn't have a bus, and getting me there would mean one of them would have to drive me into Charleston every day. "I suppose your idea of charity doesn't apply to the free rent you got from Daddy all those years."

"You watch your mouth, girl." Uncle Charlie was leaning across the table toward me, his eyes flat and dangerous. "There's no such thing as charity in a family. Families do for family. It's just how things are."

"Like you do for Daddy," I said, knowing that neither one of them had visited him even once in the hospital.

"Your daddy is a thief," Ruth spoke up. "He's shamed us."

"Besides that, he's a vegetable," Uncle Charlie added. "It's no more good talking to him than it is talking to a corn plant."

I felt the tears begin to burn in my eyes. Not wanting to give them the satisfaction of seeing me cry, I shoved my chair away from the table and ran up to my room.

Three

The next morning I woke early, got dressed, took my book off the nightstand, then snuck downstairs as quietly as possible. I fixed a quick bowl of cereal, and when Rufus saw me eat, he rapped his hard tail on the kitchen floor, so I hurried to get his breakfast before his racket woke anyone else. We both ate fast, even though I ate slower because nobody can eat as fast as a hungry Lab. I grabbed a couple carrots from the fridge, and we both slipped out of the house before we could bump into Uncle Charlie or Ruth.

It was a typical South Carolina summer morning on Leadenwah Island. A crystal-clear blue sky overhead, the air as heavy and damp as the inside of a shower stall, full of early warmth and the scent of flowers and damp earth and the promise of more heat to come. Overhead two herons were flying toward the river to begin stalking the shallows for fish. Couldn't have been a more perfect day for my first day of work.

Rufus and I walked across the yard and then down the dirt track that led between the corn and soybean fields to the main plantation drive. Several large horse pastures ran along the other side of the road, and on the far end of the nearest pasture I could see my old gray Welsh pony grazing alongside the two old carriage horses.

Rufus and I slipped through the fence and headed across the dew-soaked grass toward the horses. They turned their heads at our approach, and the pony nickered once, then trotted toward us. He nuzzled his head against my chest and then started to sniff at my pockets, where he smelled his carrots.

"Good morning, Timmy," I said as I slipped one of the carrots out of my pocket and let him have it. He chewed contentedly and followed me as I gave a carrot to each of the carriage horses.

Once everyone had gotten their treat, I put my arms around Timmy's neck, then slipped onto his back.

After a good look around just to make sure no one was out watching, I grabbed a handful of mane and gave a slight squeeze with my legs. We trotted for a short distance and then began to canter.

We went around the field like that for a while, and at one point I reached forward, slid my arm along Timmy's neck, tightened my grip on his mane, then let my body slide off his back. I kept slipping until I was pressed hard against his side, and my one foot on his rump and my arm around his neck was all that kept me from falling off. It was a trick move I had seen in some old movie on TV, and I was teaching myself to do it just in case someone came along while I was riding and I needed to hide. I hadn't met the new owners of the plantation, but I suspected that they might not approve of me riding Timmy without permission. Of course, Uncle Charlie had told me that I was never allowed to ride Timmy again and that if I ever got on him, even once, I would be severely punished, whatever that meant. Even so, I tried to tell myself that I was doing the right thing by giving him some exercise. After all, it's important to keep horses and ponies in shape to prevent injuries.

I rode Timmy for a little while longer, until we were both sweated up, and then we headed toward the barn. The summer job that Uncle Charlie and Ruth had arranged was for me to feed and water and generally care for the new owner's horses every day, muck out the stalls, and clean and oil the tack. I think they expected me to complain because the work was hot and sweaty, but for me it was perfect. I didn't have anything else to fill my time. My old friends from Miss Walker's all lived far away, so I had no way to see them. Besides, since Daddy had been accused of being a thief, most of them didn't know what to say to me, so they didn't say much at all.

Also, the day Timmy was sold had been one of the saddest days of my life. Even though I didn't own him anymore, having a job where I could spend time with him and take care of him and make sure he was okay took away some of the hurt.

The new owners of Reward lived in Atlanta. I hardly knew a thing about them, other than their name was also Force, just like mine, but apparently we were not related. Uncle Charlie had handled the sale of the plantation, but I don't think he had ever met the people, just their lawyers. Supposedly Mr. Force was a very wealthy businessman who traveled all over the world visiting his various investments. He was so busy that he hadn't even come to see his new plantation since he'd bought it the previous winter.

The one thing that made me think Mr. Force might be a nice man was that he had adopted the two old carriage horses. According to the man who had brought them here a few weeks earlier, Mr. Force and his daughter had been on a trip when she had seen the old horses and felt sorry for them. Supposedly she had asked her father to buy them and give them a nice place to retire, and he had done it right on the spot.

When Timmy and I reached the barn, I turned around and looked to make sure the two carriage horses were following. Their names were Clem and Lem, which seemed perfect because of their slow way of walking and doing everything else. I twisted the tap above the watering trough and filled the big galvanized tub to the top. Then after the horses had a good, long drink, I opened the gate so they could walk to the barn and into their open stalls for their morning grain.

Once they had eaten, I took Timmy out of his stall, hitched him to the cross ties, then hosed him down and brushed him until his coat glistened. Afterward I did the same to Clem and Lem and put fly coats on all three horses, sprayed them with fly repellant, then put them out in a different pasture.

I spent the next couple hours mucking out the stalls,

then cleaning and oiling the saddles and bridles. With most of the work finished, I walked out of the barn and down the drive toward Reward Plantation Manor, the big house where Daddy and I used to live. The name made it sound like some fancy Southern mansion with tall white columns, but it wasn't. It was a pretty, old wooden house with green shutters and shaded porches on the front and back. I checked to make sure there were no cars around and that the new owners hadn't shown up unexpectedly, then I went to a window at the far end of the house and peeked inside.

It was Daddy's old library, and it looked almost the same as it had the day I found him lying unconscious on the floor and bleeding from a big gash in his head. A stepladder had been set up in the middle of the room, and when I looked up at the ceiling, I had seen that a couple of old cypress panels had been moved aside to reveal a secret storage space. There had been pieces of gold jewelry and coins and what looked like diamonds scattered around, stuff that I had never seen before, as if Daddy had been trying to get them out of the hiding place or maybe trying to hide them when he fell. Either way, they didn't belong to him.

I stared into the room for a long time, remembering the scene as if it had been yesterday. I knew what the police claimed had happened. I knew that pretty much everybody else agreed with them. But I also knew that all of them were wrong. I thought about the last year, living with Uncle Charlie and Ruth, and about last night, about the letter from Miss Walker's. And I thought about Daddy, lying there motionless in his hospital bed.

I was going to find a way to prove he was innocent, and I was going to do it this summer. I just didn't know how.

Four

Three hours later I was reading a book in the shade of a big live oak on one side of the barn when I finally saw a plume of road dust from Uncle Charlie's black pickup as he drove out the plantation drive. It was nearly eleven thirty, and I assumed he was on his way to a card game or a bar. That meant the coast was clear, so I headed back to the house with Rufus trotting at my heels.

Back in the kitchen I emptied the dishwasher from the night before, wiped off the counters, and cleaned up the spilled milk that was left from Uncle Charlie's cereal bowl. After I let Rufus lick up the rest of the milk from the bowl, I washed it, put coffee in the machine, and turned it on. Then I sat and read my book and waited for Ruth to appear. She came down about twenty minutes later, sniffing at the freshly brewed coffee and carrying what looked like an old-fashioned yellow ball gown made of some shiny stuff like silk or satin.

I could tell right away that Ruth hadn't expected to find me there, because she looked surprised and angry. "What are you doin' here?" she demanded, half turning and bundling up the the gown behind her back. She must have been embarrassed. A ball gown was totally un-Ruth. Not that I had much to brag about in the clothing department, but she tended to dress like a train wreck. All of her clothes looked like they had never met an iron, and most of them had burns from her cigarette ashes. Ruth couldn't find the department-store makeup counter with a map, and her dull brown hair was usually as tangled up as a bird's nest. She'd have looked as silly in a ball gown as I would have in a chicken suit.

"Finished my chores at the barn," I said. "So what's the dress for?" I added, unable to leave it alone.

"Nothin'. It's just a dress." As if to make her point, she tossed it onto one of the kitchen chairs, where it fell half onto the floor. She left it there and walked over to pour herself a mug of coffee.

I caught a big whiff of mustiness coming off the dress. It smelled like it had been in some attic trunk for about a hundred years. I wondered where she would have gotten it, seeing as how there's no way she owned it. But I didn't get a chance to ask any more about it, because she took her coffee out on the back porch steps, lit a cigarette, and sat there while she smoked it. When she finally came back into the kitchen, she looked around at how everything was cleaned up, then squinted at me as if she was just noticing me for the first time.

"You sure you finished your barn chores?"

"Yes, ma'am."

"Yes, ma'am," she said in a mocking tone. "You only talk like that when you want something."

I pursed my lips and forced myself to be quiet and not bug her about the dress or anything else.

"What?" Ruth asked when the silence stretched.

"I'd like to go see him."

"Who?"

"You know who. Please?"

She poured another mug of coffee, then stood at the sink for a moment looking out the kitchen window. When she turned toward me and spoke again, her voice had become softer. Unlike Uncle Charlie, Ruth was actually capable of being human at certain times. "He probably has no idea that you're there. You do know that, right?"

I bit my cheeks hard. I could not and would not accept that. "That's not what the doctors say."

"They said if your dad is gonna come out of his coma, talking might help. I'm sorry to say it, but that *if* is getting bigger every day. It's been nine months."

She did not have to tell me that. It had been eight months and twenty-seven days. That afternoon at about three o'clock it would be eight months and twenty-eight days since I had found Daddy lying on the library floor.

The doctors had told me that the best way of helping Daddy wake up from his coma was to go in and talk to him and read books to him and just let him hear my voice. They said if he could hear me, it might help him work harder to find a way to wake up again. I didn't care what Ruth or anybody said, and I didn't care how much time had gone by. I was going to visit him every chance I got and let him hear my voice.

"Please, Ruth. I'm sure you're going out sometime today. Just drop me off where I can catch the bus. Please."

Ruth took a deep breath, and I could tell that she

was weakening. She scowled, but she picked up a dish-rag and tossed it into the sink. "Fine. But don't be expecting me to drive you all summer."

"Yes, ma'am."

"You ready to go right now? I don't have time to waste."

"Yes," I said. I raced up the stairs, grabbed the book I had been reading to Daddy off my dresser, and hurried back down.

Ruth snatched her keys off the hook by the door and jerked her head for me to follow. I told Rufus to stay, and I ran into the yard behind her.

Ruth drove me to the bus stop on Johns Island and let me out, and twenty minutes later I was looking out the window of a city bus, watching the world become more and more suburban as we got closer to downtown Charleston. We went past the round Holiday Inn and over the bridge called the Old Connector, and after another block we came to a stop near the Medical University and the University Hospital.

Charleston is an old city, full of big, old buildings, many from the eighteen hundreds and even the seventeen hundreds. The Medical University is pretty modern by comparison. The campus is full of tall structures with lots of glass. If you're sick, it's the kind of place you want to be.

I got off the bus and walked toward the biggest and newest hospital building. It looked so shiny and bright that it just had to be full of hope and certain cures for its patients. At least that's what I told myself.

Daddy's room was on the sixth floor, and I took the elevator up and then pushed the button beside the hallway door. The nurses were used to seeing me and buzzed me in. I waved to them and went straight to Daddy's room.

"Good morning," I said when I walked in. I always held a magical hope that I might come in, greeting him like nothing was wrong, and he might just answer me right back. But he just lay there the way he always had, flat on his back, his face still and peaceful. He could have been sound asleep like any normal person except for the clear tube that went from a drip bag above his bed to an IV port on the back of one hand and another tube that carried food up his nose and from there down into his stomach.

"Okay, lazybones," I said, keeping my voice cheerful even though I never felt cheerful when I saw him like that. Seeing those tubes go into his body always reminded me that he was balanced right on the edge of being alive and being dead. "Let's see. I've got a lot to tell you. School got out for the year yesterday. I had a great year and got straight As, 'cause I wanted to make you proud."

I really did get straight As, but I hadn't told Daddy that I was no longer going to Miss Walker's School for Girls. I also hadn't told him that Reward Plantation had been sold or that Timmy had been sold or that I was living with Uncle Charlie and Ruth and pretty much hated every minute of it. Daddy had always raised me to tell the truth, but there was no way I could tell him the truth about my life. I was afraid that if I told him what it was really like, he might never want to wake up.

I made up some happy stories about things I had done and places I had gone with old friends from Miss Walker's, and when I couldn't think of any more good lies to tell, I took out *A Tale of Two Cities* by Charles Dickens and went to my bookmark and started to read from where I had stopped the last time.

From time to time, I would stop reading and look up at Daddy lying there so peacefully, and the picture in my brain would flash back to that day I found him on the floor of the library. I had called 911, and a police car came to the plantation along with the ambulance. While the medics took care of Daddy, the policemen looked at the jewelry that was scattered around the floor and at the secret hiding place, and then they went out to their car and came back and took pictures. Afterward, when Daddy was in the hospital, the police discovered initials on some of the jewelry that made them suspect that it had belonged to one of Daddy's clients, Miss Lydia Jenkins.

Miss Jenkins was very old and very rich and, according to everyone, very strange. Daddy never ever talked about any of his clients, but other people sure liked to talk about Miss Jenkins. They said that she didn't trust banks or paper money or insurance companies and that she kept all her wealth in the form of gold and diamonds in an old bank vault in her huge old house in downtown Charleston. According to the rumors, Miss Lydia Jenkins didn't trust her own family any more than she trusted banks. She had never married and never had any children of her own, but she thought her nieces and nephews were all just after her money.

She had been Daddy's client for many years, and he was apparently the only person in the world she trusted. Two years earlier Miss Jenkins had suffered a stroke that had left her almost completely paralyzed and unable to talk. Sometimes when I went to downtown Charleston, I would catch sight of her in her wheelchair being pushed along the sidewalk by her nurse.

The police went to Miss Jenkins's house to ask about the jewelry. Miss Jenkins's nurse identified all the pieces. And when they went to the big safe that only Miss Jenkins and my father supposedly knew the combination to, they found the safe door unlocked and the safe totally empty.

Miss Lydia Jenkins, who had hardly spoken a syllable since her stroke, got extremely upset. When the police asked if my father had stolen her gold, all she managed to say was "Stole it." She said it over and over.

About an hour later, I had finished reading to Daddy and I was walking down the corridor on my way to the elevator when I saw a familiar face coming toward me and recognized Mr. Crawford Barrett, Daddy's law partner.

"Abbey!" he said, when he caught sight of me.

Mr. Barrett was tall and thin with a straight nose, sculpted chin, and longish gray hair that he combed straight back. Daddy liked to say that Mr. Barrett was the picture everyone had in their head of an upper-class, intelligent, and honest lawyer, like the kind of person you'd see playing a lawyer on TV.

"Hi, Mr. Barrett," I said.

"Visiting your dad?"

"Yessir."

"I had some time between appointments, so I thought I'd look in on him myself. Any change?"

I shook my head. "Maybe he'll wake up for you," I said.

"I can only hope. You know, sometimes when I get stuck on something in a case, I like to come and talk to your dad just the way I used to when he was in his office. I tell him what my problem is and pretend he answers me and tells me what I should do. Maybe one of these days, he will."

"Yessir, I hope so, too."

I appreciated that Mr. Barrett would still come to visit Daddy after all these months—goodness knows it was more than Daddy's own brother would do—but at the same time I was angry at him. I realized my reasons for being angry probably weren't his fault at all, but I couldn't help it. Mr. Barrett had been the one who took over everything right after the accident, when the police formally accused Daddy of stealing Miss Jenkins's gold and jewelry. Daddy was in a coma and couldn't appoint an attorney now, but Mr. Barrett had a power of attorney that let him act for Daddy if he ever couldn't act for himself.

He talked to Miss Jenkins's lawyer and got her to agree that they would not press charges against Daddy for something called grand larceny if Reward Plantation was sold and that money, along with everything else Daddy had, was given to Miss Jenkins. I told Mr. Barrett it was wrong to sell anything until Daddy woke up and had a chance to tell us what really happened, but he said the courts wouldn't wait. And he said that the law firm, and all their partners, would be ruined if we didn't settle and sell Reward to pay back Miss Jenkins. He also said it looked to the whole world like Daddy had done a very bad thing, and while he remained certain that Daddy would be able to exonerate himself when he woke up, the town's opinion wasn't going to change one bit until that happened. He said selling the plantation was the only way of salvaging our family's honor.

I knew all his reasons, and I realize that adults probably knew a lot more about money and laws than a twelve-year-old girl, but I still thought that he was just giving up, letting everyone in the world think that Daddy had committed a terrible crime. The police and Mr. Barrett hadn't been able to come up with a single other explanation of how that loot came to be on Daddy's library floor, and, so far, I hadn't been able to come up with any answers either.

But as I watched Mr. Barrett continue down the hall and turn into Daddy's room, I made yet another promise to Daddy and to myself that I would prove he was innocent before the summer was out, or I would die trying.

Five

The next morning I woke up early again, grabbed a quick bite, and fed Rufus, and then the two of us headed out of the house and over to the horse pasture. I gave a carrot to each of the horses. Then I hopped up on Timmy's back and we spent about twenty minutes cantering around the pasture and about ten more practicing the stunt-riding move I had been working on for the past few days.

We both had a good sweat by the time we rode up to the gate that led to the barn. I slipped off Timmy's back and froze.

A girl I had never seen before was leaning up against

the fence. She was slender and pretty with skin the color of coffee with cream and long black hair, and probably an inch or two taller than me. I noticed she had her right arm in a sling and her right leg in what looked like a removable cast. A metal cane hung by its crook from the top fence post.

"Hi," I said.

"Hi," she said back. Her voice was flat, her eyes dull. She seemed angry or surly or something I couldn't put my finger on. Right away I assumed that it was because she had seen me riding Timmy. I wondered how much trouble I was in.

"I'm Abbey Force," I said, hearing the hesitation in my voice. "I take care of the barn."

I paused for a moment, waiting for her to say something. She just gave me a blank look, as if she had little interest in anything I might say.

"This pony used to belong to me," I said, filling the silence.

"Yeah, I know," she said in the same flat tone.

"That's why I was riding him."

She closed her eyes and shook her head, as if I was soooo boring. "I don't care if you ride the stupid pony."

I felt my temper flare and took a breath, ready to tell her that Timmy was probably a lot smarter than she could ever hope to be. But then she opened her eyes, and what I saw there stopped me. I realized that this strange girl wasn't being a snobby jerk. She was sad, maybe even sadder than I was, and she didn't seem to care about anything.

I felt my anger loosen and drift away on the wind. "Who are you?" I asked.

"I'm Bee."

I waited for her to say her last name, and when she didn't I asked, "Bee who?"

"Bee Force."

On hearing her last name, several things clicked. Bee was the daughter of the new owner of Reward. But that wasn't all. In the same instant I thought of something else, something that was a whole lot more complicated. I remembered a book Daddy had told me about one time. I think it was called *Slaves in the Family*, and it had been written by a man named Edward Ball, whose family had lived around Charleston for a long time and had once owned a lot of slaves, just like my family had.

Daddy said the book had hit him like "a ton of bricks," because it could have been written about our own family just as easily as about the Balls. In 1865, when the Civil War finally ended and the freed slaves went off to make their way in the world, one of the many things they lacked was a last name. Because of that, many ex-slaves took the last names of their old owners. Edward Ball's book was about how he had set out to meet the descendants of those original ex-slaves. Daddy said the book made him think about the African Americans our family had owned. While we might not be blood relatives, he said, we were certainly relatives in terms of having come from the same place, living together and having an important connection. He thought Mr. Ball had done a great thing.

Now standing in front of me was an African American girl with my last name. Force. It was a rare enough name, and now the idea that my ancestors had probably kept Bee's ancestors in slavery made my face go bright red in shame.

"Oh my gosh," I said. "I'm sorry."

I could tell that my embarrassment momentarily startled Bee out of her melancholy. She seemed to understand why I had apologized and why my face was beet red. "It was a long time ago," she said softly. "Had nothing to do with the two of us."

"No, but . . ." I didn't know how to finish the thought.

Bee rescued the situation. "What's your real name?" she asked.

"Abigail," I said. "But I generally punch anybody in the nose who calls me that."

Bee's eyes brightened, and she laughed. She had a smile that made it seem like the sun had come out from under the clouds, and her laugh sounded nice and easy. "Mine is Beatrice, and I do the exact same thing to anybody who calls me that."

I held out my hand, and she took it. "Nice to meet you, Bee."

"Nice to meet you, too, Abbey."

I glanced at her sling. "What happened?"

"Car accident," she said, the pain coming back into her eyes.

"Well, I guess it could have been worse," I said.

"Um, right . . ."

I realized that was a lame thing to have said. Breaking your arm and leg couldn't have been any fun. I let my eyes wander around the pasture, watching the morning mist rise from the grass and the sun coming up over the live oaks, and I tried to think of something else to say so I didn't look like such a dork. "Good place to get healed up," I said at last.

Bee gave me a flicker of a smile. "I guess."

I was thinking that Bee Force seemed a lot like me. I could see that she was very sad about something, but underneath that sadness I was betting that she was smart and tough, had a good sense of humor, and maybe even a little bit of a wild streak. Suddenly I thought my horrible, boring summer might actually be looking up. Out of nowhere, it seemed that I had found someone who had as many problems as I did.

Bee stayed down at the barn while I did chores. She watched for a time, and when I started mucking out the stalls, she grabbed a spare pitchfork and tried to help. But she was pretty useless at that, with one arm in a sling, so I showed her how to clean and oil tack.

"What's your dog's name?" she asked as she lathered a bridle with saddle soap.

"Rufus."

"So where do you guys live?"

I dumped a forkful of straw in the wheelbarrow and hooked my thumb in the direction of the tenant house.

"Is Charles Force your dad?"

I had caught something in Bee's tone that told me she already knew Charles Force was a jerk, and I barked out a laugh. "Uncle," I said.

"Oh." She sounded relieved, but then the silence stretched, and I felt her unspoken question hanging.

"My dad's in the hospital," I added.

"Oh."

"Well, thanks to your help, I've done everything I need to do today," I said, wanting to change the subject. "Want to get out of here? You okay to walk with that cast?"

She looked up from soaping the bridle. "Kind of hot for a walk. Where do you swim around here?"

Now she was talking. A swim sounded perfect. But then I thought about Ruth. "I need to get a suit, but if I go home my aunt will probably give me more chores to do."

"I'll lend you a suit. I bet we wear the same size."

"You sure swimming is okay for you? How can you swim with your sling and cast?"

Bee shrugged. "I can take them off. The cast is fiberglass. Besides"—Bee raised her eyebrows—"do you always do everything you're supposed to?"

I smiled. "Course not. Have you gone in the river yet?" I asked.

Bee wrinkled her lips. "That gross brown water?"

"It's great. Trust me."

Bee laughed, and the sound was like a wave washing in from the ocean and covering over her sadness.

"We just got here last night," she said. "So the only places I've spent any time are the house and the barn.

But if you say the river is good for swimming, let's do it."

We put away the tack, and Bee and Rufus and I left the barn and headed down the plantation drive toward the big house. I'd looked in the windows probably a hundred times, but the idea of actually going back inside made me feel weird.

I could close my eyes and see every single one of the rooms. They were comfortable and high ceilinged, the downstairs rooms paneled in warm cypress that had been cut and planed from trees on the property. The floorboards were wide and ancient and worn in places from hundreds of years of foot traffic. I knew the smells, the stairs that squeaked, the sound the wind made around the eaves on a stormy night.

Thinking about it brought a lump to my throat, because it reminded me of the happiness I'd had there with Daddy. I started to feel a little bit of panic, wondering if I could really make myself go inside.

Only right then Bee stopped. "You know, if we go inside, Grandma Em might see us."

"Who's Grandma Em?"

"My grandma. She sort of takes care of me."

"What about your parents?" I asked.

Bee hesitated, just for an instant. Then she said,

"My dad is out of the country."

"Where?"

"India. He's got a software company there, but they've had some problems. He's had to spend a lot of time over there, so Grandma Em came to live with us."

"What about your mom?"

Bee shook her head and looked away. "She's . . . not around."

Once again, I had the feeling I'd said something wrong, but I didn't know what. "So Grandma Em won't let you go swimming?" I asked after a silence.

"With a busted knee and my arm in a sling, you kidding?"

I thought about Bee's injuries, how the first thing we did together might end up getting her hurt. "You sure we should do this?"

Another smile broke out on her face. "Heck yes."

Six

Reward Plantation lay along a stretch of the
Leadenwah River. The plantation's dock was
down behind the big house at the end of a long
boardwalk built over the marsh, and it stuck out into
the river where the water was deep enough for diving
even at low tide. We went to the end, and I threw a stick
for Rufus, who went sailing off and hit the water with a
huge splash. He swam out into the current, grabbed the
stick, and headed back to shore.

Before Rufus could get back up on the dock and
soak us by shaking himself, we stripped down to our
shirts and underwear. I watched Bee take the sling off

her right arm and then reach down and undo the straps on her leg cast. Even with the cast off, her knee was wrapped in some kind of tan bandage.

"You don't have any stitches or open cuts, right?" Even though I knew the river water was clean, there was no sense asking for trouble.

Bee shook her head, but as she walked to the edge of the dock and looked down at the brown water, I could tell by the careful way she moved that whatever she was recovering from, she still had a long way to go.

The plantation wasn't far from where the Leadenwah dumps into the North Edisto River, which in turn dumps into the ocean, so the water was brackish, meaning that it was part salt water from the Atlantic and part freshwater from the river. The good thing about brackish water is that alligators and snakes generally don't like the salt and tend not to show up. The bad thing about brackish water is that it's not at all clear. Trying to see into it is like trying to look through a wall.

"Probably a stupid question," I said, "but you do know how to swim, right?"

Bee looked down at the water as if she were mesmerized. She shook her head. "Nope. Sure hope it's not deep." With that, she jumped off.

I rushed over to the edge and looked down. I could

see the remnants of her splash but no sign of Bee. With panic surging, I looked downstream in the direction of the current. Nothing. I waited a few seconds, tried to gauge how far she would have drifted, and marked the spot against some trees along the bank.

I was about to dive when Bee surfaced halfway out into the river. She was laughing. "Gotcha," she said.

I smiled down at her, thinking that was exactly the kind of stunt I would pull. "You scared me half to death."

She could swim at least, but the current had already grabbed her and started moving her downstream. Just as I had feared, her right arm seemed pretty useless, and probably her bad leg couldn't do much kicking. That meant she was going to have to struggle to get to shore.

I stood there and watched her fight the current. I could tell she was trying hard, but she was getting farther and farther from the dock. She glanced up at me a couple times, but she didn't ask for help. Rufus looked at her and whined like he wanted me to do something.

When it finally looked like she was getting tired, I jumped in and swam toward her. Rufus jumped in, too, and paddled beside me. "Grab my shoulder," I said to Bee. When she did, I kicked and swam us into the pluff-mud shallows along the side of the river.

Pluff mud is the dark, gushy stuff that lines the banks of many Lowcountry rivers and smells a little bit like dead fish. It's usually deep enough that you can sink down into it all the way to your hips, which makes walking in it really miserable, even if you have two good legs. Since Bee had only one, we stayed in the shallows and half crawled back toward the dock. Rufus slogged through the mud beside us, his legs and belly covered in black goop.

When we finally reached the dock's swim ladder, Bee looked at me, a little shy. "I had no idea the current would be so strong. Thanks."

I couldn't help but smile. "You owe me one. Just remember that the next time I go off half-cocked."

She beamed. "Deal."

We went up the ladder, and when we were back on the dock we looked at each other and started to laugh. We were covered from our faces to our toes in thick, black pluff mud.

"Now we really could be the Force sisters," Bee said as she looked down at what had been her white T-shirt. "Grandma Em is gonna kill me."

"Here," I said, pulling up a rope that was tied to one of the dock pilings. I tied a loop in the end and held it out to Bee. "Keep a grip on the rope when you jump off. It will keep you from drifting, and the current will wash off most of the mud."

Bee limped to the edge. I could tell by the way she favored her bad leg that the swim and the crawl back had been painful, but she took the rope and jumped off. I stood there until I saw Bee's head break the surface. She flashed me a grin, then let herself relax and lie flat, held in place by the rope against the current.

I walked to the upstream end of the dock, jumped off, and grabbed Bee's rope as I swept past. We lay there side by side, feeling the sweep of the river's warm water against our bodies as it cleaned off the mud.

"So, Bee Force," I said, "are you gonna come here for vacations or live here year-round?"

"Year-round."

"So you'll go to school here?"

"Grandma Em says I'm going to go to a place called Miss Walker's. You know it?"

I felt a twinge of sadness but tried not to let it show. "Yeah, it's a good place. I used to go there."

"Not anymore? How come?"

"It was time for a change," I told her.

We were laughing as we climbed up the swim ladder onto the dock, but it only lasted until we heard the sound of someone clearing their throat. It wasn't an I-have-dust-in-my-throat cough either. It was the other kind.

A booming voice followed. It was female, deep, and full of authority. "What do you girls think you're doing?"

We both spun around. The woman was smaller than I would have guessed. Judging from that voice, I had expected somebody as big as a marine drill sergeant, but the woman waiting for us was tall and thin and dressed in a pair of navy blue slacks, a striped shirt, and nice flats. Her hair was going gray, but I sensed that she had enough energy to power Charleston for a week. I could tell that she would be pretty when she wasn't angry.

"We . . . got muddy," Bee said. "And we jumped in to wash off."

"Uh-huh. And you never heard of a garden hose or a shower?"

"Well, we just thought—"

"You didn't think anything. If you'd thought, you'd have remembered what the doctor said: 'Take it easy. No unnecessary activity. Let the joints heal.'"

With that the woman turned her attention to me. Her eyes were dark and as hard as marbles. They seemed to bore down into me and take me apart and sift through all my pieces to see what I was made of. After a few seconds, they appeared to reach a conclusion. Then, suddenly, they thawed and became as kind and warm as a gentle sunrise.

"You must be the girl who lives in the other house," she said, her voice just as deep as before but now soft and gentle as well.

"Yes, ma'am."

"What's your name?"

"Abbey, ma'am. Abbey Force."

She held out a hand, and we shook. Her fingers were long, her skin dry and smooth, and just like everything else about her, her grip had a surprising amount of strength. "I'm Bee's grandmother. You can call me Grandma Em. It's nice to meet you."

Just at that moment Rufus came up onto the dock and shook himself off, splattering water on everybody.

"Who is this?" demanded Grandma Em.

"That's Rufus," I said.

"Nice to meet you, Rufus," Grandma Em said. "But next time do your shaking farther away."

Her eyes hardened again as they flashed over to Bee, who was now strapping on her fiberglass cast. As Bee bent over her knee, Grandma Em gave her a light whack on the behind. "And next time," she said, "don't be thinking that swimming without a proper bathing suit is going to keep me from figuring out what you've been up to."

Bee mumbled a reply, and Grandma Em gave a tight nod, as if things had been taken care of. "Well, Abbey Force, what are you doing for lunch? Would you like to come join us?"

I still wasn't crazy about going into the big house, but I already realized that Grandma Em was a hard person to say no to. I nodded. "I'd like that. Thank you."

When we were dried off, we all walked up to the house. Rufus and I went last, and as I watched Bee with her metal cane, I could see that her limp was more pronounced than it had been earlier that morning. It was easy to see that our swim hadn't done her injuries any good at all, but she didn't complain.

We entered the big house through the kitchen door, and right away the familiar sights made the memories come rushing at me like hungry horses heading for the feed trough. I felt hot tears at the corners of my eyes and blinked furiously to keep them from falling. Rufus didn't seem to have any problems though. He curled up on the floor under the big kitchen table just like he'd lived there all his life.

Fortunately the smell of bacon distracted me, as

well as Grandma Em's insistence that we both go upstairs and take showers before lunch. She handed us clean towels and gave Bee a clean Ace bandage to put on her knee. We hurried up the back staircase to what used to be my room but now had new wallpaper and Bee's furniture rather than my own.

Bee started to take off her clothes, but then she stopped and looked at me. "Was this your room?"

I nodded.

"I'm sorry," she said. "It's a great room."

My throat felt thick. I nodded again because I didn't trust myself not to cry. I could tell that Bee sensed how I felt, and it made her uncomfortable. We hardly said another word as we finished showering and dressing.

I was wearing one of Bee's T-shirts and my own shorts as we headed down to lunch. At the bottom of the stairs, instead of turning toward the kitchen, I walked the other way and stopped outside the old cypress-paneled library. Bee followed without asking why we were going this way.

I stood staring into the room, and finally I sucked down a deep breath. "My daddy didn't do what they say he did," I blurted out. "And I'm gonna find a way to prove it."

Bee nodded, and I realized she must already know

the story of the accident and the stolen loot. "How are you going to do that?" she asked.

"I don't know yet."

A moment later we walked into the kitchen. Waiting for us on the table were plates of toast, fresh garden lettuce, ripe tomatoes, and crisp bacon.

"Are you girls hungry?" Grandma Em asked.

I hadn't been a bit hungry thirty seconds ago, but now I could hardly speak because my mouth was watering so hard. I just nodded. I hadn't had a lunch with real food like this since Daddy's accident.

We helped ourselves to all the fixings and made the most delicious BLT sandwiches I'd ever had, each of us eating an entire one on our own and then Bee and I splitting another between us. Afterward Grandma Em served chilled slices of fresh watermelon.

"What are you girls intending to do this afternoon?" Grandma Em asked as we finished eating.

"I was just thinking about that," I said. "Bee, if you're up for it, we could take a walk to explore the plantation."

"That would be a dry walk with no falling in the river?" Grandma Em said.

"Yes, ma'am."

She looked at Bee. "Be mindful of the cane," she

said. "It's harder to walk that way than it is to walk normally. Quit if you get sore."

We both nodded, and I could tell from looking at Bee that she was as eager to go exploring as I was to take her.

However, neither of us had a clue that what was supposed to be a simple plantation walk was going to turn into something a whole lot bigger.

Seven

After lunch Bee, Rufus, and I walked out the back door and set off to explore Reward. I made Rufus walk at heel as I led Bee toward the corner of the backyard, where a path led into the undergrowth and ran parallel to the river. We followed the path along the old raised dikes that used to mark the boundaries of the rice fields that had been the original cash crop for the owners of Reward. To our left the marsh that had once been rice fields waved with bright green sea grass.

After several hundred yards, the dikes ended and the path entered an area of wild Leadenwah Island undergrowth. It was shady and hot, without a breath of wind beneath the thick green canopy, and the air was even more humid and filled with faint, mingled fragrances of unseen flowers.

We could still see the river through the trees off to our left, its brown water glittering like hot butterscotch. To our right the heavy shrubbery of palmetto trees, live oaks, hanging drapes of Spanish moss, and tangles of honeysuckle and wild oleander and river oats and plants I couldn't begin to name cut off our view after only a few yards.

"Where did you live before you came to Leadenwah?" I asked Bee as we walked slowly along.

"Atlanta," she said.

"In a suburb?"

"Yeah."

"Leadenwah is real different from a suburb."

"Like how?" Bee asked.

I glanced over. I was keeping a careful eye on her, already realizing that she probably wouldn't complain even if her leg was really hurting. I made a promise to myself to suggest we go in if I saw her limp getting worse.

"Well, snakes, for starters. Do you have snakes in Atlanta?"

Bee laughed. "No, we have lots of houses, and in

the city we have taxicabs and cars and buses, just like in New York."

"Well, down here we have every single poisonous snake that lives in North America. We have lots of rattlesnakes. We have copperheads. We have a few coral snakes, and we have tons of cottonmouths."

I was talking so much, I didn't realize that Bee was no longer beside me. I turned to see her standing in the middle of the path, looking at me as if she half suspected I was putting her on.

I held up two fingers, close together. "Scout's honor," I said.

Bee made a face, then looked down at the ground, her eyes going to every root or dead stick that lay along the path. "I hate snakes," she said with a shudder.

"I'm not so fond of them myself," I said. "But just make some noise when you walk around in the woods and don't go too fast. Rattlesnakes and copperheads will get out of your way if they possibly can. Coral snakes are very rare."

"You didn't say anything about cottonmouths."

"They can be a little uglier," I admitted.

"What's that mean?"

"Well, they'll come after you if they feel threatened. That's the bad news. The good news is that they tend to live in swamps and around freshwater."

"Why is that good news?"

"Because we'll mostly stay away from swamps and freshwater."

"Because of the cottonmouths?"

"And the alligators."

"Next thing you'll be talking about tigers."

"Well, we do have Carolina panthers."

"The football team?"

"No, the wildcats."

"Really?"

"People say they're still around. I've never seen one."

"But you're not kidding about the snakes and the alligators?"

I heard the challenge in Bee's voice. "Nope," I said. I knew she didn't quite believe me, so when we came to a place where a narrower path branched in from the right and joined our path, I said, "Come on."

"Where are we going?"

"Change of plans."

I didn't look back, but I could sense Bee's tension. We walked up the new path until the undergrowth started to thin out and give way to lines of graceful longleaf pines. Ahead of us a pond glittered, its water silver and broken into small shards of light by the wind.

The pond was large, probably a hundred acres in area and longer than it was wide. A small dock stood along the near shore, and on it was a small fiberglass fishing canoe that had belonged to Daddy. I realized suddenly that no one had bothered to come to collect it and store it before the plantation had been sold, and I felt a blast of shame that I hadn't thought of it myself.

"It's pretty," Bee said, holding one hand over her brow to shade her eyes from the sun. "Does it have a name?"

"One Arm Pond," I told her.

"That's a weird name."

"It was named for one of my great-great-great-uncles who lost his arm to an alligator here."

"Sure," Bee said. From her tone she was certain I was pulling her leg.

I grabbed Rufus by his collar and held on tight as I led Bee out onto the dock. Rufus was pretty well trained, but he was a Labrador retriever and there was no way I could trust him to stay out of the water.

"Look over there," I told Bee.

She squinted for nearly a minute at where I was pointing along the far bank of the pond. "I don't see anything."

As she spoke, something small wriggled from a dark spot beside the bank and slid into the water. A second small thing followed. They were nearly a hundred yards away, and it was very hard to see them in the glare.

"Did you see that?" I asked.

"Yeah."

"Those are alligators."

Bee laughed. "They're barely as big as my foot. They couldn't eat my little finger."

"Those are the babies," I said. I pointed to their left at a pair of bumps in the water that were the eyes and another bump that was two close-set nostrils. About ten feet behind the nose, the tip of a massive tail gently moved.

"Right there you can see the mother." I pointed at where the tail, moving just beneath the surface, pushed up a small swell.

Bee looked at where I pointed for several seconds. "Is that little thing her nose?"

"Yes. We call her Green Alice. She's about ten feet long and probably weighs around eight hundred pounds. If we went out in the canoe right now and got close to her nest, she would attack us, because she'd think we were threatening her babies. If Rufus went in the water, she would eat him for a between-meal snack."

"That's why you're holding his collar?"

"Darn right. If Rufus got in that water and Alice started coming for him, he wouldn't be safe even if he made it to shore. A lot of people don't know it, but a gator is even faster than a dog on dry land for about thirty yards or so."

"Faster than a dog?"

I nodded. "Gators can't turn and they can't run very far, but over a short distance they're really, really fast."

Bee turned to look at me and nodded. "You're serious. You're not pulling my leg."

"Not a bit. I'm trying to tell you things you have to know here."

"Thanks," she said. I watched her hurry off the dock, limping as quickly as possible back toward the relative safety of the path.

We retraced our steps to the original path and turned right to keep exploring. The river was visible on our left, and every few yards we would get a peek through the thick vegetation on our right and see One Arm Pond glimmering fifty yards away. Every time we caught sight of the pond, Bee must have started thinking about Green Alice, because she moved a little faster.

When we were past the pond, the undergrowth began to thin as it gave way to several hundred acres of pine forest. Ahead of us the path begin to curve to the right, following the gentle bend of the river. I smiled in anticipation of what was ahead, just around the turn in the river. It wasn't really a secret, of course, but it was almost invisible to anyone boating on the river who didn't know it was there. Felony Bay tucked into the plantation in the shape of a huge teardrop. Also, unlike the pluff-mud banks that ran along almost the entire riverfront, the bay had a sand beach all the way around it.

From the Leadenwah River, the bay's entrance looked like nothing more than a narrow creek, because its sides were overgrown by aquatic plants that moved aside when a boat came through, then immediately sprang back to cover up the passage. What looked like a shallow creek was more than ten feet deep at the center. The bay itself probably didn't take up more than three or four acres. However, just like the entrance, the water was uniformly deep, which made it an excellent and totally protected anchorage, especially for people who wanted to stay hidden. It had gotten the name Felony Bay because most of the people who put their ships there over the years had been criminals.

Before Daddy's accident, whenever I had been in a really dreamy mood, I used to come down and sit on the beach at Felony Bay and think about some of the tales he had told me about it. I would close my eyes and imagine Indians slipping into the bay in their canoes to hide from enemies, or some big old sailing ship anchored there with a crew of pirates who were hiding from the British navy. Other times I would imagine the dashing captains of Confederate blockade-runners, who had brought damaged ships into Felony Bay for secret repairs.

I knew that Bee would find Felony Bay fascinating, too. I wanted her to lie in the sand right on the edge of the bay, close her eyes, and try to imagine the sights and smells and sounds as I told her its stories.

I was so busy thinking about how I wanted to tell those stories that I didn't see the signs. It was only when Bee asked, "What are those?" that I looked up and noticed them.

I felt my breath catch in my throat as I stared in utter surprise. Just ahead of us, a line of brand-new yellow signs that said No Trespassing ran from tree to tree as far as I could see, cutting us off from Felony Bay.

I stopped and stared. What I was seeing made no sense. "No Trespassing?" I said. I walked over to one of the signs and read the smaller print underneath. "Trespassers will be prosecuted to the fullest extent of the law. FB Land Company, LLC, owners."

I shook my head. "That's crazy. This land is part of Reward Plantation. This belongs to your family."

I turned to look at Bee. She shrugged. "If my father had sold part of the plantation, he would have told Grandma Em."

We stood there looking at the signs, neither one of us saying anything. Finally I said, "Even if your dad had somebody put these up, he wouldn't mean for you to keep out, would he?"

"No."

We nodded to each other and stepped inside the line of No Trespassing signs. As we went a little farther, we began to hear the sound of machinery. It sounded like a truck or bulldozer growling back and forth, or like somebody using an excavator to dig a hole.

We continued up the path another hundred yards until we could see light coming through the trees, and beyond that the warm glow of Felony Bay's mud-colored water under the early-afternoon sun. The machinery sound was much louder here, and as we went forward, I could see something moving down the beach.

For a few seconds I thought that Bee's father might have hired contractors to build something here, maybe a guesthouse or a boat shed, and maybe the contractors had put up the signs to keep people out while they worked. It seemed like there had to be a normal explanation, so we started to walk out of the undergrowth and into the open.

The first thing that came into view was the old, abandoned cabin. It was off to our right, and it was in bad shape. Its roof had started to sag in several places, and the walls of the rear section were starting to lean to one side.

"What's that?" Bee asked.

"It belonged to the family of a friend of mine, Skoogie Middleton. His grandparents used to live there, but then his grandpa died, and his grandmother moved out. It was a long time ago."

"But you said this was part of Reward."

"It is, but . . . I don't really understand much about it," I admitted. "All that stuff happened before Daddy and I came here to live. Skoogie and his grandma live in a trailer down the road now."

"Did she move because the house was falling apart? That seems kind of crummy to let that happen."

I glanced at Bee, wondering if she was accusing Daddy of something. "It happened back when Uncle Charlie was running things on the plantation. My grandfather was still alive, but he was sick and in the hospital. Daddy was a lawyer in New York City then, so he didn't have anything to do with Reward. Besides, I was really young and my mother was sick with cancer."

Bee scrunched up her face. "I wasn't saying your dad did anything bad, but from what I hear from Grandma Em, your uncle Charlie sounds like a jerk."

I let out a laugh, and I might have told her a whole lot more about Uncle Charlie, but at that point the machine we had heard a minute earlier suddenly belched out a loud roar that made us look to our left. We stepped farther into the open to get a better view, and I spotted one of those small digging machines with a bulldozer blade on one end and a little steam-shovel bucket on the other. It was digging a hole in the sand a few yards from the water, one of about twenty holes that dotted the shoreline of Felony Bay. Maybe the foundations for a bunch of boat docks? I wondered if Bee's dad was trying to start a marina and hadn't bothered to tell her. Whatever was happening, it was a lot of development.

Just about then the man who was driving the machine spotted us. He brought the bucket to a sudden halt, jumped out of his driver's seat, and ran toward us. "Hey!" he yelled. He was big, with powerful-looking arms and a dirty T-shirt. His hair was short but still managed to look messy, and a couple inches of scraggly black beard covered his cheeks and chin. I recognized Bubba Simmons, Leadenwah Island's part-time deputy sheriff. Not to mention the father of Jimmy Simmons, the kid who had tried to choke me to death.

"What y'all think you're doin' here?" he demanded. His voice was low and full of menace. "Can't y'all read signs?"

Rufus was on my left, his neck hair bristling, a low growl coming from his throat. I grabbed his collar to keep him from doing anything I'd regret. Bee came up on my other side and pulled herself erect. "We can be here if we want. My father owns this land," she said.

"Like heck he does. This ain't part of that plantation," he said, pointing in the direction of Reward. "Y'all, git!"

"I know who you are, Mr. Simmons," I said.

"Yeah, and I know you, too."

I stuck out my chin. "This land has always been part of Reward," I said.

He looked at me, and his face grew red. "Well, it ain't anymore. So I'm tellin' you for the last time, you git off this property! You don't move right now, I'll arrest you both."

I stood my ground. "If this isn't part of Reward, who owns it?"

"None a your business," Bubba growled, and started toward us.

He was the kind of person who looked half crazy when he got angry. Bee and I started to edge back toward the path as Bubba kept coming. We were almost running, and I could hear Bee sucking air between her teeth and I knew her leg had to be hurting bad.

Bubba followed us all the way out to the No Trespassing signs; then he stayed there and watched as we headed back toward the big house. I walked behind Bee, going as slow as she needed to as she limped along on her cane. I felt like a dog who was running away with its tail between its legs. It made me mad to get chased off, but it also made me curious. Something weird was going on at Felony Bay. If the land wasn't part of Reward anymore, I wanted to know why. Also who had bought it, and why were they digging holes and chasing everybody off?

When we got back into the yard by the big house, Bee turned to me. "Let's not say anything to Grandma Em about that guy."

"Why?"

"She'll just tell me I'm never allowed to go near that corner of the property again. Trust me. I know how she thinks."

"Okay." I shrugged and followed her into the

kitchen, where we found Grandma Em cutting up a fresh chicken for that night's dinner. She glanced at us over her shoulder. Maybe she saw the way my eyes went straight to the chicken, or maybe she knew how much I had loved her BLT sandwiches, because she asked, "Bee, you want to ask your friend to stay for dinner? We have plenty of food."

Bee smiled and looked at me. "Want to join us?"

I nodded. "Thanks." My mouth was already salivating at the prospect of having two home-cooked meals on the same day.

"She's going to stay," Bee said.

Grandma Em let me use her phone to call Ruth and let her know I wouldn't be home for dinner. The two of us started to walk out of the kitchen, but then Bee stopped and said, offhanded like, "Hey, Grandma, when we were walking around, we saw No Trespassing signs on some trees, but Abbey was pretty sure it's our property. You know anything about that?"

Grandma Em shook her head. "The only thing I really know about is this house and the grass that's right around it. Best ask your daddy when you talk to him."

Bee went on. "But he wouldn't have sold some of the land without saying something, would he?"

Grandma Em put her hands on her hips and gave

her head a shake. "Honey, that son of mine is too busy on that company he bought in India to think about anything else." She turned toward the sink, and I heard her mutter, "Including his own family."

Bee and I walked out of the kitchen, and Bee motioned me upstairs. "Okay," she said. "So if my dad hasn't sold any land, what do you think is going on? Did your dad sell that land to somebody else and not tell you?"

"No," I said.

"You sure?"

"Positive."

"I hate it when some rude person tells me something is none of my business," Bee said.

"So do I."

Bee nodded. "So we ought to figure out what's going on."

I smiled and grabbed a pen and a pad of paper from her desk. "Let's write down what we need to know. I'll make the list."

Bee nodded. "First, if part of the plantation got sold, when and how did it happen?"

"Great question," I said, writing it down. "The problem is Uncle Charlie was the real-estate agent who sold Reward to your dad."

"You can't just ask him?"

"You have to know Uncle Charlie," I said. "I don't think he'd tell me if my clothes were on fire."

Bee laughed, but then I saw her give me a searching look, as if she had as many questions about my life as I had about hers. Neither one of us was giving much away.

"Another question," Bee said, after a few seconds. "If my dad didn't buy Felony Bay, who did?"

I nodded and wrote the question down.

"And why do you think they were digging those holes?" Bee asked.

I wrote down *Holes?*

"They sure had dug a lot of them," Bee said. "But that reminds me. Who was that man?"

"Bubba Simmons," I said. "He's a part-time deputy sheriff on Leadenwah Island, but he's somebody you want to stay away from. Daddy used to say that Bubba's naturally mean, and when he's drunk he's even meaner. Daddy also said that Bubba drinks a lot."

Bee smiled, but her face became serious. "We have to figure out if my dad was cheated when he bought this place." She reached for the list I had made and started looking it over.

While she did that, my own thoughts wandered back

nine months earlier to when I had made a similar list, writing down the questions that needed to be answered to prove Daddy's innocence. I still had the list beside my bed, folded up in my diary. I hadn't looked at the questions in a long time, but I didn't need to because I knew them all by heart.

Daddy was strong and healthy and never a klutz, so how did he end up falling off the ladder?

The ladder was in the middle of the room, far away from his desk, so what did he hit his head on to get hurt so badly?

If he stole Miss Jenkins's jewelry, when did he do it and why were there so few pieces left? What happened to all the rest?

Daddy had plenty of money in the bank, and his accountants could show how all the money came from his law practice. So if he stole Miss Jenkins's gold and jewels and sold them, where was the money?

Daddy was always totally honest in all the things he ever did. If he didn't need the money, why would he choose to steal from Miss Jenkins?

If Daddy didn't steal the gold and jewels, who did?

If someone else did, how did they steal it?

Is it possible that Daddy was framed so that somebody else could get away with the crime?

I had taken my list of questions to the police and to Mr. Crawford Barrett, Daddy's law partner. I had asked them to help me get answers, but now, nine months later, not a single one of my questions had ever been answered.

Bee looked up when she finished reading and then handed the list back to me. I folded the piece of paper and put it in my pocket for safekeeping. "Tomorrow," I said, "we're going to start getting some answers."

Eight

I walked back to Uncle Charlie and Ruth's house that night after eating the most delicious roast chicken dinner with roasted baby potatoes and garden-fresh broccoli. Rufus trotted beside me, full from his own dinner of chicken scraps. The moon was nearly full, rising over the trees in the eastern sky and giving plenty of light to lead me home.

The piece of paper with all the questions Bee and I had written down bulged in my back pocket, and the need for answers was burning in my brain. How was it possible that Felony Bay had been sold to somebody else? Reward Plantation had been in my family from the early seventeen hundreds to nine months earlier, roughly three hundred years. Daddy never would have broken up the land unless he'd been desperate. So who had done it, and how had it happened, and why? Those No Trespassing signs at Felony Bay made me angry, as if a chunk of our land had been stolen right out from under our noses.

One thing I was sure of was that Uncle Charlie had at least some of the answers. I wanted to march right into the house and demand that he tell me what was going on. Who had bought the land? Had he had something to do with it? Why had he let that happen, and why hadn't he said anything? Did Bee's father know that part of the original plantation land had been sold to someone else? There were so many questions and no answers.

I also knew that I needed to be careful. Uncle Charlie was strange about a lot of things, and giving up information was definitely one of them. Daddy always said that liars are the most suspicious people of all, always convinced that someone's trying to put one over on them, since they're always doing the same. That was Uncle Charlie, all right. Every time I asked him something, he looked at me like I was trying to trick him. That was especially true when he'd been drinking, which by this time of night was guaranteed.

I walked up the dirt track toward the house so deep in thought that at first I didn't notice the pickup truck parked out in front. But Rufus saw it. Down by my side, he started to make a low growl, and I put my hand on his head and hushed him, pulling him away from the center of the track, where we were outlined in the moonlight, over to where the field of corn whispered in the night wind. The stalks had already grown higher than my head, and I could stand inside one of the rows surrounded by the sweet, toasted smell of growing corn and look out at the car and the vague shapes of two men standing in the yard just beyond it.

I crept down the row and found a place where one of the stalks had fallen and I could cross silently to the next row. There I found another fallen stalk and crossed another row, pulling Rufus along beside me, patting his head each time he started to growl. The hiss of wind moving through the corn blanketed any sound we made.

When I reached the last row of corn, I moved back toward the house and stopped. From here the voices of the two men were a little clearer, and I could make out the occasional word. I heard Uncle Charlie say, "Machine," and then another voice say, "Keep 'em out." That second voice I recognized because I had heard it just that afternoon. My stomach froze, and I felt both sweaty and cold at the same time.

A second later the truck door opened, and then its engine started. It was louder than a normal engine; it must have had a busted muffler. I squatted in the corn beside Rufus as the truck backed up and made a K-turn. For a second its headlights panned across the cornfield and outlined the rows of stalks in sharp relief, and then they were pointing down the driveway. As the truck drove past, I caught a quick peek at the driver, with his messy hair and black whiskers. My suspicions were right. There was no mistaking Bubba Simmons.

I continued to hold on to Rufus's collar until Uncle Charlie's footsteps on the front porch and then the slam of the door told me he'd gone back inside, but when I let go, Rufus didn't move a muscle. I realized that he didn't like Uncle Charlie any better than I did, and I gave his ears a scratch.

We waited for a couple more minutes, then circled the house and walked in the back door, where Ruth was reading a magazine at the kitchen table. "Where you been?" she asked, as if she didn't remember that I had called earlier to tell her I would be having dinner at Bee's.

"The big house."

She sniffed. "Don't get used to it. You don't live there anymore, and you got dishes to do here, girl."

I bit my tongue, tied on an apron, and started rinsing dishes and loading them in the dishwasher. There was no use trying to talk to Ruth when Uncle Charlie was home. I had realized some time ago that even if Ruth was nice on occasion, she was just as mean as Uncle Charlie when he was around.

As soon as I'd finished the dishes, I walked to the doorway of the small den, where Uncle Charlie was watching television and drinking a beer. He glanced at me, and his face darkened.

"What?"

"Good evening to you, too," I said.

My heart was bucking in my chest. I told myself to calm down, but I had a hunch that I was about to open a big can of worms.

"I was out walking today," I began.

Uncle Charlie stared at the TV, not bothering to acknowledge that he was listening.

"Up toward Felony Bay, I saw a bunch of No Trespassing signs strung up on the trees."

"Uh-huh," he said.

"What's the story?" I asked.

Uncle Charlie's eyes got smaller. I could tell from

his expression that he was trying hard to be cagey. "What're y'all talking about?"

"I mean why are signs there?"

"'Cause maybe the new owners don't want y'all walkin' on their land."

"Mr. Force is the new owner. His daughter doesn't know anything about this either."

Uncle Charlie gave me a pained look. "He might a bought the plantation, but he ain't the new owner of Felony Bay."

My jaw dropped, but I quickly picked it up. "How's that possible?" I managed after a few seconds.

"Simple. Felony Bay was a separate piece of property."

"No, it wasn't."

Uncle Charlie's cheeks grew red. "Don't argue with me, girl. If I said it was a separate piece, it was a separate piece."

"Since when?"

"Long time."

"So . . . who owns it now?"

"If they wanted y'all to know, I guess they would a come over and introduced themselves."

"But you know who they are."

Uncle Charlie's eyes glimmered with his secret

knowledge. "Maybe I do."

"And you're not going to say."

"Ain't none a your beeswax." Then Uncle Charlie said something that I didn't expect. He looked at me and smiled. "But you'll find out soon enough."

I went to bed a few minutes later, but I lay awake for a long time watching the moon through my window and wondering about Felony Bay and what Uncle Charlie was up to.

Nine

In spite of staying up a lot of the night tossing and turning with questions I couldn't answer, I woke up extra early the next morning when Rufus stuck his wet nose in my face. As if that wasn't enough to drag me out of sleep, Rufus gassed me with his Labrador retriever breath. It was almost strong enough to kill.

I ate my usual bowl of cereal and fed Rufus, then the two of us snuck out the back door and headed to the pasture. Since the moment I'd opened my eyes, I had been thinking about the same things that had kept me up the night before—the No Trespassing signs, the holes, Uncle Charlie, and Bubba Simmons.

The temperature had dropped a bit overnight. Heavy dew lay on the grass, and thick fog drifted off the river, lending everything a mysterious quality that only sharpened my hunger for answers. Timmy and his fellow horses, Clem and Lem, looked as indistinct as ghosts where they stood against the fence. As soon as Timmy caught my scent, he nickered and came over to nuzzle me. You could barely see twenty feet in front of you, and Timmy's back was dripping with dew and drifting fog, so rather than try to ride, I led him to the barn.

I fed and watered the horses, and when they finished their grain, I dried their backs and put on the fly coats they would need when the sun burned through. I did other chores, and once the fog started to lift, I let them back out in the pasture.

A yell came from back behind me. Bee was limping down the track on her way from the big house. "You done already?"

"Couldn't sleep thanks to Rufus, so I decided to get an early start."

"I was coming down to help," she said, sounding disappointed that she hadn't gotten there in time. A second later her thoughts seemed to shift, and she brightened. "Guess what! My dad called from India last night, and I asked him about that property."

"What did he say?"

"He got on his computer and looked at the survey he received when he bought the plantation. He says there isn't anything on the property that looks like a bay. He also said that while lots of parts of the plantation have names, there's no Felony Bay."

I nodded. "Uncle Charlie basically admitted that the land was sold to somebody else, but he won't tell me who. Also, when I walked home last night, Bubba Simmons was at our house. I overheard him and Uncle Charlie talking about the holes and keeping us off the property."

Bee looked at me a moment. "What do you think this is all about?"

I shook my head. "I think we need to find out."

"So what are we going to do?" Bee asked.

"We need to get the facts."

"How?"

I took a deep breath. "We need to go downtown and check the property records. One of the only things Uncle Charlie said was that Felony Bay was a separate property. I'm pretty sure it wasn't, and I want to find out if he was lying. Either way, I think there are records and things we can search. If somebody bought Felony

Bay, once we find out who they are, maybe we can figure out why they did and what they're doing."

After I'd said it all out loud, the stuff we needed to do sounded really boring, and I was afraid Bee would want no part in it.

"So when do we start?"

I blinked. "I beg your pardon?"

"You do want my help, don't you?"

"Of . . . of course!" I said, unable to hide my surprise and my pleasure. "I just didn't think you'd want to."

Bee glanced at her wristwatch. "We should go up to the house right now. Grandma Em is planning to go out shopping, and it sounds like we need to get a ride downtown."

We walked up to the big house and found Grandma Em just about to get in her car and leave. Bee asked if we might come along with her.

"What do you girls need to do in town?" Grandma Em asked in her deep voice. "Please don't tell me you need to shop."

The thought of shopping made me glance involuntarily at Bee, and I felt a sudden sense of dread. What if she wanted to go shopping before we did our research? I didn't want to go into fancy stores where I wouldn't have any money to buy anything and where I'd feel bad about my own clothes. Bee was tall and thin, and I have to admit she looked pretty in her well-fitting jeans. Her top definitely hadn't come off the rack at a discount store. And her hair was straight and recently cut, and she had small gold-knot earrings that set everything off.

I couldn't help feeling shabby in my old jeans that were already too short and my Atlanta Braves T-shirt that Ruth had bought at a church consignment shop a few months back. My ears weren't pierced, because Daddy had said we were going to wait to do that on my twelfth birthday, and then he'd had his accident and Ruth couldn't have cared less. Unlike Bee's perfect hair, mine was curly and dark blond, and it only got cut when Ruth told me it looked as bushy as a palmetto tree. When it was cut short, I looked more like a boy, and when it was long, like a scruffy girl. Neither made me want to hang out in fancy stores where I couldn't buy anything anyway.

When Bee replied to Grandma Em, my worries disappeared. "We're not shopping," she shot back, as if the very idea was beneath us. "We're working on a mystery."

Grandma Em raised her eyebrows slowly in a way that oozed suspicion. "What kind of mystery?"

"A mystery about some land that used to be part of Reward Plantation but that didn't get sold to Daddy when he bought it," Bee said.

Grandma Em seemed to think about that for a moment. She looked at me. "So what are you planning to do?"

"Talk to one of the lawyers at my father's firm and go to the library."

"That's all?"

"Yes, ma'am," I said.

"Well, I'm going to be a while. I have a hair appointment, and then I have some shopping to do. You think that mystery will keep you girls busy for five hours or so?"

"Yes, ma'am," I said.

She shrugged and gave us a wave. "Come on."

We climbed into the car, and as we headed into town, I thought of one more thing. "Would you mind if we went to one other place?" I asked.

I was sitting in the backseat, and Grandma Em glanced over her shoulder. "Where to?"

"The hospital. My dad is there. It won't take long, and then we'll take the bus the rest of the way downtown."

"Have you taken the bus by yourself before?"

"Yes, ma'am. Lots of times."

In the front seat Bee's head was turned. I felt her looking at me out of the corner of her eye, but she didn't say anything. I didn't understand the look, but before I could say anything, Grandma Em broke the silence.

"I'm sorry about your dad," she said. "How long has he been in the hospital?"

I felt my stomach clench. "Nine months."

Grandma Em nodded. Bee kept looking at me.

No one said anything for a long moment. The silence was becoming awkward. I felt like something weird was going on between all of us, but I had no idea what it was or exactly what had caused it.

"He's in a coma," I said, when I couldn't stand it any longer. "I go in and talk to him because I hope maybe he'll hear me and wake up."

Grandma Em seemed to think about that for an awfully long time. She gave Bee a sideways glance, then nodded. "Okaaaay," she said, drawing the word out. "I guess we could stop at the hospital and let you go talk to your dad. Does that sound okay to you, Bee?"

I was surprised at the way she asked the question, but then I was even more surprised at Bee's reaction. She sat there, perfectly still, looking as though she was frozen. Finally, looking as if it took a lot of effort, she gave her head a tiny nod. "Yes, it's okay," she whispered.

Grandma Em drove us to the Medical University Hospital, pulled over to the curb, and gave Bee another long look.

"Okay?" she asked again.

I realized her question had nothing to do with me or my father. It had something to do with Bee, but I didn't know what.

Bee sat with the same rigid posture, staring straight ahead. She gave her head another little nod. "Yes." Once again her voice was a choked whisper.

Grandma Em reached out and gave Bee's arm a little squeeze. "Okay then."

Bee opened the car door and climbed out. I did the same.

Grandma Em put down her window and glanced at her watch. "It's ten o'clock. What are you girls doing for lunch?"

I opened my mouth and closed it again. I had been planning to skip lunch or maybe buy a candy bar, because I had only a little over a dollar to my name.

"Do you know a place you can eat near where you're going?" she asked.

"Yes, ma'am, but . . ."

Grandma Em smiled. She seemed to sense my discomfort and maybe even guessed my problem. "I forgot to tell you, lunch is my treat." She took some money from her purse and put it into Bee's hand. "Just don't eat junk."

I glanced at Bee and then I started to say, "It's okay, I—" but Grandma Em talked right over my words.

"Where do you want me to pick you up?"

"I . . . at the Library Society on King Street," I replied. "But I—"

"Library Society," she repeated, and typed the name into her phone. "Got it. I'll be out in front at about three o'clock. You girls be ready."

"Yes, ma'am," Bee said.

Grandma Em waved and drove away.

I turned and started walking toward the hospital entrance, but after a second I realized that Bee wasn't with me. I looked back and saw her. She was watching Grandma Em's car, and as it disappeared around a corner, I heard a sound almost like a sob escape Bee's lips.

Finally she took a deep breath and turned to face me.

"You all right?" I asked.

She nodded, even though she looked anything but okay.

Ten

ee and I walked out of the muggy South Carolina heat into the cool air of the hospital, and I headed toward the elevators. I pushed the button for Daddy's floor, then looked around, expecting to find Bee right behind me, but she wasn't there. I was surprised to see that she had hung back and come to a stop only a foot or two inside the front doors.

Just as she had outside, she appeared frozen. Her eyes were tilted upward, but not really looking at anything. The expression on her face made me think that something was frightening her very badly. I walked back to her, but when she didn't look at me, I touched her shoulder.

"Bee?"

She started a little, then pulled her eyes down to my face. It seemed to take a lot of effort. "Hospitals just freak me out," she said. "Sorry."

"No problem," I said. "You want to stay down here or come up?"

She seemed to think it over as her eyes roamed the waiting area with its couches and chairs. "I guess I'll come with you," she finally said.

I nodded, and we walked toward the elevators. When one came, I pressed the button for the sixth floor and we went up. I led Bee down to the doors that opened onto Daddy's hallway, hit the buzzer, then waved to the nurse, who came to see who wanted in.

"You brought a friend?" she asked.

I nodded. "This is Bee."

Bee said a quick hello. She was glancing around, looking everywhere at once, nervous as a pig at a barbecue contest.

"This way," I said, and headed toward Daddy's room. The door was open, and I walked inside the way I always did, with a loud, cheerful greeting.

"Morning, Daddy," I said. "Time to wake up. You have a guest today."

Of course he didn't move, just lay there with his

hands at his sides, the tubes carrying the liquids and food into his wrist and down his nose into his stomach.

I heard a noise in the doorway and turned. Bee was gripping the side of the door as if she was afraid she might fall down. The expression on her face had hardened. There was no mistaking that just being here struck terror into her heart.

Not knowing what else to do, I turned back to Daddy. "Our guest's name is Bee. Her last name is Force, same as ours. She's not a blood relative, but she is kin, as you'd say. She's also my new best friend."

I glanced back again at Bee. She was staring hard at Daddy, but my words seemed to have helped. She took one step into the room, then two. She stopped at the end of the bed.

"Hi, Mr. Force," she said in a very soft voice.

"Say it louder," I told her. "We want to wake him up."

"Hi, Mr. Force," Bee said, louder this time. I think she even smiled a little bit.

I turned back to Daddy. "We really need you to wake up, because we have so many questions we need to ask. Especially about Felony Bay. Uncle Charlie says it's a separate piece of property and not part of Reward. I don't really understand, but it seems like somebody bought it and put up No Trespassing signs."

ly just lay there. I glanced back at Bee. "Well, anyway, I just wanted to introduce you to my new friend and tell you that I really need to talk to you. The weather is good, and you're missing some really excellent fishing. Everyone says there are more redfish than ever. The plantation is beautiful. You really need to wake up. I love you."

I leaned over and kissed his head, and we left.

As we walked toward the elevator, Bee seemed to relax a little bit. "You made it sound like he still owns the plantation."

I nodded. "I'm afraid if I tell him the truth, he might not want to wake up. He loved Reward very, very much."

I pushed the button to call the elevator, then looked over and was shocked to see a tear running down Bee's cheek. I opened my mouth to say something when the elevator came. I glanced at it, saw that it was going up, and turned back to Bee. I was about to ask what was the matter when the elevator doors opened and I heard a man say, "Abbey, another nice surprise!"

I looked around again and saw that Mr. Barrett had just gotten off the elevator.

"Hi, Mr. Barrett," I said. "Visiting Daddy?"

"I sure am," he replied. "Have you been reading to him?"

"Not today. I just went in to say hello and introduce him to my friend Bee."

Mr. Barrett turned to Bee and held out his hand. "Hello, Bee. I'm Crawford Barrett. I'm Abbey's dad's law partner."

Bee took his hand and smiled. "Nice to meet you, sir."

"Bee's father is the new owner of Reward," I said.

"You're Bee Force, then?"

"Yessir."

"I'd love to meet your father when he has a few minutes."

"He's in India working on his business."

"Well, when he's back."

"Yessir, I'll make sure to tell him."

"That would be kind of you. So how does the rest of your family like living on Reward?"

"It's just me and my grandmother," she said in a low voice.

I knew by now it was probably best to change the subject when it came to Bee's family. "Is Custis in the office today?"

"Yes," Mr. Barrett said. "Stop on in if you're

downtown. I know he'd love to see you."

The down elevator arrived, and the doors opened. Bee and I walked past Mr. Barrett with a wave.

I took a quick look inside the elevator, checking to make sure that there was plenty of room. Besides Bee and me there was just a lady in a wheelchair, along with her nurse. I barely glanced at them as I got on, stood beside Bee, and turned around to face the doors. I had one single thing on my mind, because I knew Bee was holding back some big secret about her family. I had told her everything about my family, and while I knew she didn't want to talk about hers, I hoped she would open up one day soon.

Just then one of the people behind us made kind of a choking sound, and I turned. It was the lady in the wheelchair, but when I looked at her face and recognized her, I felt the breath catch in my throat as a red blush that was equal parts shame and anger spread over my face.

I knew that Bee picked right up on it, because she turned slightly as her eyes shifted from me to the lady in the wheelchair, then back to me.

I wouldn't normally have paid that much attention to a silent old lady in a wheelchair. However, I noticed every single thing about Miss Lydia Jenkins. She was the lady whose jewelry and gold Daddy was supposed to have stolen.

Miss Jenkins would have been tall if she had been able to stand up, but the stroke she had suffered a couple years earlier pretty much paralyzed her, and she was old and shriveled and hunched in her seat. In spite of the heat outside, her legs were covered with a crocheted cotton blanket, and her hands lay still atop it. I could see big, gross blue veins along the backs of them, and her fingers were long and crooked as sticks. They reminded me of osprey talons. Her cheeks were as pale and lifeless as lumps of dough. Her lips drooped, and a little line of spit ran from one corner of her mouth.

The only thing that showed she even knew what was going on around her was her eyes. They perched over her old, hawkish nose and glared out at the world with intelligence and a feverish intensity. They gave me the willies and reminded me of one of those horror movies where a bad person looks out through the eyes of a painting, so that only the eyes move and the rest of the face is frozen.

I would never have gotten into the elevator if I had recognized her, but now the doors were closed and we were already moving. I was trapped. I slid sideways, a little in front of Bee, wishing that Miss Jenkins's crazy eyes wouldn't find me. I totally forgot all my questions about Bee's mom, because being stuck this close to Miss Jenkins brought on all kinds of tangled emotions. Part of it was fear, as if she was a witch who had cursed my father and might curse me. Another part of it was anger that she hadn't done anything when the police had accused my father of stealing her jewelry. The other thing I felt was shame that so many people seemed to believe that Daddy could be a thief. Half of me wanted to scream at Miss Jenkins, but, to tell the truth, the other half realized that shouting at a paralyzed old woman was wrong, no matter what I felt.

I also recognized the other lady, the one who was pushing Miss Jenkins's wheelchair. It was Jimmy Simmons's mother, Esther. She was a pale woman and very thin, and her baggy housedress hung off her bony shoulders like a sack. Any time I had ever seen her I had thought she looked exhausted, just like she did now. If I hadn't known better, I would have said she looked like she had been plowing fields all morning rather than pushing a skinny old lady in a wheelchair.

Normally I would have felt sorry for someone who looked so beaten down, but I couldn't help wondering if she was part of the reason that her son, Jimmy, was such a jerk and a bully. I glanced in her direction and saw her staring at me out of her watery, unhappy eyes. Her expression was unfriendly, but that was nothing new. I couldn't imagine wanting someone like that to be my nurse, but I guessed that Miss Jenkins didn't have much of a choice, since she was paralyzed and could barely talk. Anyway, it seemed like Mrs. Simmons treated Miss Jenkins pretty well, even if she was mean as a snake to everybody else.

I turned and fixed my eyes on the light above the door as we descended at what seemed like a snail's pace. Hospital elevators may be the slowest contraptions in the world. I just wanted to get to the first floor and let Mrs. Simmons and Miss Jenkins turn one way, so that I could turn the other and get away as fast as I could.

We stopped at five. The doors opened, and two more people got on. When the doors closed again, the light changed to four. The two people got off. Finally we went to three, then two. That was when I heard Miss Jenkins starting to stir.

First she made that same choking noise in her throat again, and I realized maybe she was trying to say something. I glanced around and saw that she was moving a little, rocking her shoulders from side to side. It occurred to me that she might be choking.

Bee and I had inched over to the side of the elevator,

so Mrs. Simmons pushed the wheelchair forward a few feet until it was right in front of the doors. Then she moved around to where she could see Miss Jenkins's face. "Everything okay?" she asked.

Miss Jenkins rocked harder. The elevator light showed that we had reached the first floor. The car stopped. Slow seconds ticked by before the doors opened. Mrs. Simmons was still looking at Miss Jenkins, trying to figure out what was going on.

When Miss Jenkins got pushed forward, I had moved all the way into the corner, and Bee was now just behind me. When the doors opened, it was all I could do not to bolt out of that elevator, but with Bee crowding me from the back, I would have had to risk bumping against Miss Jenkins if I tried to get out. There was no way I was going to touch her if I could help it. I gave Bee a nudge to get her moving, thinking we might be able to go around behind Miss Jenkins and get past her on the other side, but Bee had heard the noises Miss Jenkins was making and turned to look at her.

We were all jammed up with the wheelchair and Mrs. Simmons and Bee blocking the way and nobody trying to push Miss Jenkins off. The bell dinged, and the doors started to close again. Mrs. Simmons seemed to realize what was happening, and she reached out and hit the door with her hand so that it opened again.

"'Scuse us," she said as she finally started to push Miss Jenkins out. It was early, the hospital still somewhat empty, and no one was waiting for the elevator. Mrs. Simmons got Miss Jenkins into the hallway; then for some reason she turned the wheelchair around again so that Miss Jenkins was facing the elevator.

Bee got off first. She turned to Miss Jenkins's left just as a couple of orderlies appeared from that same direction hurrying toward the elevator and pushing a patient on a gurney. "Please hold that elevator," one of them called.

Without thinking I stepped to the right, holding my arm against the elevator door to keep it open. As the gurney rolled onto the elevator, I stepped away, and that's when I felt the talons.

It was everything I could do not to jerk away and scream, but I stayed perfectly still. I thought Miss Jenkins was supposed to be paralyzed, but she had managed to reach out one hand and grip my arm just above the wrist. She was looking up at me out of those fierce hawk eyes, and for a half second I wondered if she was going to try and take a bite out of my flesh. But in the next second I saw something in her eyes very different from what I expected. Miss Jenkins seemed to be struggling as hard as she could against her paralysis, and for a couple of seconds I actually felt a little bit sorry for her.

It only lasted until she opened her mouth though. Her jaw jerked from side to side for a few seconds. Then she said what sounded like "S-s-s-stole ittt."

I barely made out the words, but they hit like a knife in my stomach. I felt a hot wash of anger and shame and grief and knew there were tears running down my cheeks. I tried to twist my arm free, but Miss Jenkins was amazingly strong.

"He did not!" I managed.

I was about to throw my whole body into jerking free when I felt Mrs. Simmons's fingers trying to pry me loose.

When the talons finally let go, I looked down at Miss Jenkins, but my eyes were so blurred that I could barely see. I turned and stumbled down the hallway in the direction of the exit. I lost track of Bee as I pushed through the doors and went outside, where I sucked the hot, humid air into my lungs and tried to stop shaking.

I started to calm down, enough to think anyway, and I turned to find Bee standing right behind me. She didn't say a word, but the look in her eyes told me that she understood.

Eleven

As Bee and I headed down the block to the bus stop, I could feel her gaze on me and the weight of her unspoken questions. We reached the stop and stood there, watching the traffic pass. Finally, knowing I had to say something, I turned.

"That lady, Miss Jenkins, thinks my father stole her money," I said. "I don't care what she said. He didn't steal anything from her, but he can't defend himself. And I don't understand how she just grabbed me like that. I thought she was paralyzed, but she held on like a monkey."

Bee looked at me, her expression serious and

thoughtful, as if she had something she wanted to say but was holding back. Finally she gave a nod. "Is she in that wheelchair because she had a stroke?"

I nodded.

"But she managed to tell the police that your dad stole her money?"

I shook my head, then paused. "Well, sort of. When my dad had his accident, the police found some of her jewelry in our house, and when they've asked her about it, all she's ever said are those two words, 'Stole it.' Everyone assumes she means Daddy."

"Sometimes, when people have strokes, it messes up their brain. It happened to my grandfather before he died, and Grandma Em explained it to me. People who've had a stroke might forget how to talk or eat. It might mess up the connection between what a person wants to say and what actually comes out of their mouth. Could be the same story with Miss Jenkins."

"I think she's a mean old witch."

"I watched her eyes. They weren't angry. I think she was struggling."

I wasn't so certain, but I didn't want to argue about it. It would have been nice to believe that she was right, but for Miss Jenkins to finally be able to say what she meant and for Daddy to miraculously wake up and be able to prove his innocence . . . it was a fairy tale.

Bee didn't say anything else, just put her arm around my shoulder. She seemed to be telling me that she believed in me, and in my father, no matter what. Maybe I didn't believe in fairy tales anymore, but it sure was nice to be able to believe in my friend and have her believe in me.

Twenty minutes later Bee and I were on Broad Street in downtown Charleston, heading toward Daddy's law office. Broad is one of the main streets in the city, and the corner of Meeting Street and Broad is called the Four Corners of Law. That's where the old post office, the county and federal courthouses, and City Hall are located. Like most of Charleston, nearly all of the buildings date back to the late seventeen hundreds or early eighteen hundreds, and they are almost all perfectly restored with polished brass and fresh paint.

Bee and I got to the four-story stucco building with the brass sign that said Force and Barrett, Attorneys at Law. Those names, of course, stood for my dad and Mr. Barrett. The building looked the way it always had, with its tall windows and mahogany door. I led Bee into the waiting room expecting to see Ms. Leland, the white-haired lady who had been the receptionist ever since Daddy had opened the office. To my surprise another lady sat behind the desk. She had red hair and bright red lipstick and a smile that wasn't anywhere near as friendly as Ms. Leland's.

"Can I help you?" she asked, looking at me as if a kid my age could not possibly have any reason to be there.

"I'd like to see Mr. Custis Pettigrew, please."

She raised her eyebrows. "Does he know you?"

"Yes," I said. "I'm Abbey Force."

The woman's eyebrows shot up. "The daughter of Rutledge Covington Force?"

"Yes."

"I see," she said, sounding slightly more polite but no happier than she had at the beginning.

"And this other young lady is with you?"

"Yes."

"And her name, please?"

Bee took a step forward. "Bee Force."

The woman looked back and forth between us, clearly curious, but I wasn't about to explain. I just looked at her and waited.

Several long seconds of silence went by while the woman stared and tried to wear me down. Finally I raised my eyebrows as if to say, *Let's get this show on the road.*

The woman's nostrils widened. She cleared her throat. "Let me see if he is in," she said. There was enough ice in her voice to cool a drink on a hot day.

She picked up the phone and dialed an office extension. When someone answered, she said, "Two young ladies named Abbey Force and Bee Force are here to see Mr. Pettigrew. Is he available?"

She listened for a second, then put down the phone. "Someone will be right out."

I recognized the next person who came into the room. Her name was Martha, and she had been Daddy's legal secretary for years. She was thickly built, with dark hair that was starting to go gray, soft brown eyes, and a face that seemed to fold naturally into a smile.

"Abbey!" she said, hurrying across to enfold me in a big hug.

After we hugged and said hello, I introduced Bee. Martha shook hands with Bee, then asked, "You need to see Custis? Is it urgent? He's got a pretty busy day."

I nodded. "I promise we won't be long, but we're not just here to say hello. We need to ask him about something." I nodded toward Bee. "Bee's father bought Reward Plantation, but part of the plantation got sold to somebody else. We need to ask Custis about it."

Martha raised her eyebrows. "I see. Well, come on back."

We followed Martha through the mahogany door on one side of the waiting room and down the hallway to the lawyers' offices. We passed several open doors, where young lawyers were either typing on their computers or reading thick stacks of documents.

At the end, where the hallway turned to the left, Martha and Bee kept going, but I stopped and looked inside the open door at the empty corner office. The lights were turned off, but you could see enough in the sunlight coming in through the slats of the half-closed venetian blinds.

My heart caught in my throat as I looked at Daddy's desk, the blotter now clear of the big piles of legal folders that used to be stacked there. His pens and a few perfectly sharpened pencils were sticking out of his University of Virginia mug the way they always had. On the credenza behind his desk I could see the pictures that had always been there. There was one of my mother taken at their wedding and another of her holding me as a baby. There she was skiing, just a year before she died. Then there were lots of pictures of me swimming, playing tennis, and riding Timmy.

Right there, seeing his office as if nothing had ever

changed, I could imagine that he had just stepped away and that any second he would come striding down the hall. I could imagine that he and I would get in his car and drive home to Reward and have dinner together the way we had almost every night.

My thoughts were interrupted when I felt Martha's hand on my shoulder. "You okay?" she asked softly.

I nodded.

"I miss him, too," Martha said.

"I know." Then I turned and looked up at Martha. "He'll be back," I said. "He didn't take anything."

Martha looked at me, and her expression hardened. All her softness seemed to bleed away, and she nodded. "I know he didn't," she said, her voice very firm.

"Thank you for believing in him," I said.

Martha shook her head. "Don't thank me. I know what your daddy's made of."

Bee was waiting a few steps farther down the hall, and when Martha and I caught up, she gave me a smile. Whatever was going on with her family, it seemed to help her understand what I was going through with mine. I was grateful for that.

Martha knocked on the door of an open office and stuck her head inside. "Two young ladies to see you about some free legal advice," she said.

I heard Custis's voice boom out, "Send them in, Martha."

By the time Bee and I stepped into his office, Custis was already up out of his chair and coming around his desk. He was tall and lean, with black hair that curled just over his ears and twinkly blue eyes. He had his coat off and wore a white shirt rolled up to the elbows and a bow tie.

"This is a great surprise," he said, giving me a big hug.

I introduced Bee, and he shook hands with her and waved us to his couch. Martha asked if we would like anything to drink, then walked away to get two Cokes for us and a water for Custis.

Custis sat in a chair across from us and crossed his legs. "I understand you need a little help with some problem," he said.

One of the many things I have always liked about Custis is that he never talked to me like I was a little kid. Another reason I had come to see him was because Daddy always liked Custis the best out of all the lawyers in the firm. He and Custis used to go fishing for redfish and hunting for doves and wild turkey and quail on the weekends, and Custis used to come over to our house for dinner a couple times every month.

Daddy and Custis had both gone to the University of Virginia, and when they talked about it, they called it The University, as if there wasn't another university in the United States that was worth mentioning. In the fall Custis would usually come over on Sunday afternoons when the Cavaliers were playing on television, and in the winter he would come over on nights when he and Daddy could watch basketball. They would laugh and cheer together when the Cavaliers occasionally won a football game or had a good basketball season, and they would mope around when they lost.

I knew Custis well enough to know that if I ever decided I liked boys enough to marry one, I wanted him to be like Custis—handsome, funny, honest, and a good friend. I started out shooting straight because I trusted him.

"You've heard of Felony Bay, haven't you?" I asked.

Custis nodded immediately. "Of course. I mean, I know it by name. It's part of Reward, isn't it?"

I nodded. "Well, it *was* part of Reward. Apparently it's not any longer."

Custis cocked his head and gave me a confused look, so I went on. "Bee's father now owns Reward."

Custis looked at Bee and nodded. "You're lucky. It's a very beautiful place."

"Yessir," Bee said.

I went on. "When I was giving her a tour of the plantation, we found a whole line of No Trespassing signs over by Felony Bay. We thought it was some kind of mistake, so we ignored them and kept going. Then Bubba Simmons spotted us. He's the Leadenwah deputy, but I guess he was off duty. He threw us off the property."

"That's odd," Custis said when I finished. "Our firm handled the closing on the Reward sale. I didn't work on it myself, but I think if the property had been broken up, somebody would have said something, just because it's so historic."

"Is it even legal to break up a place like Reward and not tell the new owner?"

He looked at me for a few seconds, then stood, went to his desk, and typed a series of search terms into his computer. As he read what came up on his screen, he raised his eyebrows.

"Interesting," he mused. "It says the Felony Bay tract wasn't actually a part of Reward. It was held under a separate deed."

"What does that mean?"

"That Felony Bay could be sold separately without affecting Reward Plantation. Technically it's a separate property."

"Since when?" I asked.

Custis was quiet while he typed some more. "Huh!" he exclaimed as he read what came up on his screen. "Apparently it's been that way since your father put it into a separate holding."

"Daddy? When?"

Custis looked at the screen again. "Ten months ago."

I tried to hide my shock. I couldn't imagine a reason Daddy would have broken up Reward and not told me about it. "Do you remember why he did that?"

Custis screwed his eyes closed and scrunched up his face as he tried to think. "I should, but your dad and I were working on so many other cases around that time." He opened his eyes and rapped his knuckles on top of his desk. "Was there a lady who had lived on that piece of property for a long time but then moved off?"

I nodded. "Her name is Mrs. Middleton. She moved when I was really little, and now she lives up the road."

Custis nodded. He looked back and forth between us. "I remember now. Have either of you ever heard of something called heirs' property?"

We both shook our heads.

Custis went on. "Okay, a little history lesson. At the end of the Civil War, the Southern economy had been destroyed. The slaves had been freed, but they had no money, no education, and no business skills, and the plantation owners didn't have much money after the war either, so they couldn't hire them to do the agricultural work they had always done. So the plantation owners developed a barter system where they offered their ex-slaves plots of land so they would have a place to live and raise their own crops. In return the ex-slaves would help the plantation owners farm their land.

"In many cases, it wasn't really clear who owned the land. The legal title to the land remained in the plantation owner's name, and there was no formal paperwork showing that it had been given to the ex-slaves. However, that land was very often handed down from the ex-slaves to their children and to their children's children and so on. In a lot of cases, it's still happening. Because that land has been handed down over and over from generation to generation, it's called heirs' property. In most cases that land still doesn't belong to the occupants in a strictly legal sense, because there has never been a formal title. However, when cases have come up, the courts have tended to rule that the land does in fact belong to the heirs of the ex-slaves, and they have been granted legal title."

"Is that how Mrs. Middleton's family lived at Felony Bay?"

"Yes," Custis said, nodding his head. "Now it's all coming back to me. Your dad found out that Mrs. Middleton had been born in that little cabin on Felony Bay and lived there for almost her whole life, and that her ancestors had lived there, too. Like a lot of people who have heirs' property, Mrs. Middleton was never certain whether she owned the property. And if my memory serves me correctly, everything that upset your dad happened at the time when your grandfather was still alive and still owned Reward. Your grandfather was very sick and in the hospital, and your uncle Charlie was running the plantation for him. You would have been maybe a year old, and your mom was sick and your dad was still lawyering up in New York City.

"Now, I wouldn't swear to this in court, but if I'm remembering correctly, your dad found out that your family had never charged the Middletons rent, but your uncle Charlie started to when your grandfather went into the hospital. Mrs. Middleton couldn't afford what he was charging, and since she probably figured she didn't actually own the land, she moved out."

I glanced at Bee, because she was the one who'd asked why Mrs. Middleton left her old cabin and moved into a trailer. "Typical Uncle Charlie," I said. "When did Daddy find out about it?"

Custis shook his head. "Not till years later, and that's when he decided to break Mrs. Middleton's old land into a separate parcel. If I had to guess, I'd think he was planning to give the land to Mrs. Middleton, because he thought it was rightfully hers."

"And that was just before his . . . accident."

Custis nodded. "Pretty close."

I was already starting to see red. I wanted to go back to Reward and kick Uncle Charlie in the knee or maybe even a little higher.

"But that never happened?" I asked.

"No," Custis said. I could tell by the way he closed his lips and squeezed them together that he had more to say.

"Why not?" I asked. "If Daddy thought that Mrs. Middleton should have gotten that land, then it shouldn't have been sold to anybody else, right?"

"Well," he said with a shrug. "Not in a perfect world, but things happened."

I could tell he didn't want to say any more. "You can say it," I told him. "Bee knows about everything that happened."

Custis looked at Bee, but when he turned his eyes back to me, I could tell that he was still struggling with how much he could say. "The firm had to repay Miss

Jenkins for all her lost gold and jewels."

"But Daddy didn't steal them."

"I agree with you, but since your dad was the legal guardian of Miss Jenkins's wealth, and some of the jewels and gold were found in his possession, he and the rest of this law firm were legally responsible for the loss. Because your dad hasn't been able to help us figure out who did commit the theft, Mr. Barrett felt he had no choice but to raise the largest possible amount of money from the sale of Reward. I'm certain he felt as badly about it as I did."

"In other words, the land that my father wanted to be given to Mrs. Middleton because he believed it was hers got sold to somebody else?"

Custis shrugged. "Mr. Barrett is the managing partner now, and he handled everything. I'm not familiar with the details, but yes, from what you're saying it sounds like that's what happened. I'm sorry. But you need to understand that it was all done in the hopes of preserving as much of your father's name and standing as possible."

I sat back and thought about this. I guessed maybe it was true that Daddy would have been in even more trouble without the entire plantation being sold, and I also knew it wouldn't have been fair for the other lawyers in the firm to have to pay for a crime they didn't commit. I didn't know what Bee and I could possibly do to make things better, but it just felt so wrong, I couldn't stand it. I tried to calm down and think about the problem the way Daddy would have. I knew the first thing he would have done would be to get as many facts about what had actually taken place as possible.

"Could we find out who bought the Felony Bay property?" I asked.

"Unfortunately I can't disclose anything about business matters we handled for one of our clients," Custis said.

My face fell. "Then how can we ever find out?"

"You didn't let me finish," Custis went on. "Fortunately for you, it's a matter of public record."

"Who do we have to ask?"

He stood and held up a finger. "Just sit tight. I think you should be able to get it off the computer."

He grabbed a pad and pen from his desk and walked out into the hallway.

Martha brought our Cokes while we waited, and then after another minute Custis was back. "I just had to get the parcel number for Felony Bay," he said as he walked around his desk and typed a few words. He waved us over. On the screen I could see a page called County Tax Records.

"Like I said, it's public information."

He hit the Enter key, and a second later the property description appeared: twenty riverfront acres on Leadenwah Island. It showed the appraised value and the annual taxes. The owner's name was something called Felony Bay Land Company, LLC.

"What's Felony Bay Land Company?" I asked.

"Probably an investment partnership," Custis said. "Real-estate developers often use names like that."

"That sounds about right to me." I told him how Bee and I had seen Bubba Simmons using one of those excavating machines on the beach and about all the holes he had dug.

Custis considered this for a moment. "Sounds like it could be a developer testing to see if he could put some septic systems in, but from what you're describing, those holes are way too close to the water to be the foundations for houses or anything like that."

"Why else would they be digging those holes?"

Curtis smiled. "Did your dad ever tell you the old stories about Felony Bay?"

"You mean like how pirates and blockade-runners used to hide out there?"

He nodded. "There's one particular story about the *Lovely Clarisse*."

I thought for a moment and shook my head. "I don't think Daddy ever told me that one."

Bee and I sat down again as Custis leaned forward in his chair, like he was telling us a secret. "The legends say that during the Civil War, a blockade-runner named the *Lovely Clarisse* tried to sneak out of Charleston Harbor loaded with a cargo of gold and cotton. The Union navy, which was blockading Charleston Harbor to keep supplies from going in or out, spotted the ship as it sailed out under cover of darkness. In the pursuit and ensuing battle, the *Lovely Clarisse* was badly damaged, and her captain steered her into the shallow coastal waters south of Charleston—eventually, folks say, into the Leadenwah River and right into Felony Bay. Having survived the battle but needing more extensive repairs than could be managed in the small bay, the captain decided to offload his heavy gold to make the ship as light and fast as possible. He and his officers supposedly buried the gold somewhere along Felony Bay and then set out once again to sneak past the Union navy. They were unsuccessful, and the *Lovely Clarisse* went down with all hands about fifty miles off the South Carolina coast."

Bee and I shared a look. Custis paused for a moment, then continued. "When news of the sinking reached Charleston, the Confederate army dispatched crews to the area around Felony Bay to try to recover the buried gold, but they were never successful. Other treasure hunters tried after the war, but they didn't find anything either, and in the intervening years most people have come to assume that the stories of the Confederate gold were just tall tales."

"Did Uncle Charlie ever hunt for the treasure?" I asked. "Daddy said he did a bunch of treasure hunting before I was born."

"A number of years back, he apparently became obsessed with the *Lovely Clarisse* treasure. When your grandfather was still alive, he even tried to get him to deed Felony Bay over to him."

"How come Daddy never told me?"

"You know that he and your uncle Charlie never got along."

I nodded.

"Since you have only one uncle, I think your dad was trying not to make things worse than they already were."

"Do you think Deputy Simmons was digging for treasure?" I asked.

Custis shrugged. "Hard to say for sure, but it sounds possible. Maybe the property was bought by a developer who thinks he's going to get paid twice — once when he finds the gold and again when he sells the land." He made a note on his legal pad. "I'll sniff around and try to learn more. No guarantees. If it's public information, I'll be able to tell you, but if it's not, I won't be able to divulge it."

I nodded, knowing better than to object. Daddy had always told me that one of the most important things a lawyer does is protect the privacy of his or her clients. "How much do you think they paid for the land?"

"Based on the assessed tax value, I would guess maybe around two million dollars."

"And you said Mr. Barrett handled it?"

Custis nodded. "And he's the firm's senior partner . . . at least until your father comes back."

"There are a few more things we need to know," I said.

"Okay. If I can tell you."

"Was Uncle Charlie the real-estate agent?"

"That's certainly not private information," Custis said. "I'm pretty sure he was. I know he listed Reward, so I assume he also listed the smaller parcel. I'll check to make sure." He made another note.

I tried to think of other questions Daddy would have asked. "When real-estate agents sell property, don't they do write-ups to describe what they're selling?" I knew they had done it for Reward Plantation, because I had seen a copy of a fancy brochure.

"Yes."

"Was there a Felony Bay brochure?"

"I'll find out." Custis nodded as he jotted that down. "What else?"

I thought about how to express my next question, but I also knew that Custis wasn't going to like answering it.

I chose my words carefully. "If Daddy had decided that Felony Bay belonged to Mrs. Middleton, and if he was right, then wouldn't it have been like stealing for people to have sold that land to somebody else?"

Custis sat back and thought for a long moment. "Wow," he said at last. "You really are your father's daughter. The honest answer is that I don't know the answer, but I'm inclined to say no. Your father was operating on a certain moral perspective, not necessarily a legal one. The fact is that Mrs. Middleton moved off the property some years back, and so technically her claim under heirs' property was no longer valid."

"From what you said before, she got driven off

because Uncle Charlie charged her too much rent."

Custis nodded. "But the fact that she moved off is still the primary issue. Your father was doing something because he thought it was the right thing, but it certainly wasn't anything he had to do in a strict legal sense."

I thought about that. Then I nodded to Bee and stood up. "Thank you very much for your time, Custis," I said.

I was disappointed at some of the things I had learned, but I couldn't really be angry at Custis or Mr. Barrett. I understood that Mr. Barrett had probably had no choice but to sell every single bit of Reward in order to repay Miss Jenkins. He probably didn't know that Daddy was maybe going to give the land to Mrs. Middleton. He only knew that the Felony Bay property was worth two million dollars, and that he and the other lawyers needed the money. I also realized that Custis wasn't going to make himself any friends and might even get himself in big trouble with the firm's other lawyers if he started digging into things like this.

However, I did not work for Force & Barrett. I was going to push as hard as I could.

"I'm going to try and find out exactly what happened here," I told Custis. "I need to know what my daddy was planning to do when he broke up the land, and if I can prove that he was going to give it to Mrs. Middleton, I'm going to try and make sure that's what happens."

He looked at me and smiled. "If there's any twelve-year-old in the state who can do it, it's got to be you."

"How soon do you think you might be able to get us the answers on those other questions?"

Custis raised his eyebrows and thought about that. "I'm pretty busy, but I ought to be able to get them in the next day or two."

"Thank you," I said.

He nodded. "Just for the record, Abbey. I'll help you, but if you make this thing a big problem for our clients and for the firm, I won't be able to talk to you anymore. At least on anything that concerns Felony Bay. It doesn't mean I don't personally support what you're doing, and it doesn't mean we're not friends. It's just professional. Do you understand that?"

I nodded. For the first time ever, I felt like Custis and I were going to have to be careful about what we said to each other.

Twelve

After we left Custis, we walked up State Street, past the old brick houses of the French Quarter, through the market, and onto Anson Street. We turned onto Pinckney Street just past a barn where big carriage horses were being harnessed to a wagon, and we ate lunch in a little white house called Cru Café that has maybe the best French fries in the whole world. Unfortunately I wasn't very hungry.

I was pretty sure I understood at least part of what was going on, and every single bit of what I understood made me angry. It seemed obvious to me that Daddy had been working to get Mrs. Middleton her land back before his accident. But considering everything that had happened since then, I was starting to wonder if the two could be connected. If they were, it was tough to figure out where to start. We had run into a wall, and to get around it we would need more help than Custis could give us. I knew he didn't want to break any lawyer rules, and he didn't want to get himself in trouble with Mr. Barrett. I really couldn't blame him.

Neither Bee nor I had spoken much during lunch. We were about to ask the waitress for our check when Bee finally let out a sigh and asked, "How much more can we really do?"

I looked up from playing with my French fries. "Daddy always said you have to dig and get the facts. He said until you have the facts, all you have is an opinion, and that opinion is only worth something in a newspaper."

"Where do we get more facts?"

"The Library Society."

Bee looked suspicious. "Sounds boring."

I shrugged. "No getting around it," I said. "Just like lawyers, we have to do our research."

We walked over to King Street and headed south. I saw Bee slow down several times when we walked past stores with windows full of bright fall clothing.

I could tell she wanted to go in and look around, but I kept urging her along. The last thing I wanted to do was waste my time shopping when I barely had a dime to my name.

We finally came to the rambling headquarters of the Charleston Library Society. Daddy told me it's the second oldest private library in the United States, established in 1748. They have lots and lots of old books, and many of them are all about Charleston and the South Carolina Lowcountry. Bee and I asked one of the librarians to help us find information relating to Confederate blockade-runners, rumors of buried treasure, and also heirs' property.

She walked us around to different parts of the collection and helped us gather a stack of books. She also gave us a couple notepads to make notes. I offered Bee the books on blockade-runners and treasure, because I thought they would be more interesting, while I took the heirs' property stack.

A couple of hours of reading the dry-as-dust books about heirs' roperty convinced me that I had guessed right about which books would be boring. I had to put my fingers up against my eyelids to keep them open, while across the table Bee kept oohing and aahing as she read about Blackbeard and Stede Bonnet and other pirates who had sailed the waters around Charleston, and then she oohed and aahed even louder when she read about the *Lovely Clarisse* and other tales of buried gold.

"Abbey," she whispered at one point, her eyes glittering with excitement. "It says the captain of the *Lovely Clarisse* sailed her into a 'secret bay' when he buried the gold."

"Sounds like they're talking about Felony Bay, doesn't it?"

Bee nodded, her eyes large. "Isn't that exciting?"

I shrugged. "I think it's just a story. People want to believe it, but it's too good to be true."

"Maybe. But it doesn't matter if it's real. It just matters if the people who bought Felony Bay believe it, right?"

She had a point. I nodded and went back to my boring book.

The one thing I discovered out of all the gobbledygook about heirs' property was that most of the cases where heirs were given legal ownership of their properties had been based on the idea of "continuous occupation." If somebody moved off the property and later tried to claim it, their claims were usually refused. Unfortunately it looked like Custis was right. Without someone willing to give the land to her, Mrs. Middleton's right to Felony Bay likely wouldn't be honored.

I was falling asleep for about the fiftieth time when Bee kicked me under the table. "Look at this!" she said. She had six or seven different books spread out on the table, all of them opened to the inside cover, where the library glued its little envelope that showed who borrowed a book and for what dates.

I looked at all the books and shook my head, unable to understand. "What?"

"Look! Every one of these books has been borrowed by Charles Force. That's Uncle Charlie, right?"

I shot up and grabbed the first book and slipped the card out of the envelope. It showed that Charles Force had borrowed the book about ten months earlier. I went from book to book, checking the cards, and they all showed the same thing and roughly the same dates.

"I didn't know Uncle Charlie could read," I said.

"Weird, huh?" Bee said.

An idea that had been circling around in my brain started to take a little more shape. It horrified me and at the same time made me so angry, I could hardly see straight.

"Is it possible that Uncle Charlie bought Felony Bay?" I asked.

Bee shrugged. "That's what I'm wondering."

The idea didn't make any sense, because Uncle Charlie never seemed to have enough energy or money to do anything. Just looking at his falling-apart old pickup or Ruth's rusted Toyota, it was hard to imagine that he could have scraped together a couple million dollars to buy twenty acres of riverfront land. The same thing was true even if Deputy Bubba Simmons was in on the deal as well.

Bee looked at her watch. "It's almost three o'clock. Time for us to meet Grandma," she said.

We took our books back to the librarian and thanked her for her help, then walked out of the library, sat on the steps, and waited for Grandma Em. It was hot, the sun still high in the sky, and I could feel sweat starting to trickle down my back. After a minute an old red pickup truck rumbled by. I only noticed it because it had a busted muffler and sounded strangely familiar. There was an open parking place just past where we were standing, and the truck pulled up and backed into the spot.

The side windows of the truck were down, which must have meant the air-conditioning was broken along with the tailpipe. I glanced toward the truck, and with no reflection to blur my view, there was no mistaking that the driver was Bubba Simmons. Bee and I were high up on the steps, and Bubba was busy getting into his parking place, so he hadn't noticed us.

I grabbed Bee's arm and pulled her all the way to the top of the steps. We tucked in behind a stone urn, where we were mostly out of sight. Bubba finished parking and turned off his engine, but he didn't climb out. Instead he turned toward his passenger. I couldn't see the passenger or understand what they were saying to each other, but I knew it had to be an argument, because I caught scraps of Bubba's angry voice as it drifted through the open window.

Bee and I leaned out from around the urn to get a better view, and we saw Bubba take his right hand off the wheel and start to slap his passenger. We stood a little taller and moved all the way to the side of the steps until we were literally hanging over the railing. I could see Bubba's passenger now, cowering against the far door. He was holding his arms over his head and trying to roll into a ball. Bubba's slaps kept coming, and Jimmy Simmons's voice came through the window begging his father to stop.

After a few more seconds, Bubba finally got out of the truck, looked back in, said something in a low, angry voice, then walked away. He never turned his eyes in our direction.

Several moments went by, and then Jimmy climbed out. Bee and I were still on the steps as he came around the back of the truck, and I could see rage and humiliation in his eyes and in the set of his lips.

Just at that moment he looked up and caught sight of us. His face was red and swollen as if he had been crying, and he quickly wiped his eyes on his sleeve. I saw something pass across his face when he looked at me, and even though I knew what it was, I didn't feel angry. I watched him start up the library steps toward us, his face set in a scowl, but I couldn't help feeling sorry for him.

"Do you know that kid?" Bee whispered.

"Yes . . . unfortunately."

"Is he coming up here?" She sounded nervous.

"'Fraid so. Move away from me."

Bee stepped to one side as Jimmy continued up the steps, his eyes never leaving my face. He was trying as hard as he could to look mean and scary, I'm sure because he thought if he could frighten me like his father had done to him, then he might feel better. I stood my ground but glanced around, hoping there would be other people on the sidewalk and their presence might keep things from getting ugly. Unfortunately there was no one nearby.

"Hey, girlfriend," Jimmy said in a soft, sinister

voice when he got close. His nose had a scab on it, and I was pretty sure it was from my fist.

"I'm not your girlfriend. And I don't want to fight."

He had kept coming as he talked, and now he was very close, just one step away.

"Jimmy, I just said I don't want to fight you."

"You don't, huh?" He reached out and gave my shoulder a hard shove. "You miss me?"

I could feel sorry for somebody for just so long. The shove finished it. "I didn't miss you the last time," I said, looking at the scab on his nose. "Want another scab?"

Jimmy laughed. "You don't wanna fight 'cause you ain't got that old crippled lady to protect you. She hit me with a shovel. I ain't forgetting that."

"Then you won't forget this either," I said, and I hit him four times, twice in the mouth and twice in the nose. I really am faster than a scalded lizard, but I'm even faster when I'm mad. Jimmy never saw any of them coming.

I saw blood on his face, but I couldn't tell how badly I had hurt him because his arms came up and he grabbed for me. Knowing he would choke me if he got the chance, I jumped back and dodged sideways, thinking I'd run back into the library. The only problem was that my foot slipped off the edge of a step.

I caught myself, but as I straightened up, Jimmy was on me. I felt his hands around my neck and felt a jolt of fear as I remembered the last time he'd gotten me in a choke hold. I tried to tell Bee to run away and call for help, but Jimmy's grip was already too tight.

I heard Bee's voice, not from far away where she should have been but from up very close. "Hey," she said, "let her go."

Jimmy kept squeezing my throat. I was trying to get a grip on one of his fingers and bend it back, but he was too strong.

"Let go!" Bee said again. Only this time her voice was followed by a loud, hollow thump. I knew it was the sound of her cane landing on Jimmy's flesh.

Jimmy's fingers relaxed, and I pulled in a deep breath and then used all my strength to break away. I staggered sideways until my hip hit the other railing, and then I looked at Bee, who was holding her cane cocked over her shoulder like a baseball bat.

Jimmy was bent over, holding his hand over the top of his head and making a sound that was someplace between a moan and a snort of anger. I also knew he wasn't done fighting. Jimmy Simmons wasn't going to get beaten by two girls, never ever, not if he could help it.

"Nice shot, Bee," I said. "But you gotta get out of here."

I heard the sound of a car horn just as Jimmy straightened up. "You're dead, Force," he growled, fixing his angry eyes on me. "You're both dead." The horn sounded a second time. It was close by. I risked a glance down toward the street and saw that Grandma Em had pulled up in front of the library. She had her window down, and she was looking up in anger and amazement.

I looked back at Jimmy, who was coming at me again. I faked like I was going to try to escape down the steps, then I threw a quick jab into his nose as I jumped away from the railing.

Jimmy started to go for my fake, but he managed to slam my shoulder with a wild punch as I dodged. It sent shock waves of pain all down my arm.

The horn honked a third time, longer, this time followed by Grandma Em's voice, loud and clear and deep and full of authority. "Stop right there, young man! You girls get in this car right this second!"

Jimmy stopped and glared down at Grandma Em, and I could see the energy flow out of his shoulders. My arm was killing me, but I made a point of giving him a smile as I went past.

"Bye-bye, boyfriend."

Bee and I walked down the steps and climbed into the back of Grandma Em's car. I didn't say anything as we drove away, but when we stopped at the traffic light, Grandma Em turned and stared at us.

"When I was a young lady, it was generally frowned upon to hit a young man," she said after a long silence.

"Yes, Grandma," Bee said.

"Yes, ma'am," I said.

"However," she said, her eyes starting to twinkle, "in the event it was necessary, it was thought to be important to throw a good punch. Nice jab, Abbey."

Thirteen

At dinner that night, Uncle Charlie seemed as full of whiskey breath and unpleasantness as ever. His small eyes touched on me as I sat down, but appearing to see nothing on which he needed to comment, they went to his food. Just as they had the other night, Ruth brought a bottle of wine out to the table, and they clicked glasses and shared a private smirk.

I watched out of the corner of my eye as Uncle Charlie shoveled his dinner, thinking about how he had tried to talk Grandfather into giving him Felony Bay, and failing that how he had kicked Mrs. Middleton off the property when Grandfather was dying, and how a year ago he had taken out all the books from the library about Felony Bay and the *Lovely Clarisse* gold.

I also thought about the wine and the smirking and the Bubba Simmons late-night visit, and I was starting to realize that something inside Uncle Charlie had changed. He was feeling very cocky. Whatever his secret was, it certainly wasn't making him any nicer, which might have been the reason I hadn't noticed it earlier.

I ate Ruth's warmed-up, canned slop as fast as I could, then asked to be excused. I took my plate and started to head toward the kitchen, and that's when it happened. As I walked past him, Uncle Charlie turned in his chair and gave me a smack on the back of my head that was so sharp, it brought tears to my eyes. I spun around, wanting to smash my plate over him and barely holding back.

"That's what it feels like to get sucker punched, Squib. Didn't like it, did you?"

"What are you talking about?" I managed, trying not to let him see how close I was to tears.

"You think I don't know what you do? I'm talking about Jimmy Simmons. You sucker punched the boy again, didn't you? You and that rich black girl you hang around with."

"You don't know anything," I said. Then I turned and went to the kitchen and let the door swing closed behind me. I stood with my hands braced against the sink and got my breathing under control, then I wiped away the tears that had gathered in the corners of my eyes and started to do the dishes. I used the mindless activity to swallow my anger and hold back the questions and accusations that had been trying to boil their way off my tongue all through dinner.

I was dying to tell Uncle Charlie that I knew about the Felony Bay land and that he wasn't getting away with anything. I wanted to ask him how he could have thrown a poor, defenseless woman off land that was rightfully hers. I wanted to ask him how he could lower himself to work with somebody as crude and cruel as Bubba Simmons. And I wanted to ask him how he was ever going to live with himself if he actually found a treasure that by all rights ought to belong to someone else.

The next morning I woke up as sweaty and wrung out as if I had run a couple of miles. It was because of the dream I'd had, which had made me feel like I hadn't slept at all. In it, Bee and I had snuck back to Felony Bay, and as we crept along the path that led to the beach and the old cabin, we had heard the sound of the same machine we'd heard the other day. But when we got to the end of the trail where we could see the beach from the edge of the undergrowth, there hadn't been any machine. Rather, we had seen Uncle Charlie and Jimmy Simmons and Jimmy's father all using shovels to dig a line of gigantic holes. They were working like crazy people and yelling at one another to hurry up.

But that's when I saw they weren't just digging. They were also burying two objects that lay on the ground beside one of the holes. One of the objects moved, and when I looked more carefully, I could see Mrs. Middleton and Skoogie tied up and gagged. It didn't make any sense, but dreams don't have to make sense. I was scared to death. I knew time was running out and that Bee and I had to stop the diggers from getting whatever they were after and from burying Mrs. Middleton and Skoogie.

Despite how hard everyone was focused on digging their holes, every few minutes Jimmy's father would stop and put down his shovel. Then he would walk over and slap Jimmy on the back of the head. Jimmy would try to protect himself and start to cry. As it kept happening, I could see that Jimmy was getting angrier and angrier, but there was no way he could stop his father. And just like earlier that day outside the library, I actually felt sorry for Jimmy.

When I finally opened my eyes, I realized one other thing about the dream. It had been in color, and the main color had been red. I remembered the last two times I had seen color in my dreams, and the bad things that had happened soon after to a person I loved. Only this time I had a feeling that something was different. This time I was pretty sure the bad thing was going to happen to me, and whatever it was, it was going to happen pretty darn soon.

If that was true, there were two things I needed to think about. First, if I was going to keep myself from getting hurt, I had to keep looking over my shoulder and be extra alert in everything I did. Second, I had to figure out what to do about Bee. I wasn't going to let her get hurt for trying to help me. Finding out what had really happened to Daddy, and discovering the truth about what was going on at Felony Bay, were my jobs, not hers.

I had learned the previous afternoon as we drove back to Reward from Charleston that Bee and Grandma Em were flying to Atlanta this morning because Bee had doctors' appointments over the next two days for her knee and shoulder. That would keep her out of harm's way for now, but when she returned I would need to come up with some way to keep her safe. All I could think of was to tell her we couldn't hang around together anymore, but I hated the idea, because it would hurt her feelings and because she really was my new best friend. Which was worse, I wondered, hurting my friend's feelings a little or maybe letting her do something where she might get hurt in a lot more serious way?

I rolled over onto my stomach and pulled the pillow over my head. For several minutes I considered trying to go back to sleep in hopes that I could have another dream. If I had a normal dream, I might be able to forget my first one. And maybe if that happened, the first one wouldn't come true.

But then I thought about all the questions and accusations I'd been choking back the night before and the risk of running into Uncle Charlie at breakfast if I slept any later. If I saw him, I knew I wouldn't be able to keep my mouth shut, but my dream had taught me that keeping my mouth shut around him was even more important than usual.

Because of that, I forced myself to sit up and put my feet on the floor, trying to wake up. Rufus helped by coming over and giving me a big lick, and I finally managed to get my eyes all the way open and get dressed.

Rufus and I snuck downstairs, bolted our usual quick breakfasts, then headed to the pasture to get the horses and do my chores.

On our way to the barn, Rufus raced through the corn and sniffed for scents in the early dew. I was glad that at least one of us was feeling cheerful this morning. In addition to being dead tired, I was also feeling lonely and already missing Bee.

I was trying to convince myself that having her gone was actually a good thing. Maybe I could get everything figured out by the time she got back, I told myself, but I knew it was just wishful thinking. The more thinking I did, the more complicated everything seemed.

For example, when I thought about the dates when Uncle Charlie borrowed the books from the library and when Daddy had filed the separate deed for Felony Bay and then the date of his accident, I couldn't help but see how close together they were. But did it mean anything? Try as hard as might, I couldn't see any real connection between Miss Lydia Jenkins's jewelry and gold and the *Lovely Clarisse* and Mrs. Middleton. Even more, if I managed to figure everything out, what was I going to do about it?

For starters, if Daddy really did want to give Mrs.

Middleton's land back to her, how was I going to help with that? What adult was going to help make that happen? Custis? What about his job working for Force & Barrett? I was pretty sure Mr. Barrett wouldn't like him helping me. After all, the law firm had only been able to stay in business because they'd been able to pay back Miss Jenkins. If something I did made it look like the Felony Bay land should never have been sold, a lot of lawyers were going to be unhappy, maybe even Custis.

I shook my head, trying to clear out the mental snarls that seemed to form every time I thought about how complicated everything was. One thing was clear. If I was going to get anywhere, I needed to do things just the way Daddy would have. I needed to get more facts. I would use the time while Bee was gone to get back into town and see if Custis had gotten the answers he promised. Also I wanted to talk to two more people who I thought might be able to help me work the plan that was slowly forming in my brain.

I thought about all those things as I mucked out the stalls. I was just finishing when I looked up and saw Grandma Em framed in the bright sunlight at the opening of the barn. For a second I worried that something bad might have happened to Bee, and I trotted straight toward her.

"Morning," Grandma Em said.

"I thought you and Bee had left already," I said. "Is everything okay?"

"Everything's fine. We leave in just a few minutes. Bee's up at the house getting packed."

I nodded, but I was confused. If everything was fine, why was she here?

"I don't mean to stop you from your work," she said. "Please keep on."

I nodded and started spraying the horses with fly spray. Grandma Em sat on an old folding chair nearby.

"You just came down here to watch me?" I asked.

She shrugged like there was nothing special on her mind, but I could tell that there was. I worked and let the silence stretch.

Out of the corner of my eye I watched her scrunch up her face, look off in the distance for a long moment, then nod as if she'd just come to a decision. "You know," she said, "I just wanted to come down here this morning to tell you how pleased I am that you and Bee have become such good friends."

"There's no need to thank me. We just like each other."

"I know. . . . I'm just saying I think it's great."

I turned and looked at Grandma Em as she tried

to figure out what to say next. I realized that she felt terribly awkward about something, but I had no idea what it was.

"I know that sometimes, when you're twelve or thirteen, friends can be moody or fickle. Someone can be your friend one day and not the next. They can—" Grandma Em pursed her lips. She took a deep breath and blew it out. "The reason I thought I should talk to you today has to do with Bee's family. Did she ever mention her mother and brother?"

I shook my head.

"I suspected as much. Perhaps I should let her tell you this in her own time and in her own words, but I also think for her own good that I should tell you now."

She glanced up at me, then away again into the distance. "Something very tragic happened to Bee, and I think you may be able to relate, because I know some hard things have happened in your own life."

I felt anxious all of a sudden, as if I was about to discover something I might not want to know about my friend. "Go on," I said.

Grandma Em nodded. "One day last March, Bee's mother was driving both Bee and Bee's brother when she had what the doctors later said was a massive heart attack. She probably blacked out immediately. Anyway, the car went across the median into the oncoming lane and was hit by a large truck."

I shook my head. "That's terrible," I managed.

"Yes, it was. Bee's brother was killed instantly, and her mother was in a coma for several days before she died. Bee herself was badly injured."

My heart was beating very fast. I was thinking of everything I had lost in the past year, but how Bee had lost even more. At least my father was still alive, even if he was in a coma.

"Bee was extremely traumatized by what happened. Apparently she and her brother had been having some kind of fight when the accident took place, and she blamed herself for what happened. That's nonsense, of course, and I've told her so, so many times. But she still feels guilty."

"That's why she won't talk about her mother?"

"Yes. Bee had always been a very happy young girl, but after the accident, something changed. She even stopped talking altogether for several months. I think her father bought Reward so quickly because he wanted to give Bee a pleasant new place that would allow her to get away from her old memories. When Bee agreed to go to the hospital with you the other day, I don't think you can understand how much courage that took on her part. It was a reminder of what happened to her mother and brother."

I nodded, remembering how Bee had become strangely silent on our way to visit Daddy. "You never said anything at the time."

"No."

"Why doesn't Bee's father ever come here?" I asked.

Grandma Em let out a snort, as if she was laughing at something that wasn't really funny. "He's my son, and I've asked myself that same question many times, why he hasn't been with his daughter much at all since the accident. I don't know for sure, but here's what I think: I think that when certain people suffer terrible losses, like losing a big part of their family in a car accident, it can make the world start to look like a place of danger and fear rather than a place of joy. I think my son has lost so much that he lives in fear that another terrible thing might happen and that it might happen to Bee. Right now, I don't think he could survive that, and I think he has been staying very busy with his new company in India so that he doesn't have to confront his fear."

"In other words it's easier to stay away from Bee than to be with her?"

Grandma Em nodded. "Even though he loves her very much. Or better said, because he loves her so much. Like a lot of people, my son believes that by giving Bee a lovely home and a safe and beautiful place to live, he is giving her everything she needs. He believes that all the money makes up for him not being around. He is wrong, of course, and I have told him as much. But he needs to come to that realization on his own."

I thought about what she was telling me and also what she had left unsaid. "Nothing bad is going to happen to Bee's and my friendship," I said.

Grandma Em smiled, and I could sense her relief. "I just didn't want you to misinterpret Bee's actions if she becomes silent or gets very sad."

"She hasn't been that way, except the first day we met and at the hospital."

Grandma Em nodded. "Yes, I know." She rubbed her hands together and sighed. "Well, I just wanted to let you know how important it has been for Bee to have such a good friend. I hope you guys keep hanging out together. And I hope you will keep this between us and not share it. I wouldn't want Bee to think that I go around talking behind her back, but I thought it would be good for both of you if you knew a few of the facts."

I nodded. "I'll keep it to myself."

"Thank you, Abbey."

She got up out of her chair and began to walk out of the barn. I watched her go, but then I cleared my throat. "Grandma Em?" I waited until she turned to look at me. I was thinking about the fear she said Abbey's father had. "Do you think my father is afraid to wake up?"

Grandma Em looked at me for several long seconds, then shook her head. "No. I think your father is definitely going to wake up. I'm not a doctor, but that's what I think."

My heart started coming back down to normal. I smiled. "Thanks."

Grandma Em glanced at her watch, then gave me a wink. "I have to get us to the airport," she said as she turned again and headed back toward the big house.

I watched her walk away, wondering why she had chosen now to tell me all that stuff. It seemed almost like she had managed to read my mind. How could Grandma Em have known that I'd been thinking about telling Bee that maybe we shouldn't hang out anymore? She couldn't have, I decided, but she had also told me in no uncertain terms how important it was for Bee to have my friendship. Grandma Em had talked to me because she cared about Bee's happiness. But did she also realize that what made Bee happy might also get her hurt?

I thought about that for several moments, but then I thought about something else as well. Everything Grandma Em had told me about Bee was also true for me in spades. Bee's friendship was the best thing that had happened to me in a long, long time, and I wasn't going to do anything to screw it up. No way.

I hurried out in the direction of the big house. I got there just as Grandma Em and Bee were putting their overnight bags in the car.

I called out to them as they climbed into the car, and Grandma Em turned toward me. "Make it quick, young lady. We have a flight to catch."

I grabbed the back-door handle, pulled open the door, and climbed inside. Bee turned around in her seat and gave me a surprised smile.

"What do you think you're doing?" Grandma Em demanded.

"I have to go to the hospital to see Daddy. Would you drop me off at the bus stop on your way? You go right by it when you leave the island."

"You're not doing anything on the mystery, are you?" Bee asked. "You can't without me. We're only going for two days."

"Don't worry," I said, lying through my teeth.

"Does your uncle or your aunt know where you're going?" Grandma Em asked.

"Like they care."

Grandma Em gave me a look, but she started the engine and put the car in gear, and we headed down the drive. Ten minutes later she dropped me at the bus stop, and I thanked them and said I'd see them when they got back.

Forty minutes after that, I got off the bus in front of University Hospital.

I headed up to Daddy's floor, rang to get in, and waved to the nurses at the main desk as I hurried down to his room.

"Okay, lazybones," I called out in my cheeriest voice when I walked in. "Time to wake up. It's your daughter."

I sat on the edge of his bed and held the hand that did not have the tubes going into it. My heart was hammering, and I was holding my breath. I had come because I'd decided I needed to tell him at least a little bit about what was happening. Since all my months of happy talk hadn't had the slightest effect, telling the truth was a risk I needed to take. What Grandma Em had said to me had made me realize that I had to be honest with Daddy, at least a little bit.

"Listen up," I said, giving his limp hand a squeeze.

"I need to tell you about some things that are going on at Reward because I really need your help." I told him about Felony Bay and the No Trespassing signs. I didn't tell him that the rest of the plantation had been sold because I didn't want to give him too much bad news all at once. Also I told him I believed that he had intended to give Felony Bay to Mrs. Middleton, because he knew it was heirs' property and rightfully hers. I also told him that the people who had bought the land had no intention of giving it to Mrs. Middleton.

"I really need your help on this, Daddy," I said. "I'm pretty sure Uncle Charlie had something to do with it, and also Bubba Simmons. I think they're digging for treasure out at Felony Bay because of all those holes. And I keep wondering if all this stuff has something to do with your falling off the ladder, and with Miss Jenkins's gold and stuff. I've got Custis doing some research for me, and he's supposed to get back to me today or tomorrow, but he's afraid of Mr. Barrett and the other lawyers getting mad at him if he does too much. I need more help than Custis can give me. Everything is so complicated that my brain gets tied in knots just thinking about it."

I stopped and looked at his face to see if my news was having any effect. Nothing. He was sleeping so still that he almost looked dead. But when I looked really closely, I could see he was breathing, the same shallow breaths as always.

"Also," I went on, "I had another one of my dreams last night. I've never told you about my dreams—actually I've never told anyone—but I had one before your accident that was like a warning that something bad was going to happen. I had another one last night, and now I think something equally bad is going to happen at Felony Bay. I just don't know what it's going to be, and I don't know how to stop it."

I looked down at his face again and gave his hand a squeeze. "Come on!" I said. "Wake up. I really need your help."

He just kept sleeping, his mouth slightly open, his body still. The tubes dripped. I wanted to scream at him and shake him, but I knew it would do no good. A tear broke from my eye, ran down my cheek, and splashed down on his wrist. For the first time since the accident, I felt my hope starting to fail me. I wondered if it was possible that Daddy might never wake up.

Fourteen

I left the hospital, caught a bus heading downtown, and told the driver where I needed to go and asked him how to get there. He let me off at Broad Street and told me to ride the DASH bus up Meeting and get off when the bus made its turn to go south on King.

I did what he told me: got off on King and walked north a few more blocks. The neighborhood got seedier, the buildings more rundown, but I finally spotted the sign I was looking for. Charleston's daily paper, the *Post and Courier*, was located in an ugly, windowless building that looked more like a fortress than a newspaper company.

I stood on the sidewalk for several moments and thought again about whether I should go inside. Daddy had always told me about what he called the Law of Unintended Consequences. It's sort of like when you think that slugging some jerk in the nose will settle an argument, but then you do it, and instead of ending things, you have a fight on your hands where you risk getting your butt kicked. I thought this might be one of the places where that law comes into effect.

Still, I needed more facts than I was going to get all by myself or through Custis, and newspapers were places where people dug up the facts, even though sometimes they also twisted them. I crossed the street, went inside, and asked the lady at the small reception desk if I could speak with a reporter named Tom Blackford.

I had never actually met Tom Blackford, but he was the reporter who had written most of the articles about Daddy's accident and all the unanswered questions. He had even written pieces about my family, about how my ancestors had been wealthy planters and later on phosphate miners, and about how Daddy had been a bright student and gone to the University of Virginia and Harvard Law School.

The articles also talked about how my grandfather

had left Reward to Daddy and the family phosphate business to Uncle Charlie, and how Uncle Charlie had proceeded to lose the company's money and shut it down. The problem with the articles was that the facts were true, but Blackford sort of twisted them up to suggest that Daddy was partly to blame for what happened to the family business.

The articles also talked about Miss Lydia Jenkins, how she had inherited a fortune from her father while much of the rest of her family was poor. There was also an even more mysterious story, about how, as a young woman, she had heard glass breaking in the middle of the night but thought nothing of it, but in the morning found two bullet holes in the headboard of her bed. The police never found out who fired the shots, but Miss Jenkins had decided that someone in her family had tried to kill her to inherit her money. From that point forward she had distrusted everyone around her, including bankers and most everyone else. She had even insisted on keeping most of her fortune in the form of cash and gold in the vault in her house. Even after her stroke, she had continued to keep everything in her vault. Until it was stolen, that is.

I looked up on the walls in the waiting room, where various articles had been posted. The one right near my head was one of the last articles Tom Blackford had written about the "accident." He reported that Daddy had been the one person Miss Jenkins really trusted. He claimed Daddy was the only one besides Miss Jenkins who knew the combination to her vault, and supposedly Daddy had kept careful records every time he went into the vault and removed any part of her fortune to sell it for her. The articles didn't actually say it, but they made it sound like Daddy had been stealing from Miss Jenkins for years and that it was karma that he had fallen off the stepladder and gotten caught after he had finished cleaning her out.

I felt myself getting steamed about the articles all over again but forced myself to calm down. Daddy always said that hating newspaper people because they wrote vicious articles was like hating rattlesnakes for biting. Neither one could help what they did, he said, and the best course of action where either was concerned was to avoid them. I had tried to follow Daddy's advice, but every time a new article about Daddy or Miss Jenkins or Reward came out, my curiosity would get the best of me, and I would read it and then try hard not to cry. I had finally picked up the phone one day and called Tom Blackford and told him that he was writing a lot of terrible lies because my father was innocent. Tom

Blackford had told me that he was sorry, but he was an investigative journalist and his job was to report the facts and then interpret them the way he thought best. I got mad and told him that his best thinking obviously wasn't very good, because he'd only gotten part of the facts and he was either too lazy or too stupid to get the rest of them. That's when he told me that I wasn't the most polite young lady he'd ever spoken to, but he hoped that Daddy would wake up soon because he would really like to hear what he had to say in his own defense and then write that part of the story, too. My phone call hadn't made a bit of difference, and Tom Blackford had gone on writing his articles and saying the meanest things about my father that anyone could imagine.

Now I wondered if Tom Blackford would remember my phone call and refuse to see me. I hoped that wouldn't be the case, because while I would have dearly loved to kick Tom Blackford in the shins as hard as I could, what I really needed to do was talk to him. The stories he had written had made him the most well-known reporter in the city, and I had to count on the fact that he wanted more great stuff to write about and would help dig up some of the information I so desperately needed.

Of course that was where the Law of Unintended Consequences came into play. If he found new facts, would he "interpret" them to help Daddy or hurt him? And if he learned anything important, would he share it?

I suddenly realized that the woman at the reception desk had tipped her glasses down to the end of her nose and was looking at me strangely. "Young lady, I asked you if Mr. Blackford is expecting you," she said, sounding like a teacher when someone isn't paying attention.

"Sorry," I said, snapping back to the present. "No, he's not expecting me."

"And why do you want to see him?"

"I have things to tell him about Reward Plantation he might want to know."

She raised her eyebrows and gave me a look. I gave her a look right back, and she finally picked up the phone and dialed an extension. "A young lady is here with information about some place called Reward Plantation," she said to whoever answered.

She listened for a second or two, then nodded. "Yes. Hang on." She put her hand over the receiver and looked at me. "Your name?"

"Abbey Force."

She repeated my name, then listened. "No, she hasn't got a gun to my knowledge," she said, raising her eyebrows and giving me a careful look.

"I don't want to shoot him," I said. "I just want to talk to him."

She repeated that into the phone. "He wats to know if that's a promise."

"Yes."

She told him. "He's coming down," she said after she hung up.

She gave me an adhesive label and told me to write my name on it and stick it on my shirt. She also made me sign my name and the time of my visit in a book on her desk. I did what she asked, then waited by the locked glass doors that led to the interior of the newspaper.

I didn't know what Tom Blackford looked like, but he had gotten so much publicity for his articles on Daddy that I imagined he would be handsome and cool, like Robert Redford in an old movie that Daddy and I had watched once. Whatever I expected, it wasn't the person who got off the elevator a couple minutes later.

Tom Blackford was short with tired eyes and a horseshoe of limp dark hair around the sides of his head. He had two halves of a mustache that didn't quite meet in the middle, and narrow shoulders, and even though he was mostly skinny, he had a gut that stuck out over his belt.

He looked at my name tag, then at me. His eyes

weren't very friendly. "Well, the rude young lady I spoke to on the phone. You wanted to see me?"

His voice was high-pitched and nasal, different from the way it had sounded on the phone. He must have been eating when the lady called, because he had bits of food stuck between his teeth.

"I have something you might be interested in," I said.

"About your dad?"

"No."

He raised his eyebrows in mock surprise. "I thought you were going to tell me you had new information that proved your father's innocence."

I bit the inside of my cheek to keep from telling him once again what a pea brain he was. "There's stuff going on at Reward that I thought you might want to know about."

He wrinkled his lips as if that whole subject was too boring for words. "Like what?" he said in a tired voice.

"Like part of the plantation was sold to somebody other than the person who thought he was buying the whole thing."

Tom Blackford looked at me a moment, considering. Then he let out a sigh, as if what I'd just said had triggered barely enough interest to justify a conversation. He jerked his head for me to follow, held his ID card to the lock that opened the glass doors, and then pointed me inside the elevator. We went up to another floor and got out in a room full of people who were sitting at desks typing on computers. I assumed they were the other reporters.

Mr. Blackford led me to a very small office along the side of the room. It had no window, but the walls were hung with pictures of him and framed copies of what I assumed were his most famous articles. Sadly, the first one I looked at said "Wealthy Attorney Accused of Stealing Millions," and I felt my face start to color with shame and anger.

I sat in a chair he pointed to as he went around and plopped down behind his desk. He took out a pad of yellow lined paper, flipped to a fresh page, and grabbed a pen.

"Okay, so Reward was sold."

"Yes."

"Who bought it?"

"William Ellington Force."

"Another relative?"

I shrugged. "In one sense." I thought about telling him that William Ellington Force was a descendant of slaves who once lived on Reward, but I didn't think it was fair to bring Bee's family into this without asking their permission.

"But another part of the plantation was sold to somebody else?"

"Yes."

"And this is important because your relative thought he was getting the whole thing?"

"Well . . . yes. Or, no. I'm not sure, exactly."

"That's it? That's what you came here to tell me?" Blackford threw down his pen and shook his head. "That's not news. Sorry."

He started to stand.

"It's news because I'm pretty sure that right before his accident my father had been about to deed that same property over to an African American lady who lives in a trailer down the road. Daddy thought it was heirs' property and that it was rightfully hers, but she had been kicked off by my uncle Charlie."

Blackford looked at me. "Heirs' property, huh?" His lips bunched and worked back and forth beneath his pitiful mustache. "I assume this lady's not the new buyer?"

It was my turn to treat him like he was dumb. "You're not supposed to have to buy what's already yours, are you?"

He gave me a look. "So, who did buy it?"

"Something called Felony Bay Land Company,

LLC. I don't know who owns it, but I'm trying to find out."

"What are they, real-estate developers?"

"Well, I don't know if they're developers, but they've been digging a lot of holes."

"A lot of holes?"

"Yessir. I think maybe they're looking for treasure."

He threw down his pen again. "Why're you fishing me with this story, kid? What's in it for you? People buy land all the time around here. They dig holes for perk tests so they can put in septic. Or they dig holes as foundations for houses. Or they dig holes to dig holes. I don't know, and I don't see any story here."

I was feeling desperate. "Don't you think taking land away from a poor, disabled lady ought to get people interested?"

Blackford raised his eyebrows and seemed to think about that. Then he gave his potbelly a little rub and stood up. "Yeah, maybe. Thanks for coming in."

I felt a sense of failure as he walked me out to the elevator. I didn't have the slightest idea what he would do with the information. Probably nothing, I decided. I left without even kicking him in the shins the way he deserved.

Fifteen

I took another bus south, going back toward where I had started earlier, getting off at Calhoun Street and walking east several blocks to East Bay, to the offices of the Coastal Conservation League. I didn't know very much about the CCL, only that they got involved in protecting land and water from polluters and developers and others who wanted to do things that screwed up the environment.

I didn't really know what I expected them to do or even what they could do. I just had a vague notion that if they thought somebody might be doing something bad to the environment, they might start trying to find out who they were and why they were doing it. Maybe they could find out who the people were behind FBLC LLC, even if I couldn't. Maybe they would think it was bad that so many holes were being dug so close to the water. Maybe they would tell them they needed a bunch of permits and at least slow down whatever was happening at Felony Bay. I knew I might be grasping at straws. These people might laugh at me. But what other choice did I have?

I got a better feeling as soon I went into their offices, because the lady behind the desk was about five times nicer than the one at the *Post and Courier*. She actually smiled at me.

"What can I help you with?" she asked.

"I need to talk to someone about what might be an environmental crime," I said.

The woman raised her eyebrows, but she was being serious, not trying to treat me like a dumb kid. "What kind of environmental crime? It will make a difference as to which one of our people I call."

"Somebody is digging a bunch of holes along the shore of the Leadenwah River."

"Big holes?"

"Yes, ma'am. And real close to the water."

She nodded, dialed an extension, and told the person who picked up, "Someone is here to report what might be illegal digging." She paused, nodded. "Okay, I'll tell her.

"Sheila will be right out."

Sheila turned out to be a middle-aged woman with light brown hair and a happy face with deep laugh lines around her eyes. She shook hands and asked me to come back to her office. On the way she got us both glasses of water, and I explained why I was there.

"You saw somebody digging holes near the water on the Leadenwah River?" she asked as we sat down in her office.

"Yes, ma'am. They were big holes, and right down near the water's edge."

"Were the people burying anything in the holes?"

"You mean like waste?"

"Yes."

For a second or two I thought about lying and telling her that I'd seen all kinds of horrible things being buried there, but in the end I said, "No, ma'am. I don't they were burying anything, just digging."

"Were they digging on land or in the water?"

"I think just on land."

Sheila gave me a sad smile. "I'm afraid, based on what you're telling me, even though it sounds a bit suspicious, that they probably aren't breaking any laws."

"Can you go out there and check it out? Aren't there some kind of permits they need?"

"Is there something more that you can tell me?"

I let out a big sigh. "It's not really environmental," I said, and then I told her about Mrs. Middleton and heirs' property.

Sheila looked at me sympathetically. "I can understand why you would want to stop this. But we're an environmental organization. I'm afraid there's nothing the CCL can do. I'm sorry."

I thanked her for her time, but I couldn't disguise my disappointment. I had started off the day with what I thought were two really good ideas for getting to the bottom of what was happening at Felony Bay. Now I realized that neither one of them was going to work.

There was only one thing left for me to do in town. I walked outside and started toward the Force & Barrett offices to see if Custis had finished getting the answers he had promised yesterday. Even if he had, I knew it would probably be all the information I could get my hands on. My dream had convinced me that time was running out, but I still didn't have enough facts. I just knew something was about to happen and that it was my job to stop it.

I wished so badly that Daddy would wake up so I could ask him what I should do. I wanted to know how a twelve-year-old girl could possibly stop anything.

Sixteen

When I reached Force & Barrett, I told the
red-haired lady in the reception area that I was
there to see Custis.

"Please have a seat," she said. She gave me a cool
look and dialed an extension. "The Force girl is here,"
I heard her say.

Then she hung up the phone and looked at me.
"Someone will be right out."

I sat and thumbed through a magazine while I
waited, expecting to see Martha's smiling face come
through the door at any moment. Even so, I couldn't
get rid of the feeling that something wasn't right. Several

minutes went by, and when Crawford Barrett suddenly appeared, I understood why things had felt weird.

"Abbey," he said, giving me a big smile.

I stood and nodded. "Hello, Mr. Barrett. I was actually here to see Custis."

"Yes, I know," he said. "But when Custis told me what you had asked him to do, I decided to sit down with you myself."

I tried to fight down a sense of helplessness that verged on panic. "Custis isn't going to talk to me?" I asked, hearing the tremor in my voice.

Even as I fought for control, part of me felt deeply hurt that Custis would have betrayed my confidence and gone to Mr. Barrett. The other part of me felt an ice-cold anger.

"I'm afraid he's not able to," Mr. Barrett said. He sat down in the chair beside me and motioned for me to sit again. "A matter came up with one of our clients today. I asked Custis to deal with it, and it required him being outside of the office."

"Is Custis in trouble?"

Mr. Barrett smiled, as if nothing could be further from the truth. "Absolutely not!" he said with a laugh. "But I know you've raised some questions about the sale of the Felony Bay parcel, and I thought, since I'm the one closest to the issue, that it would be best if I tried to answer them."

"Thank you, sir," I said with a smile, since it was obvious that I didn't have any other choice. I have found that with certain adults if you say *sir* and *ma'am* often enough and smile when you talk to them, they think you agree with them, no matter what.

"I believe you asked Custis how it was that what we refer to as the Felony Bay tract came to be sold separately from the rest of Reward. Is that correct?"

"Yessir," I said.

"Well, the fact is that while the rest of the plantation has always been a single tract, your father had broken out the Felony Bay tract as a separate parcel."

"Do you know why he did that, sir?" I asked.

Mr. Barrett made a little movement with his hands. "I don't think the reason really matters now. The point is that when the plantation had to be sold, the members of the firm who were overseeing this on your father's behalf were able to sell Felony Bay separately, for a higher price per acre."

"Because you needed to pay back Miss Jenkins, sir?"

Mr. Barrett gave me a sad look and nodded. "That's right."

"So who bought it, sir?"

"A partnership."

I smiled and nodded. Mr. Barrett smiled back. "Who are the partners?" I asked, forgetting my *sir*. Since Daddy was a lawyer and didn't have anybody else to talk to at the dinner table all those years, I was a lot smarter about legal stuff than most twelve-year-old girls. It had probably also made me more persistent in asking questions. Daddy had joked that I sometimes had a tendency to "badger" my witnesses.

But if Mr. Barrett felt badgered, he didn't show it. "I wish I could help you, but the names of the partners were not disclosed in the transaction. Under the law there is no reason they need to be."

"But there has to be a head person."

Mr. Barrett nodded. "Indeed, young lady! You're a sharp one. It's called a general partner," he said. "And it is true that the general partner's name has to be disclosed on the deed. However, in this case, the general partner is not a person. It is another LLC. That stands for 'limited liability corporation.'"

"I know what LLC stands for, sir," I said. "This law partnership, Force and Barrett, is an LLC. My father is the managing partner."

That last part had probably not been the smartest

thing to say, but it just seemed to pop out. It made Mr. Barrett's smile bunch into something more like a bruise than a happy expression.

"I know that, Abbey. But he can't manage very well from his hospital bed, can he?" Mr. Barrett was trying to keep his voice light and easy, but his cheeks were tinged with red. He glanced toward the receptionist, but she appeared to be busy typing on her computer.

"So," I said, "bottom line. The land that my father was going to give to Mrs. Middleton because it was heirs' property and rightfully hers got sold to some partnership."

Mr. Barrett held up a hand to stop me. "Hang on there, Abbey. Heirs' property is a very complicated topic, and 'rightfully hers' is as well. We know that your father broke Felony Bay into a separate parcel. Perhaps he believed that Mrs. Middleton might at one point have been entitled to claim that Felony Bay was heirs' property, but perhaps the reason he never recorded the deed is that he changed his mind. After all, she had moved off the property—"

"Do you know when that happened?" I interrupted.

"I believe it was when your grandfather was still alive."

"And do you know how it happened?"

"According to my knowledge, your grandfather was too ill to handle his own affairs, and your uncle Charlie had something to do with it."

I nodded. "Mrs. Middleton's family had lived in that house for more than a hundred years, and in that whole time they'd never been charged rent. Mrs. Middleton was a widow, and Uncle Charlie started charging her way more than she could afford. She had no choice but to leave."

Mr. Barrett leaned closer to me. "That may be true, Abbey. But, sadly, it doesn't matter now. What matters is the fact that Mrs. Middleton moved. By moving, she effectively negated her claim. That means that when it came time to sell the property to repay Miss Jenkins, there was no valid outstanding claim by another party."

I felt my own face getting red. I knew I should have buttoned my lip five minutes earlier, but now it was way too late. "So the letter of the law was satisfied but not the intent of the law," I said. "A poor, handicapped lady's land got sold to somebody else, but it was legal. Daddy always said that when a lawyer did his job the right way, the intent of the law was what was honored. Sir. Daddy was going to set this right, to give Mrs. Middleton what she deserved, and, after his accident, it didn't happen."

Mr. Barrett glanced at the receptionist. His teeth were clamped together, and his lips were slightly open. If the red-haired lady hadn't been there, I think he might have tried to bite me.

"I have continued to try to be a friend to your father because of his circumstances, but let me be very clear about something," he said, his voice just above a whisper but shaking with anger. "Because of what he did, this law firm found itself saddled with shameful damage to our reputation and a tremendous debt to one of our clients. We did not worry about the finer points when we sold Reward. We worried about recovering enough money to repay Miss Jenkins. We worried about salvaging what we could of the company your father and I built together. Without your father around to help, this is work I've been doing all on my own. I know how tough things have been for you since your father's accident, Abbey, but you weren't the only one who was hurt that day, the only one left trying to put the pieces of your life back together, alone."

I was speechless. I knew that Mr. Barrett and Daddy were friends, but I hadn't before considered how he might have felt about what happened.

Mr. Barrett stood up and brushed off his pants as if my questions were like dirt that had somehow gotten

on him. "I believe we have discussed this matter suf-
ficiently, and I hope this can be our last conversation
about it. I will also tell you that Custis is a junior lawyer here, and it is not beneficial for his career for you to
be coming in during business hours and taking up his
time with personal matters that are antithetical to the
interests of this firm. Good day, Abbey."

He started to walk back toward the door that led to
the offices.

I stood up. "What's about to happen at Felony
Bay?" I asked.

Mr. Barrett came to a stop like he was a car and
somebody had just slammed on his brakes. He turned.
"What did you ask?"

"I think you heard me, sir."

His eyes narrowed. "There's nothing that's about
to happen at Felony Bay," he said. "But if you go onto
that property, or make trouble for whoever now owns
it, I must tell you that no one here, not Custis or I, will
be able to help you." He watched me to see if that was
sinking in.

"I don't think I should need to tell you this," he
went on after a few seconds, "but given what happened
with your father, a judge would not look kindly upon
you breaking the law."

By the time he finished, my cheeks were burning, and tears were bunching in the corners of my eyes. I told myself I would not cry in front of Mr. Barrett, no matter what. I started to say something to excuse myself, but it was unnecessary. Mr. Barrett opened the door leading back to the offices. He walked through and disappeared without looking back.

The red-haired receptionist was watching me, her face unreadable. I said nothing to her as I walked out the front door and down to the sidewalk. What Mr. Barrett said had hurt, but it wasn't nearly as upsetting as the fact that, once again, I was all alone in trying to figure out what was really going on.

Seventeen

It was almost five o'clock, and I was in a black mood as I caught the bus back toward Leadenwah. I felt utterly defeated, because every single place I'd gone seemed to be a dead end. The city turned to suburbs, and the suburbs turned to country, but my eyes didn't register anything, and when I got off I used the pay phone to call Ruth to ask if she would pick me up.

"What are you doing at the bus stop?" she demanded. I could hear the television in the background.

"I went to see Daddy," I said, leaving out the other meetings.

"Well, I'm very busy."

"I know. I'm sorry to ask you."

She muttered something under her breath, then said, "Okay, I'll be there when I can get free. It's going to be a while."

I knew it meant that she'd come when her show was over, but having no other choice, I thanked her and sat down to wait.

As I was watching the early-evening traffic roll by, I was surprised to see Grandma Em's car go past. Instinctively I raised my hand to wave. I saw Grandma Em turn her head in my direction, and a second later her brake lights went on as she pulled over to the shoulder. Bee climbed out of the passenger seat with a big smile. "Want a ride?" she called.

I was already on my feet heading in her direction. "Please," I shouted back.

When I climbed into the backseat, I asked, "What are y'all doing home so quickly?"

Grandma Em turned. "Bee's doctors' appointments went so smoothly that we had no reason to stay. She told me we had to get back right away, so I changed our flight."

"You want to have dinner with us?" Bee asked. "Grandma got flank steak and fresh corn on the cob, and she's going to make tomato-and-mozzarella salad."

I hadn't had lunch, and my stomach growled at the mere mention of Grandma Em's food. "Thanks," I said. "I'd love to."

I was dying for Bee's company and her help with all my jumbled-up ideas, but I also knew I wouldn't be being a good friend unless I found a way to tell her that I needed to go after the mystery of Felony Bay on my own. I had no idea how I was going to do that, but every time I thought about my dream, I became more convinced there was something dangerous going on. I was increasingly certain it had to do with both Daddy and Mrs. Middleton, and I knew I had no choice but to keep digging. I had to find a way to explain all that to Bee, and a good meal might help me think.

On the way back I borrowed Grandma Em's cell phone and called Ruth to tell her I didn't need a ride after all. She sounded relieved and didn't even ask how I was getting home.

When we drove into Reward, I got out of the car at the foot of Uncle Charlie's drive and walked up to the house. Rufus ran off the porch to greet me, and we walked around the house and found Ruth in back, now reading a book in the shade of a live oak. The book was one of those paperbacks with a shirtless guy with long hair and a woman with a low-cut dress on the cover.

She managed to hold back her sorrow when I told her I wouldn't be around for dinner.

"You still need to do the dishes when you get home," she said. "Just because you don't eat here doesn't mean you can skip your chores."

"Yes, ma'am."

"And I told you before: Don't get used to it. You don't live there anymore."

I didn't even try to come up with a response. I went up to my room to change my clothes and heard Uncle Charlie come home just as I was ready to leave. Instead of walking out the front and taking the chance of meeting him on the porch, I went along the hallway to the kitchen and out the back door.

Rufus and I jumped off the back porch and started around the side of the house. I was planning to skirt the edges of the yard, staying in the shadows where Uncle Charlie wouldn't see me, and we were halfway around when I noticed Uncle Charlie's pickup truck was parked in a totally strange place.

On most nights he parked the truck out in the open to keep from getting leaves and bird poop on his windshield, which usually happened if he parked beneath one of the live oaks. However, tonight he had not only backed the truck all the way under a tree, but he had gone so far back that the truck bed was jammed into group of oleander bushes.

At first I suspected that Uncle Charlie had come home even drunker than usual. My second theory was that he'd backed into some car and driven away without reporting it, and then parked that way to keep anyone from seeing the truck's damaged rear end.

Curious, I pushed into the oleanders to check out the back of the truck. At first I was confused, because there was nothing visible, not even a fresh scratch or a tiny new dent. But then I noticed the big tarp in the truck bed and the large object underneath it. With a fresh surge of curiosity, I wondered if there was something under the tarp that Uncle Charlie was trying to hide. With him just around the corner having his whiskey on the porch and Ruth in the kitchen heating up canned slop for dinner, I knew it was risky, but I also wanted to find out what was under that tarp.

Being as quiet as possible, I put one foot on the rear tire and stepped into the truck bed. I got down on my knees, took one last look up at the house, and lifted the edge of the tarp.

At first it was too dark to see. I could only make out what looked like a very rough, square object, so I pushed more branches aside and pulled off more of the tarp. My heart started to beat faster, because I could now see that what was underneath was an ancient crate. There was a hasp on the crate's lid with a very old-fashioned, rusty padlock on it, which was hanging loose.

My very first thought was that all the stuff about the *Lovely Clarisse* was true and Uncle Charlie had somehow discovered the gold. But almost right away I realized that a few things didn't make sense. First, if the chest had been buried for many years, it would have been damp and covered with dirt. This one was clean and dry as a bone. Also, knowing Uncle Charlie, if he had found treasure, he would have been yelling and screaming his head off. But he wasn't doing that. So what was in the crate, and why was it hidden?

I slipped the padlock off the latch and raised the lid a few inches. A musty smell hit me, as if the crate had been closed for a long time. I tried to see inside, but with the sun going down, the tarp mostly covering the crate, and all the oleander branches, there wasn't enough light. I pushed the tarp off completely, hoping Uncle Charlie wouldn't pick that moment to come around the side of the house and check on his truck.

When I raised the lid a second time, I felt a rush of disappointment. The crate was completely empty. But if that was the case, why bother to jam it into the bushes like this and try to hide it?

None of this made sense, but I certainly couldn't ask Ruth or Uncle Charlie. I let down the lid, put the padlock back on the latch, and smoothed the tarp back over it so it looked undisturbed. Then I slipped off the truck and cut around the side of the yard, my head pounding with questions. Rufus trotted ahead of me, sniffing hard and at one point chasing a rabbit out from the high grass along the track. The night was hot and still, and as I walked I felt sweat break out on my skin. Mosquitoes were buzzing around my head and face, but I ignored them and focused instead on the fact that the more I learned, the less I knew.

Uncle Charlie, Ruth, and Bubba Simmons all seemed to be deeply involved with whatever was going on. Also, Mrs. Middleton and her heirs' property were part of the mystery, but probably small pieces in a bigger puzzle. For the life of me, I could not imagine what purpose the wooden crate could have, but I knew that if it was worth hiding, it had to be important and it probably tied into everything else.

The more I thought about the crate, the more I started to suspect that it wasn't going to stay in Uncle Charlie's truck for long. That plus the warning Mr. Barrett had given me to stay away from Felony Bay had convinced me that I needed to get back over there soon. I was more positive than ever that time was running out.

When I got out onto the plantation drive, I was surprised to see someone walking toward me through the gathering dusk. It was Bee; only I noticed what I had missed in the car earlier, namely that the sling was no longer on her right arm, and her knee was no longer in a fiberglass brace.

"Hey, what's up?" I said as she came up to me.

"I had a lot of time to think about Mrs. Middleton and all that heirs' property stuff while we were waiting to see the doctors," Bee said. "I realized that she's the one person we haven't talked to yet."

I looked at her, and then I shook my head, feeling really stupid. "You're right," I said. "I can't believe I didn't think of that."

"I asked Grandma Em if we could eat a little later than usual. Maybe we could walk over there before dinner?"

"Okay," I said.

For almost a full day now, I had been puzzling over what I was going to say to her to try to convince her that I should be pursuing the Felony Bay mystery on my own. I had even rehearsed the speech I wanted to give, but now, as we turned and started to walk toward Mrs. Middleton's trailer, all I told her was the simple truth.

I told her about the dream I'd had, how in it all the people were digging out at Felony Bay and how they were doing something bad to Mrs. Middleton and Skoogie, and my feeling that they were also just about to discover something terribly important. I explained that I'd had the same kind of dream only twice before, once before we found out about my mother's cancer and the second time just before my father's accident. I told her I was afraid it meant that something bad was going to happen. I was afraid it was going to happen to me, and I told her that I was afraid something bad might happen to her as well.

She listened without interrupting, and when I finished, she said, "Are you saying you don't want my help?"

I shrugged. "I just don't want anything bad to happen."

She stopped and turned to look at me. "You did more stuff today, didn't you? And now you've hatched some kind of idea. What are you planning to do?"

I let out a sigh. So much for my ability to keep Bee

out of this, I thought. As I started walking again, I told
her how I'd spent my day and all the dead ends I'd run
into at the newspaper, the CCL, and not being able
to get any more help from Custis or Mr. Barrett. But
then I also told her about the crate I'd found in Uncle
Charlie's truck.

"What do you think it is?" she asked, her voice
growing excited. "Do you think they already found
some treasure?"

I shook my head. "The box didn't have dirt all over
its sides like it would if they had just dug it up. Also it
was empty."

"That's weird," Bee said. I could see from her
excitement that my attempt to warn her off had done
just the opposite. "You think the crate has something
to do with all the holes?"

"I don't know why it would, but none of this makes
sense."

"We really need to understand why they're digging
those holes, don't we?" she said.

"Yeah."

"So what are you planning? There's something
you're not telling me. I know it."

"I'm going to sneak over to Felony Bay tonight
after Uncle Charlie and Ruth are in bed."

"Really?"

"But you don't need to come if you don't want to," I added.

"Are you kidding?" Bee clapped her hands. "This is the best thing that's happened to me in a long time. No way I'm letting you have all the fun by yourself."

I could see the happiness in her eyes, and I knew that just as much as it was probably a bad idea to let her come tonight, her joy was also just what Grandma Em had hoped to see. Bee was back in her life. She was excited, and she was really looking forward to something. How could I possibly say no to that? Besides, if I was honest with myself, I really didn't want to.

We found Mrs. Middleton and Skoogie out behind their trailer on a couple of folding lawn chairs. They were sitting inside a small enclosure that looked like a tent covered with screening and reading books by the light of a battery-powered lantern. Like on a lot of South Carolina summer nights, the air was humid, as sticky as drying glue, and while the biting sand gnats that came out at dusk and dawn were starting to go to bed for the night, the mosquitoes were fierce and they weren't going anywhere.

I had to admit that since Daddy's "accident" I had

come to realize that I had used to take a lot of things for granted, like having good food, a wonderful private school to go to, spending money when I needed it, and nice new clothes. Even living with cheapskate Uncle Charlie and Ruth, we always had air-conditioning. And in the South, air-conditioning had become one of those things most people couldn't live without.

Only now I realized Mrs. Middleton and Skoogie didn't have any. Or if they had it in the trailer, they only ran it when they absolutely couldn't stand not to have it on, because the extra electricity was something they probably couldn't afford. That was the only possible reason they would have been sitting out on a night that was over eighty degrees, trying to read in the fading light as the sun dropped behind the treetops.

"Hi, Mrs. Middleton," I called from the gathering shadows. "Hi, Skoogie."

Mrs. Middleton put down her book and squinted in our direction. "Who's that? Is that you, Abbey?"

"Yes, ma'am."

"Well, come on over here and visit."

"I hope you don't mind us interrupting you," I said.

"No, no, no. Y'all come on inside this screen and get out from those mosquitoes. What y'all girls doing all the way down here?"

Bee and I opened the door in the side of the shelter and ducked inside. "I just wanted to introduce my friend to you," I said. "This is Bee Force. Her father bought Reward."

Mrs. Middleton held out a gnarled hand. "A pleasure to meet you, young lady." She shot a glance at Skoogie. "Git on your feet, boy, and remember your manners!"

Skoogie stood up, clearly embarrassed. "Hi," he said, giving Bee a wave.

We stood around and made small talk for a few minutes; then I gave Bee a look and got down to business.

"Can I ask you a question, Mrs. Middleton?"

"Certainly, child."

"Before my father's accident, do you know if he had any plans to sign the land around the old cabin over at Felony Bay to you?"

Mrs. Middleton's expression changed. In the dim light I saw the sadness in her eyes. "Why do you want to know?"

"Please, I don't mean to pry, but I'm trying to understand some things about what happened to Daddy. It's important to me."

She took a deep breath. "Your daddy was a blessed

man and a saint. Ain't no way he did what they accused him of. No way, child."

I stood there waiting for more, but after a few seconds I realized she had answered my question. Daddy had been about to give her back the land.

"Do you think . . . do you think it had anything to do with what happened to Mr. Force?" Bee asked.

Mrs. Middleton was quiet for a moment, then looked at us hard. "I sure hope not, my dears. But the more I think about it, the more I wonder."

"I'm sorry you didn't get your land back, Mrs. Middleton," I said.

"I keep praying on it."

We excused ourselves, saying we had to get back for dinner. After we left, Bee and I were quiet for a time as we walked along the township road toward the Reward gates. We didn't have to talk about what Mrs. Middleton had said. She had all but confirmed what we both suspected. Whatever was going on over at Felony Bay and whatever had happened to my father were connected. We just didn't know how.

"You still want to come tonight?" I asked at last.

"Darn right," Bee said. "I'm so mad about what happened to your dad and that poor woman and her grandson that I could spit nails."

"Then we better make up a plan."

As we walked up the plantation drive to the big house, we went over everything we would do later that night. A few minutes later, we sat down to a wonderful dinner of flank steak, corn on the cob, and mozzarella-and-fresh-garden-tomato salad.

Afterward I thanked Grandma Em for inviting me, and when Bee walked me out onto the porch to say good night, I reminded her to bring a couple flashlights, since Uncle Charlie kept his in the bedroom where I couldn't get to them. Both of us would go to sleep now and set our alarms for one thirty. We would meet at the barn at two, and that would give us plenty of time to do our reconnaissance.

I walked home smelling the perfume of night-blooming flowers and gazing overhead at a sky that was completely clear of clouds. The moon had been full just a couple days ago, so later tonight I was pretty sure we'd have plenty of moonlight for walking the path to Felony Bay.

When I reached the back door and looked through the glass panes, I nearly did a double take. Ruth was in the kitchen, and to my great surprise she was actually washing the dishes. That was always my job, and I couldn't remember a time when Ruth had done them for me. To my even greater surprise, she was smiling and humming a tune as if she was in a great mood.

I stood a moment and watched, and in the next instant, something even more amazing happened. Uncle Charlie walked into the kitchen, something he almost never did. Every night when dinner was over, instead of helping clear the table, he would get up and head into the den, where he would drink whiskey and watch television until it was time for bed. Also he never fed Rufus, cooked anything, made his own sandwich for lunch, or even fixed himself a bowl of cereal. And he always made Ruth or me get his drink, so there was never any reason for him to go into the kitchen. Only, as I watched, that was exactly where he showed up.

He had two glasses of wine in his hands. He went over to the sink, put one on the counter beside Ruth, then slapped her on the butt. She turned with a warning look, but he gave her a goofy smile and raised his glass for a toast. She wiped her hands on a towel, picked up her glass, and clicked with his.

It was obvious that they were celebrating again, and I was sure it had something to do with the crate in the back of Uncle Charlie's pickup. My curiosity was on fire, and I couldn't wait to sneak out and get over to Felony Bay.

Then I had a terrible thought. What if Uncle Charlie and Ruth weren't planning to go to bed at the regular time? What if they planned to stay up all night drinking toasts? It would be terrible luck to be stuck here and unable to sneak out and meet Bee. I just hoped, if that happened, she would have the good sense to go home and go back to sleep.

My fears were put to rest in the next instant as Uncle Charlie glanced at his watch, downed the rest of his wine in two gulps, and said loud enough for me to hear through the glass, "I'm heading up to bed. We need to catch a little sleep while we can."

I felt a renewed surge of excitement on hearing this. As I opened the back door and walked inside, my heart was beating fast with the expectations of the adventure Bee and I were going to have. If I had paid a little more attention to what Uncle Charlie had said to Ruth, and to the fact they were in such good moods, I might not have felt nearly as good about things.

Eighteen

My alarm went off at one thirty sharp, and I rolled out of bed and hit the Off button as fast as I could before it woke up Ruth or Uncle Charlie or, more importantly, Rufus. I pulled on blue jeans, socks, a dark T-shirt, and hiking boots; then I stopped to think about what else I might need. After a second I grabbed a can of bug spray, gave my arms, legs, neck, and face a good coating, and opened my top drawer and took out the hunting knife Daddy had given me for my tenth birthday. With the tooled leather sheath strapped to my belt, I put my ear to the door of my bedroom to listen for the sound of Uncle Charlie's snoring.

To my surprise, I heard nothing, so I opened my

door a crack to see if I could hear any better. Again nothing, which was unusual, because Uncle Charlie snores like a warthog. Finally I put my head into the hallway. I could tell by the darker square at the end of the hall that Uncle Charlie and Ruth's bedroom door was open, which was also unusual. In the next instant, I caught the barest hint of light coming from the downstairs.

I held my breath even as my pulse began to pound. I could hear soft footsteps moving through the downstairs. They were followed by the unmistakable sounds of the kitchen door opening and the squeak of the screen.

I eased my bedroom door shut and tiptoed to my window, pulling it open, pushing out the screen, and climbing onto the porch roof just as I heard the engine of Uncle Charlie's pickup come to life. Rufus got off his dog bed, came over to the window, and started to whine. I told him to be quiet and stay, then lowered the window and pushed the screen mostly back into place.

Uncle Charlie's pickup was coming around the side of the house, the tires snapping twigs as they rolled slowly across the ground. The truck's headlights were off, but the moon was bright enough to illuminate the dirt track. I dropped to my belly and lay on the flat roof to keep the moonlight from outlining my silhouette in case Uncle Charlie glanced toward my bedroom window.

I was being very quiet, because I didn't know if Ruth had stayed behind. However, as the truck went past, I spotted the outline of a second passenger in the glow of the dashboard lights. It had to be Ruth, I thought, and I wondered where they could be sneaking off to at nearly two in the morning. A half second later, I had a pretty good idea.

I got up, crossed to the tree limb that stuck out over the porch roof, and climbed on top of it. I slid along the branch to the trunk, climbed onto the opposite branch, shinnied out along it, and dropped to the ground. There was no longer any reason to worry about waking up Uncle Charlie or Ruth, so I ran down the dirt track to the plantation drive, then went through the fence and across the pasture.

The horses were sleeping, but Timmy woke and trotted toward me as I came across the field. I gave him a quick nose rub, then continued on my way. Timmy, and soon after Clem and Lem, fell in behind me and followed me over to the gate, all of them hoping for a midnight snack.

Bee was already waiting for me, and I told her about

Uncle Charlie and Ruth sneaking out in the pickup.

"You think they're going to Felony Bay?" she asked.

"Where else?"

"So they are behind what's going on there."

"Looks like it."

"Maybe we'll find out what they're doing with that crate."

I nodded, thinking exactly the same thing. "Got the flashlights?" I asked.

Bee handed me one. She had another for herself. I was about to lead the way out of the barn, but I stopped.

"We have to be *really* careful," I said. "If they're at Felony Bay like we think they are, and if they happen to hear us or see us, we have to hightail it as fast as we can."

"Why?"

"There are only three ways to get out of there: up the dirt track toward the township road, back on the path toward the big house, or out past One Arm Pond and through the pastures to the plantation drive. Uncle Charlie knows that, and if we're not quick, he'll be able to trap us."

"We have to run in the dark?"

"If they hear us." I nodded. "Fast as you can. Don't

worry about anything else."

"Snakes?"

I shook my head. "Just run."

Before she could ask any more questions or get any more upset, I led the way out of the barn toward the big house, where we would find the path that would take us to Felony Bay. On the way I found an oleander bush and cut a long stick that was thick enough to be sturdy and forked at one end. I used my knife to cut the forks about four inches long.

Bee didn't ask what the stick was for, and I didn't offer to explain. I figured she would find out soon enough if we ran into a problem.

We reached the big house, skirted the edge of the yard, and checked for unexpected lights that would show that Grandma Em had heard Bee sneaking out. The house was as dark as a crypt.

We got to the back corner of the yard and quickly found the trail that led to Felony Bay. As we stepped into the woods, the night seemed to envelop us. To our left the river glowed through the trees, its surface the color of honey as it reflected the moonlight. The air was thick with the scent of early-summer flowers and vines, heavy with mock orange and honeysuckle; and up ahead the trilling of hundreds of frogs populated the night.

We went slowly, our flashlights off, using the moon and the light reflected from the river to guide us. We had decided that, on the off chance that Grandma Em was awake and looking out her bedroom window, we would not use flashlights until we were well away from the big house. When we finally thought it was safe, we flicked them on, and I felt relieved to have the powerful beams light our way.

I took the lead and kept my light aimed at the ground, examining the thick, dark roots and vines that coiled and ran through the dead leaves, making sure none of them was a snake out searching for a meal. The night breeze moved gently across my skin, while overhead I heard the harsh cry of a night heron on its way to the river to hunt fish.

We moved faster with our lights on, but we would turn them off well before we reached Felony Bay in order not to give ourselves away. We would also need to give our eyes time to once again adjust to the moonlight.

After about fifteen minutes, the undergrowth on our right began to thicken, and I knew One Arm Pond had to be just ahead. The peeping of the frogs grew louder. In spite of my desire to hurry, I slowed my pace, keeping my eyes on the ground. Behind me Bee must have noticed my caution, because she said, "What's the matter? It's not Green Alice, is it?"

"No," I whispered, but I kept picking my way along with care. There was no sense in frightening Bee if there turned out to be no need.

After another couple minutes, the cacophony of the frogs had become almost deafening, so I knew One Arm Pond had to be directly on our right. I couldn't see it through the leaves, not even moonlight reflecting off the surface, but I could smell the musty odor of pluff mud. I was studying every single root, vine, or stick with great intensity now, and that's when I came to a quick stop.

Two feet ahead of me, way too close for comfort, something that looked at first like a thick black root had just crawled from underneath a layer of dead magnolia leaves. It was maybe four feet long and as thick as a beer can in the middle. The sight made my heart start to hammer.

"What?" Bee asked.

I shook my head and said nothing, just held my oleander stick out in front of me with the forked end pointed at the ground.

"What?" Bee asked again.

"Just don't move."

We stayed perfectly still, but the snake sensed my body heat or my smell. It started to coil, and it opened its jaws and gave a warning hiss. My flashlight beam lit up the inside of its mouth. It was snow white, true to its name: cottonmouth. Of all the venomous snakes that live in South Carolina, I was most afraid of the cottonmouth. It was the one snake that would attack when it felt threatened.

Behind me I heard Bee's intake of breath, and then the sound of her feet shifting backward along the path. Her motion was likely to antagonize the snake, and that meant I had no time. I waited until the snake's head moved sideways for just a second as it searched with its heat sensors preparing to strike, then I stabbed down with my oleander stick.

It was a lucky shot. I managed to knock the head down to the ground and pin it between the two forks. The snake thrashed and fought, and it was amazingly strong. Thankfully the stick was also strong and held the snake's head in place.

If it had been a copperhead or a rattlesnake, I would have picked it up by the tail and thrown it into the woods as far as I could, comfortable that it would hightail it once it landed. But not a cottonmouth. I knew there was a decent chance that the snake would hit the ground and come right back after us, most likely moving too fast to pin again. I took my knife from the sheath on my belt, leaned down, and cut off its head in one stroke.

The headless body spurted blood, but it continued to move, striking blindly in all directions. I knew it might keep that up for another five minutes or so, but I also knew we could ignore it. I wiped the blood off my knife, cleaned my hands against the bark of a palmetto tree, then turned to look at Bee.

She was standing several feet behind me, her hands to her mouth. "You okay?" she asked in a trembling voice.

I nodded. "How about you?"

"I hate snakes."

"I'm not so fond of this particular type myself."

"I can't believe you just cut off its head."

"It was either him or us."

She shuddered and shook her head. "I hope we don't see any more."

"We're almost past the pond. That's the worst place for cottonmouths."

She nodded and gave a wan smile as if that was at least somewhat encouraging news. I didn't have the heart to tell her that we were going to have to turn off our lights for good in another fifty yards or so, as we'd be getting close to Felony Bay.

We made our way past One Arm Pond without any more problems. Gradually the sound of the frogs faded behind us, and when I thought we were well clear of the pond and hopefully of more cottonmouths, I stopped walking and clicked off my flashlight.

"What are you doing?" Bee asked.

"Turn off your light."

"Why?"

"We're getting close, and we can't risk using our lights from here on, in case Uncle Charlie and Ruth are there."

I could see her expression and knew she didn't like the idea, but after a second she flicked hers off. "I can't see a thing."

"Just wait."

We stood there about a minute, and gradually I began to pick out the faint light on the path and the moonlight reflected on the river to our left. The river acted like a night-light, giving a gentle glow to everything around it.

When my eyes had once again adjusted to the dark, I could see the ground under my feet and even make out the shadowy shapes of roots and sticks. I could also see the path winding up ahead of us as it snaked its way through the undergrowth. We started moving again, more slowly than before, and we soon came to the line of No Trespassing signs on the trees that marked the boundary of Felony Bay. I pointed them out to Bee, and she nodded.

A little farther, I began to hear the sound of the excavation machine. It grew louder as we moved forward. The undergrowth gave way to the horseshoe beach, and I could look through the leaves and see a pair of bright lights moving in tight, jerky motions.

At the edge of the undergrowth we squatted behind a thick bush and looked out at the beach. Bubba Simmons was on the same small excavator he had been operating the other day. Its headlights were aimed at the ground where he was digging a fresh hole. When he turned the machine, his headlights momentarily lit two nearby people standing beside a pickup truck. I recognized Uncle Charlie and Ruth. In spite of the fact that I had been expecting to find them there, my breath caught in my throat.

Uncle Charlie stepped to the edge of the hole, looked down, and gave a nod. Bubba climbed off his machine, and then the two of them walked over to Uncle Charlie's pickup and pulled the tarp off the crate, lifting it off the truck and dragging it over to the hole.

I hadn't seen anyone else, and I thought it was just the three of them working together, but then I heard another voice. It was a man. He was someplace out of the light. With the noise from the excavator, I couldn't understand what he said, but something about his tone was bossy, like he was the one in charge.

Uncle Charlie turned toward the voice and nodded. Then Ruth came over and opened the lid of the chest and held it while Charlie and Bubba walked over to the falling-down cabin. They both had flashlights, and they disappeared into the cabin's dark interior and reappeared a moment later carrying burlap bags that pulled their shoulders down with the weight.

The man in the shadows said something else, and Uncle Charlie and Bubba put the bags down with a loud clinking sound and went back into the cabin. Ruth started unloading the contents of the bags into the crate as Uncle Charlie and Bubba brought two more bags. The process continued until Uncle Charlie and Bubba had brought out five bags each. Once all the bags had been unloaded, Ruth closed the top of the crate and hammered the rusty lock closed.

Finally Uncle Charlie and Bubba brought over two long cloth straps, which they slid under the crate.

The crate was very heavy now, and they grunted and strained as they shoved it to the very edge of the hole. Once it was in place, Bubba climbed on the excavator and backed it close to the crate while Uncle Charlie put the looped ends of the straps over a hook on the back of the machine. Then, as Uncle Charlie and Ruth shoved the crate over the edge of the hole, Bubba backed up the excavator, using the straps to lower it to the bottom.

When the crate was in place, Uncle Charlie unhooked one end of each of the straps, and then Bubba drove away from the hole, pulling the straps free. Uncle Charlie finished unhooking the straps from the excavator, dragged them over to the side of the cabin, and tossed them into the darkness. Bee and I stayed perfectly still as we watched Bubba use the excavator to put some of the dirt back in the hole.

"What do you think they're doing?" Bee whispered.

"It looks to me like they're burying the chest."

"Why would they do that?"

I shook my head. "No idea," I said, but that wasn't quite true. An idea had popped into my head, but it seemed so lowdown and preposterous that I didn't want to say it out loud.

When Bubba finished, he turned off the excavator's engine. A sudden silence settled over the night.

The man in the shadows said something, and Uncle Charlie raised his hand in a wave. A second later a car door slammed, an engine started, and headlights went on. The car made a K-turn, and its lights panned over the area, but it was on the far side of the cabin. Bee and I ducked, but it wasn't necessary, because the lights never even came close to us. A second later, we caught a quick glimpse of taillights.

As the car disappeared, heading toward the township dirt road, Ruth came over and joined Bubba and Uncle Charlie. "What a jerk," she said. "Can't be bothered to get his hands dirty."

"Thinks he's got more to lose than everybody else," Bubba growled.

Uncle Charlie gave an annoyed snort. "Let's get this place cleaned up and get some sleep."

They spent the next few minutes walking around and picking up gas and oil cans and some trash, and then Bubba loaded the excavator onto a small trailer that was hooked to his pickup. Lastly Uncle Charlie and Ruth took some garden rakes and smoothed out the excavator's tread marks.

The three of them stood together again and looked at what they had done. "Looks good enough," Uncle Charlie said. "People will be stomping it up pretty good once we bring them out here."

Ruth nodded. "Let's go. I'm dead tired."

They climbed into the trucks, and a second later I heard two engines start. Uncle Charlie pulled out first and then Bubba, and they both drove out toward the township road.

Bee and I waited two full minutes, letting the night sounds settle around us. Bugs buzzed and chittered, frogs peeped from One Arm Pond far behind us, and the occasional heron or other night bird cried out, but otherwise the night was silent. There were no voices, no rumbles of car or truck engines to signal anyone coming back.

I looked at my watch. Two fifteen. We had more than two hours until sunrise, and I thought it was a good bet that nobody else would come around. It would give us plenty of time to check things out and try to figure out what Uncle Charlie and the others were up to.

"Ready?" I asked.

Bee nodded and pushed out of the bushes and down onto the flat sand beach of Felony Bay. I followed, and we walked over to where Uncle Charlie had been standing just a short time ago and shined our lights down on the fresh pile of sand that now covered the crate.

"I wonder what's in there?" Bee said.

"Sounded heavy," I said.

"Yeah," Bee said. "Like iron or steel . . . or maybe gold. But why would they bury it here?"

"Because I don't think they're trying to hide it," I said. "I think they want to pretend they found it."

"That doesn't make any sense."

"Yes, it does," I said, finally putting voice to the ideas that had been taking shape in my brain. "It makes sense if it wasn't your gold to start with. It makes sense if it's not really old Confederate gold but gold that you stole."

Bee looked at me, and she got it right away. "You think your uncle stole Miss Jenkins's gold and blamed your dad? But how could he have gotten to it, if it was locked up and only your dad knew the combination?"

"I don't know, but I can't think of any other reason why he would do this. And since we know my dad didn't steal Miss Jenkins's gold, this would explain where it went, wouldn't it?"

Bee sighed. "Okay, so how do we prove it?"

Bee's question stopped me cold. We might know what was going on, but we couldn't prove anything. It was going to be our word against Uncle Charlie's and Ruth's and Bubba Simmons's and one other person's we hadn't seen. And we were just two twelve-year-old girls.

Suddenly I saw the whole thing, just the way it was going to unfold. Uncle Charlie and Ruth were going to call the newspaper and the television stations and tell them they had made an amazing discovery. They would tell them to bring their cameras out to Felony Bay, where they would show them the hole they had dug and the treasure crate they had discovered. The papers and TV stations would buy it hook, line, and sinker. The gold they had stolen would become theirs, and nobody would challenge them . . . except a couple twelve-year-olds.

I felt my spirits plummet. "We can't prove any of it," I said.

Bee poked me with her elbow. "Wait. This doesn't make sense. Miss Jenkins's jewelry would have obviously been newer than centuries-old Confederate gold, right? So even if your uncle found a way to steal it, he can't just 'find' it. I mean, he's not stupid enough to try that, is he? There's got to be something we're missing."

"You're right," I said, thinking that Bee was thinking much more clearly than me.

"Come on," she said, pointing toward the open door of the old cabin. "Let's look in there."

We went to the door and pointed our lights inside what had once been the sitting room. Vines covered the doorjamb and snaked along the floor in long tendrils. Everything was layered with dust and rotting leaves and bird poop, but I could make out a brick fireplace to our left, and to our right a doorway that led to the kitchen and the bedrooms. As we stepped all the way inside, the sweet smell of the night disappeared, replaced by the odors of mildew and rot. I held my oleander stick out in front and shined my light on the floor, cautious of snakes, until I remembered that Uncle Charlie and Bubba had been in here. Their stomping around would have driven most snakes to find a safer spot.

Other than all the leaves that had blown in, the front room was still in decent shape, but the back of the house had started to lean to one side. When I stepped over and looked into the old kitchen, I could see the night sky through holes in the ceiling and rotten spots on the floor where the boards had fallen in. It looked very spooky, like it would probably be dangerous, not to mention full of nasty creatures like snakes and spiders and centipedes.

"Check this out," Bee said.

When I pointed my light in her direction, I saw a piece of plywood in the middle of the floor that rested on two sawhorses and made a crude worktable. I went over and looked more closely. There were drops of something on the wood and circular burn marks on the end nearest the fireplace.

Bee trained her light on the fireplace. "Look," she said, as her light revealed a pot that hung from an old wrought-iron hook over the fire pit. The pot was blackened around the bottom but still had shiny metal along the outer lip, as if it wasn't very old.

I went over to the fireplace and examined the pot and also the ashes in the fire pit.

"Somebody's been having fires in here," I said.

"Too hot for fires," Bee said.

"I know, but the ashes are still fluffy and all gathered together in a nice pile. Old ashes flatten out and get hard."

Bee took the pot from the hook. She put it on the floor and shined her light down inside it. There was something smeared on the inside of the pot that looked like leftovers from somebody cooking butterscotch.

"What do you think this is?" Bee asked as she tapped her finger against it.

I used a fingernail to try to scrape some of the stuff off the inside of the pot. I couldn't get much, and it didn't look like anything I wanted to taste. "No idea."

We brought the pot to the plywood table. The burn marks on the plywood seemed to match the size and shape of the pot bottom. I pointed that out to Bee. "Looks like they took the pot when it was hot and rested it here."

Bee tapped the table around the blackened wood, where there were tiny splash marks the same color as the inside of the pot. "I think it's the same stuff," she said. "Looks like they poured it out."

I put my face down close and sniffed. "No smell." I chipped at it with my fingernail, and a small bit came free. "It doesn't look like food," I said, rolling it between my fingers. "What do you think they poured it into?"

"Who knows?"

"Keep looking," I said. "We need to find more." I had no idea exactly what we were looking for, but I was convinced we had stumbled onto something important.

We shined our lights over the rest of the plywood table and around the cabin but found nothing else. Finally my hopes started to plummet all over again when I thought about what we had: a pot with some melted stuff inside and our word against Uncle Charlie's that we'd seen him bury an old crate filled with something heavy. I knew what Daddy would say about such little evidence: that we couldn't prove a thing.

Out of desperation I dropped to my knees and

started looking around on the floor underneath the table. That was when my light caught a momentary reflection. I crawled over to where I had seen the glint, but when I aimed my light right at it, I could see nothing but old wood boards with wide cracks between them.

I tried several more times, and only when I shined my light at the same angle I had the first time did I see the glint again. "Come over here. I think I found something," I said. Bee came to my side of the table and added her light, and with the extra brightness I could see a metal object where it had fallen in the crack between the floorboards.

"What is it?" Bee asked.

"I think it's a piece of jewelry."

"Miss Jenkins's?"

I took my knife from its sheath and slipped the blade into the crack. Taking great care, I worked the tip of the knife along one side of the crack, then pressed it against the metal thing and started to work it up and into the light.

Bee gasped as it came free. The ring looked like it was made out of silver, and it had a big, clear stone in the middle. "I think it's a diamond ring!" Bee said.

"You don't think it's a fake?" I asked.

She put her light on it, and we could both see the sparkles in the stone. "I don't know for sure, but I'm betting it's real," she said.

I realized that the cabin was probably so dark even in daylight that it would have been invisible down between the floorboards and would have only shown up if somebody was really searching the way Bee and I had been. We had finally gotten a lucky break.

We were so intent on getting the ring that we didn't hear the truck engines outside until it was too late.

Nineteen

"Quick!" I said. "The flashlights!"

We clicked them off, throwing the cabin into total darkness. The caged feeling of tight space and the smells of wet wood and mold and mildew came rushing in on us. I stuffed the ring into the pocket of my blue jeans and shoved my knife back into its sheath. I reached out, groping in the dark, and found Bee's hand as the first flashlight beams approached the cabin.

". . . said you had everything," I heard Uncle Charlie say in an angry tone.

"I thought you'd gotten the stuff in the cabin when I was trailerin' the dozer," Bubba Simmons said.

"I gotta do everything myself," Uncle Charlie growled. "If I hadn't asked again, you could have blown everything."

"Well, I didn't. We're takin' care of it, ain't we?"

They were coming fast and getting close. There was only one place to hide, even though the idea made my skin crawl.

"Come on," I whispered. I tugged Bee's hand and used my other hand to feel my way toward the kitchen.

Lights from the men's flashlights were already hitting the cabin's front door when we stumbled into the back room. The musty odors of the cabin were twice as bad in there. It stank of wet, punky wood and rot. I thought of a swamp, of spiders as big as my hand, of stinging centipedes and poisonous snakes. Every surface seemed to crawl.

I heard heavy footsteps outside, and I jerked Bee to one side of the doorway. As I moved farther, my foot went through a rotten piece of floorboard. I started to fall and nearly jerked Bee off her feet as well, but I flailed blindly in the dark and caught the wall with my other hand.

My hand made a thumping noise against the wood, and I felt a sharp stab as a splinter stabbed into my palm. It was everything I could do not to cry out. My heart was pounding, and I could hear my pulse slamming against my eardrums.

Outside the cabin the flashlights stopped.

"You hear that?" Bubba growled.

"Yeah," Uncle Charlie said. "Probably just a possum or raccoon."

"Suppose," Bubba said, not sounding too sure.

A second later their flashlight beams sliced through the cabin's darkness as they came inside.

"Okay, grab one end of this plywood," Uncle Charlie ordered.

Their feet shuffled, and they went out slowly. I took a deep breath and tried to calm my racing nerves enough to think. As my eyes once again grew accustomed to the cabin's total darkness, I could see the outline of a lighter opening along the kitchen's back wall. As my eyes adjusted further, I could make out moonlight gleaming off leaves outside.

Bee and I were both still holding our breath, and I was trying to figure out if I could risk turning on my flashlight for just a second to see what was between us and our potential escape route, but I could already hear voices and footsteps as Uncle Charlie and Bubba returned to the cabin.

"I'll get one of the sawhorses. You get the other,"

Uncle Charlie said. I heard wood scrape as he grabbed one; it banged the doorframe as he went out. Bubba was just a second behind.

Once again I thought about using my flashlight, but Uncle Charlie was already coming back. His flashlight beam hit the door and then he was inside again. "Where's the pot?" he called out.

"On the hook where it's always been," Bubba answered as he came into the cabin.

"It's not." Uncle Charlie's light played around the room. "It's on the floor next to where the table was. How'd it get down there?"

"I dunno."

I could tell the hamster that powered Uncle Charlie's brain was working overtime. "I don't like this. I'll take the pot out to the truck. Check out the back room for anything suspicious."

"You check it. I never went in there. It's half falling down, and I think it's full of snakes."

At hearing the word *snake* I felt Bee stiffen beside me. Her hand shot out and grabbed my shoulder, her fingers digging in so hard, I nearly yelped.

"I'm not the one who forgot to get the table and pot," Uncle Charlie said. "You check the back room."

Bubba belted out a couple curse words and started

toward the room where we were hiding, his flashlight penetrating the darkness and illuminating a tangle of junked furniture, falling beams, and wind-blown trash. Bee and I were hidden to the left of the doorjamb, but we would be in plain sight the instant he stepped into the room. I crossed my fingers and made a wish that Bubba would be too afraid of snakes to step all the way inside.

As if he had heard my wish, he stopped just outside the room and let his beam play around the walls. Bee and I were just enough to the side to still be hidden. My heart was banging so loudly that I was sure he must hear it, but he just stood there.

"I'm waiting," Uncle Charlie prodded.

Bubba cursed again, but this time he stepped into the room. His movements were jumpy and tense, as if at any second he expected to get bitten. He turned away from us and shined his light into that corner; then he started to turn in our direction.

There was only one thing to do.

I held my breath and waited, and when his light hit us, I screamed and jumped out at him, my hands stretched toward his face.

He did just what I hoped. He bellowed and jumped back in fear and surprise, tripping over the doorjamb and dropping his flashlight. I had my flashlight ready, and I turned it on and pointed it toward the back door.

We ran across the rotting floorboards, feeling them bend and nearly break under our weight. They held just enough, and a second later we were out in the night. I turned my flashlight off, and we crept forward trying for silence.

Behind us I could hear Uncle Charlie snapping questions and Bubba choking on his anger and trying to explain that he'd just been attacked.

"By what?" Uncle Charlie demanded.

Bubba's voice came back low and heavy with shame and confusion. "I don't know. Somebody. Somebody small."

Uncle Charlie went silent. Next I heard him shout my name. "Abbey?"

Silence. Bee and I moved very slowly, pushing blindly into the wall of vegetation, trying lose ourselves in the thick undergrowth.

"Abbey? Are you out there?" Uncle Charlie shouted again.

Bubba was still blubbering about having had the life just about scared out of him.

"Stop whining and get around back," Uncle Charlie snapped.

I heard footsteps coming around the side of the cabin, and then I saw two flashlight beams stabbing through the bushes all around us. Bee and I continued to worm our way as far into the brush as we could go. Thick vines made movement difficult. They snagged us and blocked our way. Thorns stabbed our skin and grabbed at our hair, but we were so scared, we barely felt them.

Uncle Charlie must have heard us, because he stopped just about opposite of where we were. He shot his light in our direction, but the leaves were too thick.

"Abbey, I know you're in there," he snarled. "You come on out right now. Don't make me come after you."

Bee and I didn't move. Uncle Charlie and Bubba kept shining their lights all around us, but I could tell they weren't sure where we were. They walked up and down and tried to shove their way into the bushes in several different places, but they were too big to squirm between the vines and thorns.

Bubba tried three or four times to punch through the thick jungle. "I ain't going to jail because of your niece." I heard what sounded like a cocking gun. I tried to swallow, but my throat felt like it was full of sand.

"No, somebody might hear," Uncle Charlie

grumbled. He sounded sorry that he couldn't let Bubba open fire. "Come on," he said, after a few seconds. "We'll get Ruth and seal the place off, then wait for sunrise. It'll be easy to find them then." He started retreating, then called back over his shoulder, "Hope the snakes and black widows don't get you girls first."

Beside me, Bee let out a choked whimper. I patted her back to try to reassure her that everything was going to be okay, even though I had no real belief that it would. A few seconds later I heard two truck engines start and pull away, but it didn't make me feel any better because I knew exactly where they would be going. One of them would be waiting for us on the trail that led back to the big house, someplace just past One Arm Pond. It was a perfect choke point, so narrow there between the pond and the river that we could never get past them. Another of them would be on the plantation drive blocking the way to the big house, and the third would be down by the township road blocking our way off the plantation.

What made their plan perfect were the smaller ponds and marshlands around the plantation that blocked our escape in a number of directions. There were only a couple ways to get off Reward, and unfortunately Uncle Charlie knew them as well as I did. Even if we could slip past them, I wasn't sure where we should go or what we could do. After all, Bubba Simmons was the deputy sheriff for Leadenwah Island. If we asked anyone for help, Bubba was the person they would call.

Another problem, as if we didn't have enough already: Bee's leg wasn't all the way healed. Because of that we would need to move more slowly than I could on my own, which meant we probably didn't have a chance of getting to any kind of safety on foot.

"It'll be okay," I whispered to myself as much as to Bee. "I've got an idea."

Twenty

We waited. Sitting there in the dark and hearing the soft sounds all around us, listening for the slither of a snake or mistaking the light brush of leaves against our skin for the touch of a poisonous spider was almost more than either of us could take. I knew that for Bee those empty moments were even worse because she was new to all of this, where at least I had spent more than a few summer nights outside in the South Carolina Lowcountry.

Finally, after enough time had gone past that we were sure no one had stayed back to try to trick us, we moved out of the undergrowth. The moon was lower in the night sky now, its light much dimmer. Still, its dusky reflection off the water in Felony Bay gave us a sense of direction.

Bee let out a shuddering sigh when we finally crawled free of the last of the vines and thorns and stood up in the open. "We have to get back to my house and tell Grandma Em," she whispered.

"We can't," I said, finally breaking the bad news. "Remember what I said earlier. It's too easy to catch us if we go along the path back to the big house. That's what they want."

"So what are we going to do? We can't just sneak out of here and call the police. Bubba's the deputy."

"Yeah."

"Mrs. Middleton's trailer is just down the road, but . . ." Bee's shoulders sagged, and she shook her head. "We can't go there. She's poor and old, and we don't know what might happen to her if we got her involved."

I smiled, relieved that Bee had come to the same conclusion I had. "We're going into town. We'll find Mr. Barrett or Custis and tell them what's going on. They'll know what we should do next."

Bee looked at me in the dim light, and I could see the disbelief in her eyes. "We're going into Charleston?

That's ten or twelve miles. What are we going to do? Steal a car?"

I waved a hand. "Come on."

We started back along the path that led to the big house, but when we reached the line of No Trespassing signs, we cut left and followed them away from the river. The low light of the moon made it much harder to see in the woods. Fortunately the yellow No Trespassing signs acted like a set of markers to keep us from wandering off track.

To our right the steady chorus of frogs marked the perimeter of One Arm Pond. We followed the signs until the sound of the frogs faded; then I started to look to our right. When I could finally make out an end to the line of trees that were slightly darker than the night sky, it meant that we had reached the pastures. I whispered to Bee, and we headed slightly to the right, toward where I knew we would eventually find a pasture fence.

We moved very slowly, our lights still off, trying to be silent. Overhead an owl hooted from the branch of a live oak. It was answered by another owl much farther away, its cry faint as a whisper. To our left a grazing deer, alerted by our scent, blew a high-pitched huff to warn other deer.

By the time we reached the pasture fence, the moon

had disappeared completely, and the darkness was deep and nearly impenetrable. I led the way by feel through the fence and across the uneven grass, stepping with care to avoid gopher holes.

I wasn't sure of direction, having only the pitch-black shadow of the trees against the nearly pitch-black sky to steer by. We finally came to another fence, climbed through, and went to the next fence. At the third fence, we turned right and followed the fence line until it turned left.

My shin hit the watering trough before my hand felt the gate. It hurt, but at least it told me we were in the right place. We slipped through the fence and crept toward the barn. I touched Bee's arm before we stepped inside, stopping her. It suddenly occurred to me that Uncle Charlie might have guessed what we were about to do and be waiting here for us to show up. I didn't think he was that smart, but I knew it was a risk.

We stood for maybe a minute listening for strange sounds. We heard nothing. After a few seconds, I went inside and asked Bee to hold her flashlight beneath her shirt and then turn it on. Rather than throwing a hard beam, it put out a soft glow, just enough for me to find a couple of grain buckets and fill each one with a hand-ful of oats.

Bee turned off her light, and we went back into the pasture. We found Timmy and the two carriage horses against the far end, and they woke up as we approached and nickered when they smelled the grain.

As the horses came toward us, I turned and headed toward the barn. Bee went ahead and held the gate so that I could walk straight through. The stall doors were open, so each horse went into his own stall, hoping for a bucket of food.

While Bee slid the stall doors closed, put more feed in the buckets, and hung them inside the stalls, I went to the tack room and felt my way over to Timmy's saddle, blanket, and bridle, which I brought out and put on the floor outside Timmy's stall.

Next, with Bee again holding the light under her shirt, I picked out a bridle that used to belong to Daddy's old Irish hunter. He had been a very large horse, and the old bridle had a number of holes that would allow me to let it out. I hoped it would work for Clem, the younger of the two carriage horses. I took the bridle and a long coil of rope, but I didn't bother with a saddle because none of the ones in the tack room would come close to fitting Clem's huge back. Finally I grabbed a folding step stool that hung from a peg on the wall and leaned it against the wall outside Clem's stall.

In the glow of the light under Bee's shirt, we went

into Timmy's stall, where I saddled him, and then into Clem's stall, where I got on the step stool and, after about ten minutes of monkeying around with the bridle, managed to get the bit into Clem's mouth and the straps over his ears.

As I expected, Clem tossed his head and objected to the bridle, not having had anything resembling a bit in his mouth for a long time. I patted his neck and whispered to calm him and finally gave him a second small bucket of oats to make him happy.

Bee watched all the preparations with hardly a word, but I knew she had to be full of dread. "We're going to ride horseback into Charleston?" she asked.

"How else can we cover that much distance?"

"But how can we get out of here without being seen? You said they were waiting for us."

"They are, but trust me. I have an idea."

I threw one end of the rope over Clem's back, fed it twice around his huge neck, then took it down around his chest and back up. Then I cut the rope with my knife and tied the two ends with a square knot. Clem, who for many years had been harnessed to carriages every single day, stood patient and uncomplaining.

"Okay," I said to Bee when I finished. "Watch this and see if you can do it."

I brought the step stool around to Clem's side and

climbed on it again. Then I grabbed hold of the rope I had tied around his neck and chest, swung one leg up so it lay across his hindquarters, and let my other leg hang down along his side, showing Bee how it worked. I knew that if anyone looked at Clem from the other side, I would be almost totally invisible.

"Do you think you could do this on Timmy for maybe thirty seconds?" I asked as I held myself in place along Clem's side.

Bee looked at what I was doing and shook her head. "I'll fall off."

I thought for a second, then sat back up on Clem's back. Then I lay down flat on his back, getting as low as I could, putting my arms around his neck to hold on. "Can you do this?"

"I can do that," she said.

"Good, then this will be easy," I said, hoping I was somewhere close to right.

Bee shook her head. "Only one little problem. I don't know how to ride. You were going to teach me when I finally got the bandages off my knee. Remember?"

"Yeah," I said, grimacing. "Well, I guess this is your first lesson."

Twenty-one

We led Jimmy and Clem out to the mounting block beside the paddock. I had Bee hold both horses while I went back into the barn to get Lem and a riding crop. This was where the next part of my plan came in. I walked Lem out along the dirt track that led to the barn until we came to the edge of the plantation drive.

The drive was empty to the left as far as my eyes could see in the dark. However, when I looked right, I saw the dark outline of Uncle Charlie's pickup truck maybe fifty yards away.

I pointed Lem toward the pickup, stepped behind

him, and gave his rump a hard whack with the riding crop. He lurched in surprise and began a slow canter toward Uncle Charlie's truck. His canter quickly slowed to a trot, but by that time he was most of the way to the truck.

A second later the truck's interior lights went on as Ruth opened the driver's door and got out. I raced back toward Bee, wanting to clap my hands for joy, because I knew Ruth had just ruined her night vision for at least the next couple minutes.

I reached the mounting block, helped Bee into the saddle, and showed her how I wanted her to lie down as low as she could. Then I grabbed Timmy's reins and went up on the mounting block. I hopped on Clem's back, then quickly led Timmy out the dirt track toward the plantation drive.

Even before we got there, Ruth was talking to herself. "How did you get out of the corral, you crazy horse?" she asked, as if Lem could actually explain. The makeshift harness worked perfectly as I slid down along Clem's side in my trick riding position. Keeping a grip on Timmy's reins and making sure that Clem blocked most of Ruth's view of him, I nudged Clem across the plantation drive and into the soybean field on the other side. If Ruth saw anything, I was almost positive all she would see were two more riderless horses heading off to find fresh grass.

We rode across the soybean field toward the woods on the far side. We were almost to the trees when Bee whispered, "Can I sit up now?"

I glanced over at Timmy and saw Bee starting to slide off his back like a piece of melting cheese. Jumping off Clem, I shoved Bee back into the saddle, then grabbed both sets of reins and led both Clem and Timmy into the trees as fast as I could run.

When we reached the cover of the longleaf pine grove, I stopped and looked back. It was too dark for me to pick the truck out of the blackness. This gave me a moment of relief; if I couldn't see Ruth, she certainly couldn't see us. After a second I turned and started to lead the horses through the trees toward the fence line.

When we hit the fence, I turned left and walked along until I spotted what I was looking for, the back gate that led to our neighbor's plantation. The retired judge who owned the property had already gone north for the summer, but I had ridden through his property enough that I knew it almost as well as Reward. Bubba Simmons was almost certainly parked out on the township road waiting to see if we would try to escape in that direction, but he would have to be parked where he could spot us if we came out the dirt track from Felony Bay or if we came out the plantation drive. If we rode to the far end of the judge's plantation, we could come out on the township road at a point where he'd never be able to see us.

I opened the gate and led Clem through while Bee followed on Timmy. After closing the gate, I brought Clem close to the fence, then climbed onto the top rail and used it to make an easy mount. As we rode across the pasture, a quick glance at my watch showed that it was three fifteen in the morning. The ride would take us a little more than two hours, by my best guess. With any luck we could be in downtown Charleston just a little after five, when there would be hardly any traffic. I was pretty sure we had successfully snuck out of Reward and was even feeling pretty good, thinking we might have the hardest part of the trip behind us.

Bee was barely visible next to me in the darkness. "Having fun yet?"

She gave me a wry smile. "Yeah, piece of cake. Now that we're away from the snakes and gators."

We rode across another couple pastures, hugging the tree line for good measure in case someone was looking for us, went along one of the dirt tracks that crisscrossed the judge's property, skirted the open lawns around his house, and finally came to the gate that led out to Felony Bay Road.

I dismounted, opened the gate, and crept out. The night was very still, the breeze almost nonexistent, and I heard only the buzzing of night insects and the distant trilling of frogs. There was no sign of cars or lights. With a sigh of relief, I waved Bee out and onto the road, then closed the gate and once again used the fence to remount. We turned the horses in the direction of Charleston and went on without talking, the horses' hooves almost silent in the dirt.

After a ways we passed Mrs. Middleton's dark trailer, and we both turned and gazed at it. I knew Bee was wishing just as much as I was that we could go knock on the door and ask for help. We also both knew that Bee had been right a little while earlier when she turned the idea down. Involving an old lady who hobbled around on a walker would be the worst thing we could do.

After another minute the dirt path turned onto the paved county road, and for the next forty-five minutes we rode steadily alongside it toward the end of Leadenwah Island. We stayed off the road wherever we could, keeping to yards and fields. A few dogs barked, and we saw several pairs of headlights, but they went past quickly, people speeding to early jobs.

When we finally crossed the short two-lane bridge onto Johns Island, the homes became a little more suburban, but most still had good-size yards and plenty of open space. A few more vehicles came along, but we were able to get well away from the road before they reached us, and they never slowed.

We were nearly halfway across Johns Island when I looked over my shoulder as I'd been doing every few seconds and noticed another pair of headlights about a half mile behind. Unlike the other vehicles we had seen, this one was coming much slower. It was still a long way off, but it seemed to brake frequently. It also appeared that the driver was shining a spotlight out the window.

"Uh-oh," I said.

Bee looked back. "You think they figured out that we got off the plantation?"

I nodded. "They might have gone looking for Timmy and Clem and figured it out when they couldn't find them."

At that moment we were riding through a field, a little ways off the road, but since they were searching the sides with a spotlight, I knew that the horses would be easy to pick out. I felt trapped and fought a rising tide of panic as I looked around.

"We have to get farther off the road," I said.

"Gee, you think?" Bee said as she kicked Timmy into a trot.

Up ahead a narrow driveway seemed to go deeper than most of the others, curving sharply through the trees to some invisible house. Having no other choice, we turned onto it. I kicked at Clem's flanks to urge him forward, but my legs were spread so wide on his huge back that I couldn't manage more than a tap. He plodded at his carriage-horse pace. The clopping of his hooves on the gravel seemed maddeningly slow. I kept looking back, seeing the approaching high beams through the trees and the searchlight spearing into yards and fields on either side. The curve in the driveway was too far away. The lights kept getting closer. We weren't going to make it.

We reached the curve and got barely out of sight when the spotlight shot down the drive. Both horses stopped and sat perfectly still, and Bee and I didn't dare to breathe. Out on the road the truck engine idled low and smooth, as if the driver had stopped and was thinking about turning down the drive for a better look. For several seconds I worried that the spotlight had caught a flicker of Clem's tail.

The idling continued. I was sure the driver sensed our closeness, but I also knew that turning into someone's driveway at four fifteen in the morning was a good way to bring a call to the police. I crossed my fingers and toes and prayed that whoever was in the truck would be a little bit cautious.

Another few seconds ticked by, and then the truck engine grew louder. I tensed, ready to jump off Clem's back and run, but then through the trees I saw the headlights moving down the road, the spotlight continuing its search.

"That was close," Bee said.

I blew out the breath I'd been holding. "You're not kidding."

Once again we waited. The high-pitched peeping of frogs came from a nearby pond and, from farther off, the fitful barking of a dog. We didn't dare move, because we didn't know if the truck would turn around and come right back. I had to figure that whoever was looking for us would realize that we couldn't have made it much farther than this. They were almost certain to turn around in the next couple minutes and head back toward Leadenwah.

Five minutes passed, then seven, then ten, before we heard a vehicle approaching from the opposite direction. It sounded like the same truck engine, and just like before, it was going slow. To my relief the spotlight was more sporadic this time, the searching more rushed. The driver seemed to be in a hurry, perhaps eager to get back with his or her partners in crime and decide what to do next.

"What do you think?" I asked as the truck's lights faded.

"I think maybe we have a little time before they come back," she said.

"I think you're right."

"I'm scared, Abbey."

"I know," I said. "I am, too. But we can do this. Come on."

We turned back to the road and once again headed toward Charleston. A glance at my watch showed that hiding from the truck had used up over fifteen valuable minutes. The time was getting short, every minute of delay meaning more traffic and more of a risk of getting caught.

It took us forty-five minutes to cross the rest of Johns Island. As we approached the long bridge over the Stono River, I broke a green branch from a sapling and used it to whack Clem into a reluctant trot. My heart was in my mouth as we went up the long bridge and then down the other side. We would have been trapped if the pickup had caught us there, but thankfully we saw just a single car going in the opposite direction.

The bridge brought us onto James Island, where we turned off the road and trotted across the fairways of a municipal golf course that took us far from the reach of any spotlight. When the golf course ended, we went through small subdivisions and stayed off the main roads.

It was already a few minutes after five o'clock, and there was a glow in the eastern sky. Birds were singing in the trees. Lights were on in some of the houses we passed, and we even saw several joggers. They gaped at two girls riding horses in the pre-dawn. Most of the world was still far from awake, but morning was coming on way too fast. We had only a short distance to travel, but every hundred yards seemed to take forever on the old carriage horse. Light was starting to leak into the world. Dawn was going to make us sitting ducks for Uncle Charlie.

We rode through more neighborhood streets, across the campus of a school, and behind a few commercial buildings, staying out of sight as much as possible on the way to our final bridge. Even so, the world around us continued to grow lighter as we prepared to make our final dash into the city.

Finally we reached the end of James Island. The bridge was narrow and old-fashioned, with no bike lane, and we could hear it before we saw it. Early cars and trucks were whizzing across, their tires making an eerie whining on the bridge's surface.

"What's that sound?" Bee asked.

"There's a section of metal grating on the bridge," I told her.

"Timmy doesn't like it."

The pony was sidestepping and tossing his head. "He'll be okay," I said. "Just follow behind me."

Clem's years of being a carriage horse should make him okay with the metal grate, I told myself. I just hoped I was right.

"What if I get bucked off?" Bee asked.

"You won't," I said, crossing my fingers and making a wish that she really wouldn't.

Both Clem and Timmy were jumpy as we started onto the bridge, and several drivers had to hit their brakes and swerve around us. I whacked Clem's butt to urge him into a trot. We were almost home free. Two hundred yards ahead loomed the tall buildings of the Medical University Hospital, and just beyond were the old neighborhoods where we should be able to lose ourselves in the tangle of narrow streets.

We were nearing the end of the bridge when it happened. A black pickup truck going in the opposite direction slammed on its brakes. The driver's head was turned toward us, and I caught a quick glimpse of Uncle Charlie's scowl of surprise and rage.

My own eyes went wide with shock, and my heart seized in my chest. Uncle Charlie was holding up traffic. There was angry honking behind him, but he didn't seem to care. He gave me a look that made my blood turn to ice; then he floored his accelerator and shot forward, speeding toward the opposite end of the bridge, where I knew he would find a place to turn and come roaring back in our direction.

"Come on, Bee," I said, smacking Clem's flanks with my switch. It seemed to take forever, but finally he started to canter, and I held on to my slapdash rope harness for dear life.

"Where are we going?" Bee asked as we reached the end of the bridge.

"Here," I said, slowing Clem to a trot and turning into the parking lot of a fast-food restaurant. Around the back there was an exit onto a smaller road.

Uncle Charlie was close behind us—I could feel it. I kept looking over my shoulder for the black pickup, but thankfully I didn't see it. We turned right at our first intersection, then immediately left, zigzagging and winding through the twisting inner roads around the hospital.

There were a lot more cars on the road now. A number of drivers stared at us wide-eyed. There was a big risk that one of them might use their cell phone to report us to the police. We couldn't afford to let that happen, because the police would just turn us over to Uncle Charlie. We crossed another road and went into the parking lot of a small corner building. The lot went around the back and gave us a momentary place to hide while I tried to come up with an idea.

Even if we were out of sight, Uncle Charlie was still searching. He would never quit. He would drive up and down all the roads around the Medical University and poke into all the open parking lots. No place around there was safe.

It was almost full daylight, and the streetlights that had started lining the streets when we crossed off James Island were winking out. We had to get Clem and Timmy out of sight fast, but where were we ever going to hide a couple horses in downtown Charleston? Also, we needed to get ourselves to some place where there would be lots of people around, so even if Uncle

Charlie found us, he wouldn't be able to do anything bad.

The problem was that it wasn't even six o'clock. There were a few people on the street now, but hardly any places were open. I thought about Custis, but I didn't know where he lived. I knew he wouldn't be at work until probably eight thirty at the earliest, which meant we had a serious amount of time to kill. My brain was a muddle of panicked thoughts, but I tried to calm myself enough to think.

"I've got an idea," I told Bee, after I'd thought it through as well as I could. There was at least one place that was open, where we would be safe until it was time to go down to Custis's office. Also there was something I needed to do there, and I had to do it before we went any farther.

We headed out from behind the building, trusting our luck to hold just a little longer. There were only three blocks to go, and I knew a way to stay off the street for at least one of them.

We made it to the end of the first block, then turned into one of the Medical University parking lots. Lucky for us, the booths where the money collectors sat were dark because it was still too early for anyone to be on duty. Just as I hoped, Clem was heavy enough to make a ticket pop out of the machine when I walked him forward. I told Bee to get Timmy beside me; then I took the ticket and we rode through when the gate went up.

At the far end of the lot a sidewalk led to the center of the Medical University campus. We followed it and rode across the big, deserted Medical University green and out to the road on the other side.

Now there was only one short block to go. As we trotted down the deserted street, the clopping of the horses' hooves seemed terribly loud. Every second, I expected to hear the screech of tires or see Uncle Charlie's black pickup come sliding around the corner after us, but we made it to the high wrought-iron fence that surrounded Miss Walker's School for Girls without getting caught.

"Are we going in there?" Bee asked, when I slid off Clem's back and walked up to the gate.

As I looked through the fence at my old school with its old buildings, broad green lawns, and large fishpond with water lilies and fountain, I nodded. "If they haven't changed the combination on the electric lock."

They hadn't changed the combination even once in the seven years I had gone there, so I figured there was a pretty good chance that they still hadn't. I held my breath and punched in the old code. As soon as I did, I heard the magnetic lock snap, and I shoved the gate open.

We led the horses inside, took off Timmy's saddle and blanket and both bridles, and stuffed them in a sheltered spot. The horses took long drinks from the fishpond, then started grazing, seeming quite comfortable in their new surroundings.

Since school was out for the summer, I didn't think anybody would be coming onto campus for a while, and I hoped that when they did, they wouldn't be too angry to discover the horses. I would try to explain things later.

Bee and I went back out the gate, looked down the block to make sure no black pickups were coming, then trotted across the street and retraced our steps to the Medical University Hospital. Inside the hospital lobby, we headed straight for the elevators, but the guard at the information desk called out to us.

"Young ladies, it's six o'clock in the morning. You're about three hours early for visiting patients."

"We're going to see our father," I told him.

The guard eyed us as if he didn't believe me. "What room is your father in?"

"Six thirty-two," I said. "Rutledge Covington Force."

The guard punched in my father's name on his keyboard and checked the name and room number. "Okaaay," he said, drawing the word out long. "Still pretty early if you ask me. There some reason you can't wait for normal visiting hours?"

"We have to go out of town. Our flight leaves in a couple hours, and we won't be back for a week. We promised we'd visit before we left."

He looked back and forth between us as he thought it over. Finally he waved his hand and told us to go on. As we walked toward the elevator, I heard him mutter to himself about how some people today just let their kids run around like wild animals.

If he only knew the truth, I thought.

Twenty-two

bout two minutes later, we walked off the elevator onto the sixth floor and went to the locked door, where I rang the buzzer. After several seconds a startled-looking nurse came down the corridor and squinted through the glass at us a moment before opening the door.

"What are you girls doing here?" she asked, glancing down at her wristwatch. "Do you know what time it is?"

I'd never seen this nurse on the day shift, so I didn't recognize her, and she certainly didn't recognize me. "We're Rutledge Covington Force's daughters," I said.

"Both of you?"

Bee gave her a very pretty smile. "Yes, ma'am. I'm adopted."

"Oh," the nurse said. "Of course. You're here to see your father?"

"We have to fly out of town in just a short time," Bee said, smoothly picking up the lie. "We promised ourselves that we would come in to visit him before we left."

"Okay," the nurse said. She still seemed confused, but she wasn't fighting us. "Go on in."

"Thank you, ma'am," Bee said, smiling and using her best Southern manners.

The nurse got that brain-dead smile adults so often do when kids throw in lots of syrupy sirs and ma'ams.

Having no time to waste on greetings, I went straight to Daddy's bed, sat down on the side, and took his hand the way I always did. Then I sucked down a deep breath.

"Daddy," I said in a soft voice, "I have to tell you some important things. I've been telling you lies for a long time now. You've been asleep ever since last August, when you fell down in your library and cracked your head. I've been afraid if I told you the truth about what's happened since then, you wouldn't ever want to wake up. But now things are pretty bad, and I think it's time to tell you.

"When I found you and called the ambulance, the police came to the house. There was a bunch of jewelry and stuff that had spilled out of a hiding place in the ceiling, and so when the ambulance people took you to the hospital, the police collected the jewelry and looked all around the house.

"Later on they said you'd taken all the gold and jewelry that Miss Jenkins used to keep in her safe, and . . ." I stopped. Maybe it was just my imagination, but I swear I felt that Daddy wasn't in that same deep sleep he'd been in for the past nine months. For some reason I was convinced he was really trying to listen to me.

"So anyway, Miss Jenkins had to be paid back, and Mr. Barrett said the only way to do it was to sell Reward. So that's what happened. It got sold last February. The good news is that the new owners' name is also Force. Their ancestors used to be slaves on the plantation. I know if you can hear me you're sad that Reward was sold, but you're glad about who's living there now.

"My new best friend is Bee Force. She's the daughter of the owner. She's twelve, and she's right here in the room with me. And the reason we're here is that we had to run away from Reward tonight because we discovered something really bad."

Over the next couple of minutes, everything I'd been holding back, all the rest of the story, came pouring out. I told Daddy how the Felony Bay property had been sold separately from the rest of the plantation and how Uncle Charlie, Ruth, and Bubba Simmons had buried their old chest after midnight and then chased us and kept us from getting back to the big house to tell Bee's grandmother what we had seen. I told how we had ridden horses from Reward into Charleston and how we were hiding out until we could get ahold of Custis and tell him everything that had happened.

I finally stopped talking. Daddy had gone so still that it frightened me. I couldn't tell whether I'd done a good thing or a terrible thing by confessing.

"I'm sorry if I told you too much," I said, fighting back the tears that were trying to burn their way out of my eyes. Right then, I was afraid I had just made everything worse, maybe much worse. Only I didn't think I'd had any choice.

"I really, really need you to wake up," I told Daddy. "I really need you to help me figure out what we should do."

We stayed in Daddy's room until eight thirty. Neither of us had eaten since dinner the night before, and we had no money to go to the cafeteria. We sat there with our stomachs growling like angry dogs, taking drinks of water from the tap in the bathroom. We both jumped every time the door opened and one of the nurses came in to check on Daddy, because each time we expected it to be Uncle Charlie.

Bee kept looking at her watch. "Don't you think I should call Grandma Em?" she asked. "She's going to be worried sick when she realizes I'm gone."

"Okay, but you can't tell her where we are. She's going to want to come get us, but first we need to talk to Mr. Barrett or Custis."

She promised and went into the hall to borrow a cell phone from one of the nurses. She came back a minute later with a worried look.

"That's weird," she said. "There's a recording when I call the house that says the phone is out of order."

"Did you call her cell?"

"It doesn't work at the house."

"Maybe she's sleeping late," I offered, hoping it was true.

Bee shook her head. "What if she heard something last night and realized that I'd snuck out? What if she went out to find me, and Uncle Charlie did something to her?"

I shook my head, but it was mostly instinct. I didn't want to admit that Uncle Charlie would do something really terrible like kidnapping an innocent old lady. But then I thought about what he had tried to do to us in the past few hours . . . and also how Deputy Simmons had wanted to use his gun to try to shoot us when he couldn't find us. Uncle Charlie only stopped him because he'd been afraid the sound would carry.

"I hope he didn't," I said after a few seconds.

We stood there and looked at each other. "You want to call the police?" I asked after a long silence.

"Like they're going to believe me when some sheriff says I'm a liar." Bee gave a helpless shrug.

I glanced at my watch. I was feeling terrible guilt about what might have happened to Grandma Em, but I knew we needed to stay focused. "It's eight forty-five. Let's go find Mr. Barrett or Custis."

I looked at Daddy one last time. I couldn't be sure, but it seemed like he was having a dream in which somebody was telling him something he didn't want to hear.

"Good-bye, Daddy," I said. "Sorry to have to tell you so much bad news."

Out in the hallway, I stopped to tell the nurses how Daddy looked different, and they promised they would have the doctor check on him as soon as he came up for his rounds.

"I think he may be waking up," I insisted.

They nodded, but I could tell they didn't believe me.

"Would you at least call Mr. Barrett or Custis Pettigrew? Promise me you'll do that if he looks like he's waking up? They're his friends, and they'll come in and talk to him and help him. Will you do that?"

They promised they would check on him every few minutes, and if it looked like there was any change in his condition, they would call them. I thanked the nurses, and Bee and I said good-bye, then headed out the locked door that led to the elevators.

The hallway was deserted as I pushed the Down button. The elevator came a few seconds later, and the doors opened. It was empty, and Bee and I started to move inside, but then we came to a dead halt.

"Squib!" said a familiar voice from very close behind us. "I thought you might be here."

Twenty-three

I spun around in terror and looked back at where the men's room door was swinging closed. Uncle Charlie was just a foot away. There was no place to run and no one to call for help. I sucked down a deep breath, ready to scream my head off, but he grabbed me and slapped a hand over my mouth. I flailed with my elbows and tried to kick him, but he was way too strong. Bee made a move toward him, but he held up a hand and pointed at her.

"We've got Grandma Em," he said in a harsh whisper. "If either of you makes a peep, something terrible's gonna happen to her."

I was hoping Bee would run away screaming, but she was utterly frozen. Uncle Charlie's threat had done its trick. Bee wasn't going to risk anything happening to Grandma Em.

The elevator doors started to close, but Uncle Charlie muscled us into the empty car before they did. He hit the button for the first floor, then shoved me into the back wall of the elevator.

"I'm not jokin', Squib. One word, one single word outta either one of you, and the old lady is gonna get hurt." He glanced at Bee, whose terror was written across her face. "Understand?"

Bee nodded right away, and Uncle Charlie looked at me. His eyes were red from staying up all night, but there was enough meanness in them so I was afraid that for once he wasn't just being a big bag of wind. I was as scared and angry as I had ever been.

Time seemed to stand still for the next few seconds, and everything seemed totally unreal. I didn't scream or try to slug Uncle Charlie or hit the emergency Stop button, even though I wanted to do all three of them at once. Instead I looked at Bee. The fear in her face was terrible to see, and I realized that having lost her mother and brother, there was no way she could survive losing Grandma Em. So I just stood there and let

Uncle Charlie think he had won. Which wasn't hard, seeing as I had no idea how we were going to get out of this one.

The elevator finally came to a stop, and the doors opened. Uncle Charlie took a tight grip on each of our arms and started to steer us out, but someone in a wheelchair was blocking our way. It took me a second or two to realize that I'd stepped right in front of Miss Lydia Jenkins. I couldn't believe I was seeing her again, in the same place, twice in one week. Behind Miss Jenkins, five or six other people were also waiting to get into the elevator, including Esther Simmons.

"Remember what I told you," Uncle Charlie whispered.

In that moment before everyone started to move to let us off the elevator, Miss Jenkins and I locked eyes. Right away she started doing the same thing she had done the last time I'd seen her, moving her head back and forth, struggling, and keeping me pinned in place with her eyes.

Esther Simmons turned Miss Jenkins's wheelchair slightly, and I felt Uncle Charlie start to steer me out of the elevator. Before I could step clear, Miss Jenkins's hand shot out, just like the last time, and she grabbed my wrist.

Uncle Charlie tried to force me to take a step, but Miss Jenkins's grip was strong for such an old lady. The harder Uncle Charlie tried to pull me, the harder Miss Jenkins squeezed. Just like the last time, Miss Jenkins's eyes were intense and jumpy, but there was something different in them, too. I realized that her eyes were trying to tell me something that she couldn't express any other way.

As Charlie jerked me harder, her lips started to tremble. "Ddddddd," she said, then shook her head the way somebody would in a charades game when another player makes a bad guess. "Dddddon't ddddddon't gggggo wwwwww—"

Esther was trying to push the wheelchair past us, either not noticing that Miss Jenkins had a death grip on my wrist or not caring. Uncle Charlie had Bee all the way out of the elevator now, and he was pulling me to follow. The arm Miss Jenkins was holding was straight out from my side, but she kept her ferocious grip.

Finally Uncle Charlie jerked even harder, and Miss Jenkins let go. Even as I was pulled away, she was still struggling to say something. A second later the elevator doors closed, pinching off her words, but just before she disappeared from sight I heard what sounded like "Wwwwwwithhim."

"Nosy old bag," Uncle Charlie muttered.

Uncle Charlie steered us out of the exit and through the parking lot to where he had parked his truck. He opened the passenger-side door, looked around to make sure nobody was nearby, then pulled our hands behind our backs and used a roll of duct tape to wrap them and then our feet.

"You keep your mouths shut, or I'll tape them, too," he said, forcing us both to lie on the floor.

As we pulled out of the parking lot, he picked up his cell phone and punched in a number. "I got 'em . . . yeah, at the hospital. I told you, didn't I? Be there in twenty minutes."

I was still just as angry and scared to death as I had been when he snuck up on us in front of the elevator, but I actually fell asleep for part of the drive. After all, Bee and I had been up all night, and I was totally exhausted. I was sure Bee was as tired as I was. If we were going to have a chance of escaping, we needed to get all the rest we could, even if it was only for a few minutes.

I woke when Uncle Charlie hung a turn onto the township road and the wheels slammed into a pothole in the dirt. My head banged hard on the floor, and I struggled to push myself up onto the seat.

"Did I tell you to get up there, Squib?"

I didn't answer him, but I stayed where I was.

He reached over without slowing down and tried to shove me back down, but I moved over next to the door, too far away for him to grab me without stopping or swerving all over the place.

Out the side window was Mrs. Middleton's trailer, and she was in her yard. She was leaning on her walker and looking out at the road. My eyes locked with Mrs. Middleton's in the half second that it took for us to hurtle past, and then we were gone, the pickup's tires slamming hard into the ruts and kicking up a huge rooster tail of dust.

We were going fast, but at least the road was dirt underneath us. If I was ever going to jump out, it had to be right now. I could shout to Mrs. Middleton that we were being kidnapped, tell her to call the police. It might be our only chance.

I tried not to think how much it was going to hurt to break an arm or leg or scrape half the skin off my face. I jerked the handle as hard as I could and shoved against the door.

Nothing happened.

I pulled the handle again, and again nothing. There was no click of a lock unlatching.

"Child-proof locks, Squib," Uncle Charlie said. "We want to make sure we protect the little ones." He laughed at his own joke.

Reward's gates came up fast, and we roared into the drive and then hung another turn into the dirt track that led to Uncle Charlie's. I hadn't said a word since we'd gotten into the truck, partly out of fear and partly because my brain was racing with so many thoughts. Now, as we pulled to a skidding stop behind the house, I got my voice back.

"It was you! You found a way to steal Miss Jenkins's gold and then you blamed Daddy!" I blurted out. "He trusted you! You're his brother!"

"Your dad and I never got along too good. He always thought he was the smart one."

Bee was still on the floor, but now she rose up on her elbows. "Where's my grandma?" she demanded. "I want to see her!"

"Your grandma's probably at her house," Uncle Charlie said. "I lied. We didn't do anything but cut her phone line. She's probably worried sick about you by now. But she's not going to find you. Not anytime soon." He gave his horn a loud honk and waited. After a second the back screen door opened, and Ruth and Deputy Simmons came out. Ruth hung back on the porch steps while Bubba approached the truck.

"Well, well, what've we got here?" he said, smirking.

Uncle Charlie killed the engine and hit a button that popped the door locks. Then he came around to my side and jerked open my door. I turned and fired off a kick, getting in one good one. He grunted in pain, but he quickly recovered, grabbed my arm, and slapped me hard across the face. It stunned me enough for him to jerk me out and throw me down on the ground. A second later Bee landed beside me.

My face burned from where he had hit me, but I was too angry to even think about crying. I just wanted to find a way to get free and then slug him as hard as I could. Jimmy Simmons's swollen nose would look like nothing compared to what I would do to Uncle Charlie's. Bee craned her neck in my direction, and when our eyes met, I could tell that she was just as angry and scared as I was.

"You're even stupider than Daddy always said," I sneered, looking up at Uncle Charlie. He looked down at me, and then he pulled back one foot. For a second, I thought he was going to start kicking. I didn't care. "You may think you got him to take the blame for stealing Miss Jenkins's gold, but you'll never get away with this," I said.

Apparently deciding not to kick me, Uncle Charlie smiled. "Hate to break it to ya, Squib, but yes we will."

He said it with so much cocksure conviction that it brought me up short. "How?" I demanded.

"I'm a student of history," he said, sounding so pleased with himself. "And a student of history knows the important details other people overlook. Did you know that during the Civil War all those fine Southern ladies melted down their jewelry and tea sets into ingots and gave them to the Cause? Did you know that, Squib?

I just glared at him.

"There've been rumors about treasure in Felony Bay for years, so when we find a big bunch of buried gold, is anybody going to think it isn't from the *Lovely Clarisse*? What's your guess, Squib?"

My heart suddenly sank as everything became clear. Uncle Charlie and Bubba Simmons hadn't been cooking anything in the blackened pot in the fireplace.

"You melted down the jewelry," I said.

"Y'all ain't as dumb as you look, Squib," he said. "Made gold ingots just like the old ones. I even got the CSA stamped right into the metal, same size as the originals. CSA stands for Confederate States of America, Squib. We even got the jewels sewn up just like the real thing in bags cut from an old silk ball gown. I bought a crate and a lock that date back to that time at a flea market in Mississippi. I thought of everything. And now we're about to make history finding that lost treasure."

I closed my eyes for a second, remembering the moldy-smelling yellow gown Ruth had brought into the kitchen a few days earlier. It really did seem like Uncle Charlie had thought of everything.

"Enough talking—we're wasting time," Bubba Simmons said. He looked down at us. "We gotta finish this."

Bubba's tone sent chills down my back. I knew he was talking about Bee and me.

Uncle Charlie wiped his lips on the back of his wrist, looking uncomfortable all of a sudden. He walked over to Bubba and lowered his voice. "Why don't y'all handle it?" he suggested.

"Me?" Bubba scoffed.

"Yeah, I mean, I wasn't . . . we didn't plan on . . . you know."

Bubba's face wrinkled in anger. "We also never planned on your niece and her friend snooping. How else you gonna guarantee she don't go running off at the mouth and telling everybody what we did?"

Uncle Charlie looked scared, like he was figuring out for the very first time that he was in way over his head. "I don't know," he said, his voice so soft I could barely hear the words.

"Toughen up," Bubba said. "We can't back out now. We're gonna make it look like an accident."

"How?"

"Just trust me. Help me get 'em back in the truck."

As Bubba bent over to pick up Bee, I forced myself to speak again even though I was so scared I was about to wet my pants. "I can't believe you got sucked into doing this. You're just an idiot like Uncle Charlie."

Bubba's lips got tight. "I didn't get sucked into nothing," he said in a low, nasty voice.

"Yeah, well, this whole thing is a really stupid idea," I said, turning back to Uncle Charlie. "Nobody's going to believe you when you try to explain our disappearance."

"Wanna bet, smart mouth?" Bubba said. "Your uncle told me all about the crazy stuff y'all done in the ponds and rivers around Reward. Nobody gonna be too shocked to find out you ran y'allself into some serious trouble."

That gave me an even worse feeling in the pit of my stomach. I pinched my lips, wondering if he had thought of the same thing I was thinking of right that minute. I sure hoped not.

Bubba glanced at Uncle Charlie and jerked his head toward the truck. "Get it done," he said.

Uncle Charlie's face contorted. For a second or two, I thought he looked a little bit uncertain, maybe even guilty. But then he set his jaw, and he reached down and pulled me to my feet, then threw me over his shoulder. He walked me to the back of his truck and used one hand to unfasten the hooks that held the tailgate. I didn't even fight because, to be honest, I was pretty close to giving up, and it was everything I could do not to start crying like a baby.

From up on his shoulder, I could look toward the back door. I saw Ruth there, standing up on the back steps. She had one hand to her mouth and the other wrapped around her stomach as if she was in pain.

Once the tailgate was lowered, Uncle Charlie dumped me on it, then got up himself and dragged me farther into the truck bed. When Bubba dumped Bee on the tailgate, he dragged her back, too.

"Planning to kill your own flesh and blood, Uncle Charlie?" I asked.

He straightened up and looked at me, his voice shaking. "If you'd have minded your own business and done what I said, you'd have been fine. You got only yourself to blame."

"You really believe that?"

He refused to meet my eyes as he turned away from me, hopped off the tailgate, then slammed it into place.

"I'm so sorry," Bee whispered. "I know you stayed quiet in the hospital because of what they said about hurting Grandma Em." She shook her head. "If we'd just screamed, we could've gotten away."

"It's going to be okay," I said to her. I didn't know why I said it. I was pretty sure nothing was going to be okay, but I didn't want her to be as scared as I was. Uncle Charlie had been right, I was thinking. None of this was Bee's fault. It was all mine.

I heard Uncle Charlie open the driver's door, but before he climbed in, I heard Ruth's voice. "Charlie," she called.

Uncle Charlie's door squeaked as he held it and swung it back and forth in little arcs of nervous energy. "What?"

There was a long silence. I couldn't see Ruth, but I heard her footsteps as she walked up to Uncle Charlie.

Her anxiety was so intense, it felt like static electricity in the air.

"We can't do this," she whispered when she got close.

Uncle Charlie squeaked his door. "But we can't trust them to keep their mouths shut, can we?" he asked, when he finally stopped.

Ruth didn't say anything.

"We don't have any other choice."

I heard what might have been a stifled sob, then Ruth's footsteps as she hurried away. A second later the screen door slammed and then also the inner door. It was plain that she was upset about what was happening, but it didn't matter. She might not be a monster like Uncle Charlie, but she was a coward, which made her almost as bad.

"We best get going," Bubba said as he climbed into the other side of the truck.

Twenty-four

The truck headed out, and Uncle Charlie turned left on the main plantation drive. My heart sank. I already suspected where we were heading, so I wasn't a bit surprised when we turned right onto a little-used dirt track. As we bounced over the ruts, I began to hear bullfrogs booming out their deep croaks. My spirits crumbled as I recognized the sounds of One Arm Pond.

The truck jerked to a stop and made a bumpy K-turn, and then the engine died. I heard the doors open and close. A second later the tailgate dropped down. When I craned my neck, I could see One Arm Pond glistening like cut glass in the light wind that riffled across the water's surface. A white ibis flew overhead, its orange beak curved like a scimitar, and a small gray heron stalked the shallows along the near shore. It all looked so peaceful and beautiful, and normally it would have been—just not today.

Green Alice's nest was all the way on the other side of the pond, but even though I couldn't see her yet, I could feel her presence. The alligator was there just the same as she always was, huge and powerful and deadly, if you were stupid enough to go swimming in her pond or canoe too close to her babies.

The truck sagged as Uncle Charlie hoisted himself into the truck bed. He took Bee under the arms, pulled her roughly to the edge of the tailgate, then jumped down. Bee let out an angry snarl and fired off a kick that caught him under the ear, but she was too well taped to do anything else.

"Ouch!" Uncle Charlie cried, putting his hand to his head. "Help me out here, Bubba."

Uncle Charlie took Bee under the armpits, and Bubba took her feet, and they hauled her onto the small dock and put her down. Then they walked over to Daddy's old fiberglass fishing canoe, kicked it a few times to warn any snakes that might have found their way underneath, and took it by the ends and rolled it over.

A second later I heard a loud thump and the sound of wood cracking. I craned my head around to see Uncle Charlie holding the canoe while Bubba stomped on the thwarts. When he finished breaking the last one, Uncle Charlie rolled the canoe on its side, and Bubba began to stomp the fiberglass hull, breaking the wooden ribs.

When they finally put the canoe in the water, it was a bent, misshapen husk. While Uncle Charlie held it to the side of the dock to keep it from drifting away, Bubba Simmons grabbed Bee under the arms, dragged her over, and then rolled her into what was left of the canoe. Afterward he came over to the truck for me. I tried to kick him in the head, but he was ready for that. He reached over the side, grabbed the collar of my shirt, pulled me around headfirst, then loaded me onto his shoulder like a man carrying a sack of potatoes.

The canoe was now a big, open envelope, with its ribs cracked and the thwarts fallen in against the hull, the water easily sloshing over the lower sides. Bubba bent over and dumped me beside Bee. As I tumbled in, my head hit the gunwale so hard that for several seconds I couldn't focus.

"What are they doing?" Bee's voice penetrated my fog of pain.

As my head started to clear, I felt a sudden rush of movement as Bubba gave us a big shove out into the pond. Beside me Bee tried to sit up to see where we were going. I didn't bother, because I already knew.

Green Alice's nest was on the far shore, almost directly across from the dock, probably a hundred yards away. The shove would get us a third of the way there. After that the morning breeze would slowly do the rest. Even as I thought those things, the breeze quickened, and we started moving faster.

For a moment there was silence on the pond. Then I heard Uncle Charlie's voice. "We don't have to stay here, do we?" I could tell he was scared.

"I don't reckon we do," Bubba said. "That gator'll take care of things soon enough, and until it does, they won't be going anywhere."

"You're being real stupid, Uncle Charlie!" I shouted in as loud a voice as I could muster. "Nobody's gonna believe this was an accident if we've got duct tape all over our arms and legs!"

"What if she's right?" I heard Uncle Charlie say.

"Gators eat duct tape just like they eat everything else," Bubba said.

"Oh no, Abbey!" Bee exclaimed, the realization hitting her. "It's Green Alice they're talking about, isn't it?"

In the next second I heard the pickup's doors close and the engine rev as Uncle Charlie turned around and drove back out the dirt track. The sound of the truck quickly faded.

I was still trying to think what to tell Bee when words became unnecessary.

Something like an angry snort came from very close to the canoe's side. A second later we felt a powerful thump against the canoe's damaged hull. The blow made us roll right to the gunwale and brought a wave of pond water over the side that sloshed around in the bottom of the canoe. We had already drifted too close to Green Alice's nest.

Several seconds went by, and then she hit the canoe again. The sound of her whacking the hull was thunderous. We heeled dangerously, took on more water, and this time a long, white seam appeared in the fiberglass. The water in the canoe's bottom was already making us heavier and less buoyant, so that even if the wind changed direction, it would barely push us away.

I was in full-time panic mode. We needed to come up with some way to distract Alice or frighten her, something that would buy us enough time to get to shore and escape. But how do you distract an angry mama alligator when you can't move?

I didn't know whether Alice was hitting us with her tail or her snout or trying to bite into the canoe's side. It didn't really matter. Alice had already buckled the canoe's hull in some places. Water was leaking through the seams in the fiberglass. I jerked helplessly against the tape on my wrists and ankles. I realized that even if we didn't break apart or capsize, we could still drown right here in the bottom of the canoe.

Fortunately Bee seemed to be thinking more clearly than I was. "Abbey," she said, her voice sharp as a whiplash. I realized she had been talking to me for several moments, but I hadn't been hearing. "Slide back toward me," she commanded. "Hurry!"

Bee's voice snapped me out of my panic. I used my knees and elbows to inch backward while she moved in the opposite direction.

"Okay, stop," she said, just as Alice slammed into us yet again.

I realized that the canoe was no longer rolling as much because we had taken on so much water. Also, Alice's attacks seemed to be pushing us away from her nest but thankfully not out into deeper water. A second later I felt a soft bump and realized that the canoe had nosed into the pond's mud bottom. I raised my head and saw that we were much closer to shore than I had realized, but it wasn't going to help, because neither of us could climb out and run.

Bee was working hard to change that, pressing her face against my wrists. A second later I felt a tug as she managed to snag the end of the tape in her teeth and pull some of it free. I forced myself to hold still and felt her tug again, then a third time.

Just as I was finally starting to move my wrists, Alice hit us yet again. One of the seams cracked all the way, and for one second a long, yellow tooth poked through.

I knew it was a matter of seconds before Alice hit us again, and that it wasn't going to be long before she broke the canoe in half. Once that happened, she would drag each of us to the bottom of the pond, where we would become food for her babies. I could feel Bee continuing to work on the tape, but it wasn't coming away fast enough.

There was a big splash, and my muscles turned to jelly. It had to be Alice, preparing to smash us again. But then I heard a voice from someplace close by, and I tried to sit up and look around. Bee stopped and looked up, too.

Skoogie Middleton was standing on the shore of the pond only about twenty yards away from us. The splash I had heard was a piece of wood he had thrown that was now floating beside Alice's head.

I didn't know why he was there or how he had managed to find us, but I watched in amazement as Skoogie threw another stick. This one landed on top of Alice's head, right between her eyes. I could also see Alice's two baby gators. They were in the water, closer to Skoogie than to us, which meant Green Alice's attention was now totally focused on Skoogie.

Skoogie saw me looking at him and yelled, "Y'all get outta that canoe!"

My body was paralyzed, because I saw Alice already moving toward Skoogie, her powerful tail driving her faster than I'd ever seen her move.

"She's coming!" I shouted. "Run!"

I don't know whether he heard me. He stood there as if he was hypnotized, and I could feel the cold dread rising up in my belly as I saw what was about to happen.

Alice shot onto shore, her short legs and long, thick body skimming right over the pluff mud. She raced up the bank toward Skoogie like a green torpedo. Still, he just stood there.

I closed my eyes and waited for the screams that were sure to come when Alice grabbed him in her powerful jaws. But for several seconds, I heard nothing.

"Get outta that canoe!" Skoogie yelled again.

I opened my eyes in amazement as Alice charged him again. Just as he must have done the first time, Skoogie stood his ground and let her get close, then he jumped to one side and ran around behind her. Alice stopped and turned with slow, laborious movements. While alligators are very fast in a straight line, they are slow as molasses when it comes to turning around. Alice had charged him twice, and she already looked tired.

"Got it!" Bee shouted, and I realized my wrists were free. While I was watching Skoogie, she must have gone back to tearing away the tape on my arms. My knife was still in its sheath, because Uncle Charlie hadn't even bothered to take it away once he got my hands bound. I used it to free my ankles, and then it took only another moment to cut the tape from Bee's arms and legs.

We clambered over the side of the canoe. Our legs sank deep into the mud, almost all the way to our hips, but we slogged as fast as we could up onto the bank and through the tall grass away from Alice and her nest.

A few seconds later, Skoogie came up to us, leaving

a tired Alice to guard the bank. Her jaws were wide open in a fearsome manner, but she no longer posed any threat to us.

"I thought y'all wasn't gonna get out," Skoogie said.

"I thought you were gonna get eaten," I told him.

Skoogie smiled and shook his head. "I'm the best gator dodger on Leadenwah Island."

"But what are you doing here?" I asked as my brain started to work again. "How did you know how to find us?"

"My granny saw you go past in Mr. Charlie's truck, and she said you looked real scared like something bad was happening. My granny don't like Mr. Charlie, and she had some suspicions, and so she told me to stay outta sight but to see if anything bad was goin' on.

"I hid in the bushes by your house, and I seen plenty a bad stuff goin' on, so I followed the truck to the pond. I stayed out of sight until they left, then got some wood and went around to the right side of the pond, where I could get that mama gator to pay attention to me."

Bee suddenly reached out and grabbed Skoogie and hugged him until I thought he might suffocate. "You are my hero," she said.

Skoogie was surprised for a moment, and then a

smile broke out on his face, so big I thought it would never come off. Finally I cleared my throat. We might have gotten away from Green Alice, but our problems were still only just beginning.

Twenty-five

We moved to a spot about a hundred yards from the pond, our legs and clothes dripping pluff mud and pond water, and tried to gather our wits. Bee and I told Skoogie everything that had happened, starting with the previous night when we had snuck out and gone to Felony Bay.

Skoogie listened without saying a word, but when Bee got to the part where Deputy Simmons wanted to shoot his gun into the bushes, his eyes widened in shock. "What're we gonna do if the police are the bad guys?"

Bee looked at me. "Can't we just go find a phone

and call Mr. Barrett or Custis, and tell them what's happening?"

I shook my head. "Uncle Charlie cut the phone line to the big house, remember?"

"What about your grandmother?" Bee asked Skoogie.

"We only got a cell phone, but Grandma broke hers a couple days ago, and she hasn't been to town to get a new one."

"What about a car?" Bee insisted. "We can go get Grandma Em, and she can drive us out of here!"

Skoogie shook his head again. "Not 'less you want to get your grandma shot. They got a tractor and a manure spreader parked across the plantation drive like it's broke-down. It's blocking anybody gettin' in or out."

"So what are we going to do?" Bee asked.

"My grandma's got a truck," Skoogie offered. "She could drive us someplace."

"First we have to make sure we can get off the plantation without being seen," I said. "And that won't be easy."

Skoogie walked a few yards to an ancient live oak with branches that drooped all the way to the ground. With a practiced motion, he grabbed one of the lowest ones, swung himself onto the limb, and climbed up to a place high up in the tree where he had a view around the plantation. After a few seconds he called down to us. "You're right. That Deputy Simmons is parked on the drive near Mr. Charlie's house. Gonna be a little tricky sneaking past him."

I shook my head. To get around Deputy Simmons, we would have to sneak through the cornfield and then crawl through the soybeans. Even though the corn was high, we would be putting birds to flight the whole way through, so any experienced hunter like Deputy Simmons would know right away that someone was trying to sneak past him. Skoogie and I could move fast enough to probably get away, but there was no way Bee could with her knee. She still wasn't fast enough to take the risk.

We didn't dare leave Bee here alone, because sooner or later Uncle Charlie or Deputy Simmons was liable to come back out to the pond to make sure their little plan had worked. If they spotted the canoe over by the shore, they'd know right away that it hadn't.

As I struggled to puzzle things out, Skoogie dropped to the ground. "Might be that you don't need to sneak out," he said. "Might be that you want to be right here."

I looked at him in amazement. Skoogie had always

been quiet and cautious. "What are you talking about?"

"When I come in this morning, I seen a couple a them news trucks with them satellite dishes on top."

"Coming here?" I asked.

Skoogie nodded. "Going down the dirt road toward that little cabin where Grandma used to live."

I understood what Skoogie was suggesting, and I looked at Bee. Her eyebrows were already up like she was reading my mind and didn't like it a bit.

"Abbey, we need to get out of here. Please, no crazy ideas," she said.

I shook my head. "Skoogie's right. If we all get caught again, we're dead. We need to do something they don't expect."

I told them my Idea. It was going to be a huge gamble, but it was better than getting caught trying to sneak out. In the end Bee agreed there was no better choice.

Skoogie had to sneak back to his grandmother's trailer, because a single person sneaking has a way better chance than three. In case Bee and I failed, he would find a way to make a call to Mr. Barrett and the state police and hopefully convince one of them, as crazy as it sounded, about what Uncle Charlie and Bubba Simmons were doing. Skoogie didn't like the idea of leaving us, but he understood the sense of it and in the end he went along.

We watched him head off; then Bee and I started through the thick undergrowth that bordered the pond, heading toward the trail we had used that first day I took Bee to see Felony Bay.

I used my knife to cut another forked stick in case we ran into more cottonmouths, and I led the way. We went slow, staying low and making sure to make no noise.

As we drew close to Felony Bay, I was trying so hard to stuff my fear back down inside and not let Bee see how scared I was that I almost didn't notice that the No Trespassing signs were gone. I walked up to one of the trees where I was sure there had been a sign, but all I could see were the four staples that had been used to fix it in place.

"Somebody tore down the signs," I said.

"They're cleaning up," Bee said. "Just like they tried to clean us up."

"But they didn't," I said. Reminding myself that we were still alive and free and able to fight back brought a fresh burst of hope that helped calm the fear that bubbled in my stomach.

We started walking again, moving slower. Up ahead

we began to hear the sound of machines. They made a low hum, much softer than the excavation machine we had heard the last time. As we came closer, we started to see light through the trees and the glimmer of sunshine reflecting off metal surfaces.

"Those are the satellite trucks," Bee whispered.

"How do you know?"

"I've heard them before."

This was good. Satellite trucks meant people and cameras and microphones. With all those things around, Uncle Charlie and Deputy Simmons wouldn't be able to do anything to us. At least that's what I tried to tell myself.

We crept forward, staying behind the thick layer of undergrowth that walled off the beach. When I pushed some branches away and looked out from our hiding place, what I saw nearly made me cry out with anger.

A little wooden platform with a speaker's podium stood in front of the hole where the crate had been "buried." Uncle Charlie was standing on the platform looking almost respectable in a navy blue pin-striped suit with a red bow tie. He wore a big, happy smile like a person who had just won the lottery. A microphone was in front of his face, and I saw two big loudspeakers set on either side of the hole.

Ruth was standing in front of the platform beside Bubba Simmons, but rather than looking like it was the happiest day of her life, she looked like she was going to be sick. Anyone watching probably thought she was nervous about being onstage, but I thought the real reason she felt sick was that her husband had fed Bee and me to an alligator.

On the other side of the hole, behind a line of plastic tape, stood four different television cameramen along with their helpers. There were also photographers as well as several newspaper reporters, including Tom Blackford, all of them scribbling in little notebooks.

Uncle Charlie must have just started talking, because he was thanking everyone for coming to what he called "one of the greatest treasure finds in the past hundred years."

It was windy on the beach, and the satellite trucks made a constant roar, but Uncle Charlie's voice came booming over the speakers so loudly that nobody could miss a word.

He went on to say how for many years he had been a great student of local history in general and of tales of buried treasure in particular. He told how many people, including his own family, had pooh-poohed him, but how his belief and interest had never faltered.

When, through tragic circumstances, his family's legacy, Reward Plantation, had been put on the market, he had scraped together enough money to buy a small parcel of the original plantation that he believed contained a significant store of buried treasure. According to Uncle Charlie, his "intense and in-depth scholarly and historical research" had attracted several other investors. I had known there was no way Uncle Charlie and Ruth and Bubba Simmons could have afforded to purchase the land on their own. I was reminded of the mysterious man who had been with them the night before.

Uncle Charlie went on to say that the exploration had been "arduous," as people could see from all the holes that had been dug on the beach. "We did not hit pay dirt right away. It took us some months and much more research and excavation. But ladies and gentlemen, we kept at it with diligence, and today we are going to show you the exciting results."

He went on to tell the story of the *Lovely Clarisse*. "Up until today," Uncle Charlie said, "no one has known whether the legend was true, because on its second attempt to make Havana, the *Lovely Clarisse* was sunk with all hands. Over the years many have tried to find the gold, but no one succeeded. Until now."

Uncle Charlie had made himself sound like some

kind of workaholic rather than your basic bum, and now he pointed down at the hole where he and Deputy Simmons had placed the crate. Uncle Charlie stepped down off the stand, grabbed a shovel, and jumped into the hole. The newspeople followed with their cameras, and the photographers popped off pictures as he threw out several shovelfuls of dirt and exposed the crate. Then he grabbed a crowbar that was lying on the ground beside the hole and used it to break the rusty padlock he had put on the crate the night before.

Moving to one side of the hole, he pried up the crate's lid. The crowd made an oohing sound, and Uncle Charlie smiled up at them as the piles of gold ingots and small cloth bags became visible.

"I present the treasure of the *Lovely Clarisse*," he said to the cameras.

I knew that this was probably the only chance we were going to get. "Come on," I whispered to Bee. We moved to our right, until we were around the back of the cabin. There, safely out of sight of the crowd watching Uncle Charlie, we slithered out through the vines and brambles and into the open.

Our legs and shorts were caked with pluff mud to midthigh. We were bleeding from lots of tiny scratches and cuts from all the thorns. Our shirts were ripped, and our hair was a tangled mess with burrs and bits of twig that had caught there as we crept through the bushes. If we wanted people to believe our story, we needed to look more like young ladies and less like wild savages.

I was pulling scabs of pluff mud from my legs and brushing off the burrs when I heard someone rasp out my name: "Force!"

My blood froze in my veins, and I turned. Jimmy Simmons was standing a few feet behind me. He had just come around the back of the cabin, and he had a cigarette he must have stolen from somebody in one hand and a pack of matches in the other.

"You're dead," he hissed, tossing the cigarette and matches onto the ground and stepping forward.

My mind was racing as I struggled to think. I had no time for Jimmy Simmons right now, but I also knew he wasn't going to let me walk away without a fight. The only good thing was that he wasn't shouting out our names. It meant he probably didn't know his father and Uncle Charlie had been looking for us. Which probably also meant that Jimmy didn't know about the stolen gold. I had to hope that was the case.

Jimmy had already closed the distance between us. I glanced at Bee and saw the panicked look on her face. "We have to run," she hissed.

I gave my head a little shake.

"Jimmy," I whispered, turning to face him, "I know you think this is a chance to get back at me, but we don't have time right now. There's something a lot more important going on."

He cocked his head and looked at me with his mouth open. His big hands hung at his sides, the fingers tensed as if eager to grab my throat. "What're you talkin' about?" he asked with a sneer.

"Your father, for one. He's in big trouble."

"No, he's not."

Jimmy's voice carried no conviction, and for a second I could swear I saw something in his eyes that was far more than the stupidity I'd always thought was there. I actually thought it was the glimmer of understanding, maybe even intelligence, and it dawned on me that in the back of his mind Jimmy might have known for a long time that his dad was a crook. In that same instant I realized that I felt sorry for him, and I decided that telling him the truth was my only way out.

"Yes. Your dad and Uncle Charlie are in a whole lot of trouble," I said. "That gold they said they found, well, they didn't. They stole it from Miss Jenkins."

Jimmy's eyes squinted, and his face bunched up. For a second I thought I'd totally done the wrong thing and that he was about to go crazy and attack me. In the next moment, I watched his shoulders slump and the tension go out of his hands, and I knew the expression on his face was sadness more than anger.

"What're you talkin' about?" he said again, but this time there was no energy behind his words. What I heard was almost a pleading tone.

"I'm sorry," I said. I glanced at Bee. I wanted to turn and run, but I knew Jimmy would never let me go. Time was passing, and our window was closing fast. I had to do something.

"What about my mom?" Jimmy said, pulling my attention back. "She's not in trouble, is she? She works for Miss Jenkins."

I tried to think of the right answer, but my brain was a puddle. "I don't think she knows," I said, hoping desperately that I was right.

Jimmy lowered his head. He spoke in a dull voice that was so soft, I could barely hear the words. "She always told me that he's a loser but that he's also my dad. She makes me spend time with him."

"Abbey!" Bee whispered.

I glanced at her and shook my head again. Jimmy was still too dangerous to risk turning my back on.

"You and your mom don't live with him?" I asked.

"Not since school got out. Ever since that thing with the teachers."

"What thing with the teachers?"

He gave a self-conscious shrug. "You know how everybody thinks I'm stupid? And don't say you don't, 'cause I know you do. Well, one of my teachers said I was this thing called *dyslexic*. It means I read backward, sort of. The teacher wanted me to go to special classes for dyslexic kids. My mom wanted me to. She said I could do good in school if learned to read right, but Dad said no way. He said that being dyslexic is being stupid, and no son of his was going to ride the blue bus for the retards. They had another one of their big fights, and Dad hit her pretty good. Afterward my mom packed us up, and we went to live with my aunt."

I looked at him, conscious of the seconds ticking past but also that this kid who I had always thought was nothing but a dumb bully might actually be something different.

Jimmy's eyes flashed up, and he seemed to have recovered a little bit of spirit. "You better not be lying about this, Force," he said. "If you are, I'm gonna double kill you."

"If I'm lying, I'll let you double kill me," I said. "I promise."

"You guys!" Bee hissed. "Come on!"

I glanced at Bee, then back at Jimmy. "If your father and Uncle Charlie stop us, we may need you to call the police. I'm not joking. Would you do that?"

After a second or two, Jimmy shrugged, seeming to say that maybe he'd help and maybe he wouldn't. "What're you gonna do?"

"Forget your cigarette and go on around the other side. You can watch."

Twenty-six

As Bee and I stepped through the cabin's back door, I tried to shut out any thoughts of snakes and spiders. I know Bee did the same as we moved quickly through the ruined kitchen and into the main room. Once there, we crept up to the front door, taking care to stay out of sight.

My heart was in my mouth as I searched the crowd in front of the platform for Uncle Charlie. What if we had taken too much time and he was back at the microphone? What I saw gave me a surge of hope. Uncle Charlie was still down in the hole showing off some of the gold pieces. The press and television newspeople were standing near him, holding microphones out to catch his words as their camera people continued to shoot pictures.

"Ready?" I whispered to Bee.

"Yes."

No one seemed to notice when Bee and I bolted out of the cabin's doorway and jumped onto the platform. I stood on my toes at the podium, grabbed the microphone, and tipped it down so it would pick up my voice. A loud squealing sound came over the loudspeakers, so I knew the microphone was still on.

The screech also got everybody's attention, and the crowd of reporters turned their heads in our direction. Their expressions showed annoyance and surprise, but at least they were listening.

"Excuse me, ladies and gentlemen," I said. "My uncle and Deputy Simmons are lying to you. My name is Abbey Force, and I need to report a very serious crime."

I glanced down. Uncle Charlie's eyes were wide with shock and alarm, his lips tight with anger. As I watched, he dumped his gold ingots back into the crate and began to scramble out of the hole. He had to cover only a few feet, which meant I had to talk very fast.

"Last night, my friend and I saw Uncle Charlie; his

wife, Ruth; and Deputy Bubba Simmons dig this hole and bury this crate. It's not really treasure from an old ship. It's gold and jewels they stole from Miss Lydia Jenkins." I pointed, my words racing out. "Over there in that cabin is where they melted down everything they stole from Miss Jenkins and made it into gold bars."

Uncle Charlie was already on the platform. He grabbed my arm and pulled me away from the microphone. I tried to twist out of his grasp, but he was too strong.

"Uncle Charlie and Bubba Simmons caught us and tried to kill us by shoving us into an alligator pond," I shouted, even as he clamped a hand over my mouth and handed me off the stage to Bubba Simmons.

Bee hadn't said a word, but as Uncle Charlie dragged me away, she rushed to the microphone. "My name is Bee Force, and my father bought Reward Plantation from Abbey's father. Abbey's telling the truth. These people tried to kill us."

She couldn't say any more, because at that point Uncle Charlie pulled her away, too, and handed her down to Bubba Simmons.

Bubba was strong as an ox, and he had huge hands. He held each of us by the arm, and even though we both tried to shout, he dragged us back among the satellite trucks, where the roar of the generators drowned out everything else. I had a desperate hope that at least a couple of the press people had understood what Bee and I had tried to say and maybe believed us. If they had, I was sure somebody would call the police or demand that we be released.

I knew we'd been beaten when no one came after us, and then I heard Uncle Charlie's voice boom out loud enough to be heard over the generators.

"I've got to apologize for that interruption, but there's an explanation that'll help y'all understand what's going on. That first young lady, Abbey Force, is my niece. Her daddy, Rutledge Force, is my brother, and right now he's in a coma in University Hospital. He's accused of robbing Miss Lydia Jenkins, that same lady Abbey just mentioned, who was his client. Reward Plantation had to be sold because of that theft, and I am sorry to say . . . well, this isn't the first instance of my niece acting out or lying. I am afraid her sense of reality has been badly damaged."

Uncle Charlie turned and looked back in our direction like he actually cared. He could still see us, but we were way behind the satellite trucks now and far out of sight of the reporters. Even though we were both twisting and fighting, we couldn't get out of Bubba's iron grip. I caught sight of Ruth. She was standing a few feet behind the platform staring in our direction, and for a second I wondered if she would come over and try to help Bubba. However, she just remained where she was, with her arms crossed tightly over her chest, looking even more sick than she had before.

"Bee Force is another girl who's suffered a family tragedy," Uncle Charlie went on. "Her mother and brother were killed in a car accident last winter. Bee was the only survivor. She has been in psychological care ever since."

"Don't listen to him!" Bee and I shouted. "He's lying!" It did no good. No one could hear us.

"Now, they haven't broken any laws, even though they probably hoped they could," Uncle Charlie continued with a chuckle. "Maybe if Deputy Simmons takes them over next door where they live and tells them not to come back, we can put this behind us."

He kept talking, but I couldn't hear him after Bubba slammed Bee and me together, which knocked the wind out of both of us. Then he picked each of us up with a different arm and slapped his hands over our mouths. "I shoulda waited there and made sure that gator did her job," he said in a low growl. "I ain't gonna make that mistake a second time."

We were far enough away now that I could no longer hear Uncle Charlie's lies. But I knew it didn't matter what he was saying. In spite of everything we had tried, he had beaten us.

A second later we reached Bubba's sheriff's department car. He took his hand off my mouth, opened the rear door, and tossed me across the seat. He tossed Bee in behind me and pulled two sets of handcuffs from the pouch on his belt, clicking one set onto Bee's wrists and then another onto mine.

As I tried to sit up and put my feet on the floor, I hit something, and when I looked down, whatever hope I had died completely. Skoogie Middleton was already in the car, lying on the cruiser's floor with his hands cuffed behind his back and tape over his mouth to keep him from crying out.

Bubba climbed behind the wheel, looked back over his shoulder, and nodded. "Caught that one tryin' to sneak back to his grandma," he said.

"Why have you got him handcuffed?" I asked. "You need to let him go. He didn't do anything."

"Nice try, little lady, but he knows about the canoe."

We had worked so hard and come so close, but we were prisoners again. It was even worse than it had been the first time, because now Skoogie was a prisoner as well, and I knew we weren't going to escape Green Alice a second time.

A tear broke loose and trickled down my cheek, but I didn't care. I closed my eyes and silently told Daddy that I was sorry I had let him down. I was sorry I had let everyone down.

Twenty-seven

As Bubba started the car and pulled away from
Felony Bay, I tried to summon some hope, but it
was a huge stretch. I really believed we had lost,
but I knew we had to keep fighting to the very end.

"You know you're not going to get away with this,"
I said from the backseat. "You're gonna get caught."

I saw Bubba's hands grip the wheel tighter and his
shoulders hitch up toward his ears.

"Uncle Charlie and Ruth are back there. Everybody
saw us leave with you. You're the only kidnapper, not
either one of them. They won't go to jail, but you will."

"Quiet down!" He cranked his head around and

glared back. If there hadn't been a wire screen separating us, I'm sure he would have started hitting.

"You want to slap me, don't you?" I said. "Just like you slapped Jimmy that day I saw you together in your truck."

Bubba slammed on the brakes, and for a half second I thought he was going to get out, come around to my door, and haul me out. But when he turned around in his seat, I could see the fear in his eyes. He must have been scared, starting to wonder if he really might be hung out to dry by his partners in crime.

"You," he said in a hoarse rasp. He had dried spittle at the corners of his mouth. "Keep your trap shut 'fore I come back there and show you what slapping really is."

I glanced at Bee, who looked at me and nodded. *You go, girl*, she mouthed.

Bubba sped up again. We were playing with fire where he was concerned. If he totally lost his temper and self-control, we would have no way to protect ourselves, but at the same time his fear was all we had to work with. Our only hope was that he would get rattled and make a big mistake.

"Grandma Em knows almost everything we know," I lied. "She's gonna figure out the rest when we disappear. You gonna kill her, too?" I paused for half a second. "Jimmy knows, too," I said.

Bubba's head snapped around. "Liar."

"I just told him five minutes ago behind the cabin. He'd snuck back there to smoke a cigarette. When he saw me, he was going to beat me up, so I told him everything."

Bubba stopped the car again, but this time he didn't even turn in his seat. He just sat staring straight ahead with his hands on the wheel. After another moment or two, I heard a strange sound and realized Bubba was muttering to himself. I figured he was thinking about what I had said and trying to come up with a way to deny things to his son. I also knew there was no way he could.

Nearly half a minute went by before he started driving again, but even then he went slowly. We hadn't gone far from the cabin yet, and we were still on the dirt track that led up from Felony Bay. I could see the township road about fifty yards ahead, and I knew we were going to turn right toward One Arm Pond.

I hadn't said anything else to Bubba, because fear was scrambling my brain and I had run out of words. I closed my eyes and felt my throat clamp shut as I tried to shake off the picture of Green Alice. I only opened them again when Bubba slammed on the brakes once more, and Bee and I pitched forward, almost smashing our heads against the seat back.

"What the hey?" Bubba said to himself.

When I looked up, I saw two state police cars blocking our way on the single-lane dirt track.

"You're dead," I said from the back, finding my voice once again. "You better surrender."

Bubba turned and looked at me out of the corner of one fear-yellowed eye. "I told you to shut up," he snarled.

He jammed the shift into Park, got out of the car, and walked ahead. The driver in the front police car rolled down his window and stuck his head out, and he and Bubba talked for a moment. I caught only snatches of what the policeman said, but I did hear something about an arrest order.

When Bubba replied, his voice barely reached us through the car windows and over the sound of the air conditioner, but I heard him say something like "I don't know nothing 'bout no arrests. A couple kids started acting up. I'm just taking them back to where they live. How 'bout y'all back up into the road and let me get past."

I was hoping desperately that the state police would refuse to let him leave, but the policeman just smiled and rolled up his window, and then he and the police car behind him began to back up to let Bubba pass.

Bubba was as pale as new cotton as he walked back to the car. I knew that if he'd been scared a minute earlier, he was positively panicking now.

"What's the matter, Deputy Simmons?" I asked. "Did I just hear something about the police arresting somebody? It isn't Uncle Charlie, by any chance, is it? He's a big talker, you know. Wonder who he's gonna pin everything on? Better turn yourself in before he hangs you."

"I'm tellin' you for the last time, girl, you shut your trap."

Once the other vehicles were out of the way, Bubba started forward. We inched past the two state police cruisers, which had pulled off on the side just where the dirt track emptied onto the township dirt road. Bubba was doing his best to look relaxed and normal, but he was doing a lousy job.

We turned right, and I swung around and got on my knees and looked out the back window as the two police cars grew smaller. We had come so close, but we had failed. The state police had been our last chance. My head dropped down into my shoulders, and I felt my heart fall into my stomach. As scared as I was, though, I was also mad, and I wanted him to hurt bad for what he was about to do.

"You really think anybody's going to believe that Bee and Skoogie and I ran away from you and jumped in a canoe and paddled out to get eaten by an alligator?"

Bubba didn't answer. The car slowed, and we turned into Reward.

"Tell me you're not really stupid enough to think you can get people to believe that story."

"I'm a deputy," he said, half grunting the words. "People'll believe what I tell 'em."

"No! They're gonna believe what Uncle Charlie tells them. He's gonna say you did this all by yourself, and then he and Ruth are gonna keep your share of the money."

Bubba shook his head like he was trying to clear his brain. He'd been backed into a corner, and he knew it. The question was whether he was smart enough to realize he had choices. We were heading up the drive, toward the last turn that would put us on the dirt track that led to One Arm Pond. I felt it when Bubba took his foot off the accelerator. The car slowed, but it didn't stop.

"Even if other people believe what you say, you think Jimmy's gonna believe you?"

Bubba's neck was red as a beet, and in spite of the

air-conditioning, I could see sweat breaking out of his hair line and dripping down his neck and onto his collar.

"Jimmy's gonna know you're a murderer, and nothing you say will ever make him think different."

Bubba sagged in his seat all of a sudden. If I hadn't known better, I would have sworn he reacted like somebody who just took a hard punch to the stomach.

I was starting to feel a surprising sense of hope when a half second later Bubba's eyes went to the rearview mirror, and he stomped down on the accelerator and cranked a hard turn toward One Arm Pond. Right away I realized that what I had just said had pushed him over the edge. He was going to kill us as fast as he possibly could just to shut me up.

I felt tears burning at the corners of my eyes. I was about to tell Bee and Skoogie how sorry I was when instead of driving all the way down to the pond, Bubba cut the wheel hard and pulled into a tractor shed where Daddy used to keep his corn harvester.

The harvester was still there, and Bubba tucked his car in between it and the wall of the tractor shed. I was too stunned to say anything as I watched him lean forward against the steering wheel and watch as two state police cars went speeding down the dirt track we had been on just seconds before.

"Hey, police," I shouted at the top of my lungs. "We're here!"

The police cars were already past us, and I knew there was no way they had heard me. That wasn't why I shouted. I was trying to bother Bubba.

"Better give up, Bubba," I said. "They're after you already."

Bubba lashed his elbow back, but it just slammed into the metal screen. "Shut up," he growled.

He shoved the car into gear and shot out of the barn, spraying clouds of dust and heading back toward the township road. When I looked back, I saw that both of the police cars had turned around and were coming after us, their light bars flashing.

Bubba must have sensed them, because he turned on his own lights and accelerated even more. Anybody watching us would have thought all three police cars were heading to the same emergency. They wouldn't have guessed that two state police cars were chasing a Charleston County deputy.

We were starting to pick up serious speed. Trees whipped past. We slammed through the bumps in the dirt road. Several times the back tires bounced off the ground, and when they hit again, the car would slide to one side or the other.

As we shot through the Reward gates and onto the township road, I looked back but could barely see the police cars through the huge cloud of dust we kicked up. I knew the paved county road was just a half mile ahead, but so did Bubba. He mashed the accelerator, and I could feel the engine roar as we went even faster.

Bee and I jammed our feet against the seat back, because it seemed obvious that Bubba had no intention of slowing down when he turned onto the paved road. I glanced ahead, praying a truck wouldn't be coming along just then, and that's when I noticed the other flashing lights. There were two more police cars, and they had spread out across the road, blocking the way.

Bubba must have realized there was no way to get around them, because he slammed on his brakes. The car went into a skid and came to a jarring halt with the front end nosed into a drainage ditch. Bubba wrenched open his door and jumped out.

The two police cars behind us had already slid to a stop, and policemen from each car were already running toward Bubba. More policemen were approaching on foot from the two cars that had been stopped to block the road.

Bubba stood in the drainage ditch and stared angrily

at both groups. He made one last attempt to bluff his way out. "What the heck you boys think y'all're doing? I told you I got me some prisoners, and I'm on my way to lock 'em up. You boys best be outta my way right now."

"Deputy Simmons," one of the policemen said, "stand away from your car. Place both hands on top of your head. You are under arrest."

Bubba looked at eight guns aimed at him, and he did as he was told. "What're you boys talkin' about? Arrest me? For what?"

"Kidnapping, for starters," one of the state policemen said as he stepped down into the ditch, grabbed Bubba's shoulder, and jerked him out of the water. As they came up the bank, another policeman stepped in and took Bubba's pistol from his holster.

"Th-that's a b-big lie," Bubba stuttered. "Who told you that?"

"Right after we passed you the first time, dispatch got a call claiming a deputy sheriff was kidnapping two girls with intent to do grievous harm. At first we just wanted to ask you a few questions, but you answered them for us when you ran."

I realized Jimmy Simmons had made that call, but it had no time to sink in. The policemen were on all sides of Bubba now, and the one who had jerked him out of the water took Bubba's hands, put them behind his back, and tried to cuff him. As he did, Bubba threw an elbow into the man's stomach. The policeman grunted and took a step back, but in the same instant the others were on Bubba like flies on honey.

Bubba went down with two of the policemen on top of him. I heard some painful grunts, and a second later they dragged him back to his feet. He was cuffed and now bleeding from the nose and a cut on his lip.

After they slammed Bubba into the backseat of one of their cars, one of the policemen came over to our car, opened the back door, and looked at us. "You kids okay?" he asked.

Bee and I nodded. Skoogie grunted. I held out my hands to the policeman. "Please take these off," I said.

He smiled, unlocked our handcuffs, and took the tape off Skoogie's mouth.

I looked around at the policemen and felt a tremor of alarm, because they were acting relaxed, like they thought catching Bubba had been everything they needed to do.

One of the policemen walked toward us with a pad of paper and a pen. "I'm going to need to take some information," he said.

"There's no time for that," I said. "My uncle, Charlie Force, and his wife, Ruth, are all involved. They stole a bunch of gold and jewels from Miss Lydia Jenkins and framed my dad, and we know all about it, and that's why Deputy Simmons was going to kill us. They already tried once, but we got away."

The policemen all looked at one another and then at us, their faces wrinkled like they weren't sure what to believe. Finally the one who had taken off our handcuffs came over, squatted down, and looked into our eyes. "Those are a bunch of very serious allegations," he said. "Do you have any proof?"

My mind raced, and I opened my mouth to tell him everything. But then I thought about the blackened pot we had found in the cabin and the plywood table, and I realized they were probably buried somewhere by now. And I thought about the books Uncle Charlie had checked out from the Library Society. But even as I thought it, I realized checking out books wasn't a crime. I thought about the canoe in One Arm Pond, but what did a busted-up canoe prove?

My heart plummeted as I realized it was basically Bee's and my word against Uncle Charlie's and Ruth's and Bubba Simmons's. We had seen them dig the hole and bury the crate, but who would believe us? Who would believe me when I said I had seen the yellow ball gown Ruth had cut up to make the bags for the diamonds? Who would believe us when we said they had shoved us into One Arm Pond in a broken canoe so Green Alice could eat us?

I realized my mouth was still open, but so far no words had come out, because, of everything I had thought of, not a single shred of it was proof.

"Well?" the policeman prodded.

I felt so angry and frustrated that I thought I might burst into tears.

"What about the ring?" Bee suddenly blurted out.

I looked at her in amazement. I had completely forgotten about the ring we had found in the crack in the cabin floor underneath the plywood table. I stuck my hand in my pocket, hoping desperately that I hadn't lost it crawling through the pluff mud when we escaped from One Arm Pond, or riding Clem into Charleston, or doing any of the other crazy things we had done in the past twelve hours. At first my fingers felt nothing, and I had a feeling like panic.

But then I jammed my finger all the way to the very bottom of my pocket, down where it ended in a narrow point. I pulled it out and held up the ring for the policeman to see. "Here," I said. "We found this in the cabin where they melted down all the gold. It belongs to Miss Lydia Jenkins."

I said that as if I knew it for sure, even though I really didn't. But in my heart I was positive that I was right. There was no way that ring belonged to anybody else.

The policeman took the ring and held it up as the other policemen stepped close. "Where did you find it again?"

"In the old abandoned cabin down at Felony Bay. That's where they melted down Miss Jenkins's jewelry and tried to make it look like old Confederate gold. They're all down there right now, trying to convince the press that they found the gold from the *Lovely Clarisse*, but they didn't."

The policeman didn't say anything, because right then a couple other policemen with different uniforms showed up, and the first policeman stepped away to talk to them. When I looked to see where the new policemen had come from, I saw a couple of black-and-white police cars that said City of Charleston on the doors.

"That's weird," I whispered to Bee.

"Yeah," she said. "So's the ambulance."

I looked again, and for the first time I noticed that an ambulance was parked behind the Charleston police cars.

After he spoke with the Charleston police for a few moments, the policeman who had Miss Jenkins's ring went over to the back of the ambulance, where we couldn't see him anymore. He spent several minutes back there, and I started to worry about what was going on.

Finally the policeman came out from behind the ambulance. He told Bee, Skoogie, and me to sit tight; then he called all the policemen together and spoke to them in a voice too soft for us to overhear. When he finished talking, all the policemen turned around and went to their cars.

The car with Bubba drove off toward the mainland, but all the other police cars, including the one with Bee, Skoogie, and me, all headed toward the dirt track that led down to Felony Bay.

Twenty-eight

The policeman who was driving put the windows down, and all the way back to Felony Bay I felt the warm air blow across my face. Whenever I looked back, I could see the ambulance following us, but so far no one had said a word to explain why it was there.

In spite of the fact that I knew we were now safe, I worried that Uncle Charlie would find a way to convince the police that he and Ruth were telling the truth and that Bee and I were lying. As it turned out, I didn't need to be concerned.

We drove down and parked as close to Mrs. Middleton's old cabin as we could, given the number of other cars and news vans that were already there for Uncle Charlie's news conference. The ambulance pulled up right behind us, and the attendants opened its rear doors and set up a ramp that sloped to the ground. The sight of the ambulance made me curious, so as soon as the policeman opened the rear door for us to get out, I walked around the ambulance and spotted Miss Lydia Jenkins in her wheelchair.

My breath caught in my throat, and right away my head began to swirl with questions. Why was she here? Was she going to accuse my father of some other awful crime? Was she going to help Uncle Charlie somehow?

As I looked at her, I realized that Miss Jenkins seemed to be staring at me out of the corner of her eye. As she struggled to turn her head in my direction, the man in the doctor's coat who was pushing her wheelchair seemed to notice, and he swiveled her around so she was facing me head-on.

One of the Charleston policemen came up behind me. "You ought to go talk to Miss Jenkins," he said in a gentle voice.

I looked at him like he'd just told me to go jump off a cliff, but he put his hand on my back and gave me a gentle prod in Miss Jenkins's direction.

"It's okay," the policeman said. "She's the reason

we're here." He gave an encouraging nod. "Go on and talk to her. It's okay. I promise."

I turned toward Miss Jenkins, and when I took a halting step, she nodded, as if to say that was what she wanted. Even from a distance I could tell that something about her had changed.

Miss Jenkins's eyes were fixed on me, and they had that same intense look I had seen the other day. In spite of my reluctance I took another step forward. The policeman's hand was still on my back, but he was no longer pushing, just encouraging me.

I don't know how long it took me to walk up to Miss Jenkins, but at some point in the process I realized that Bee was right beside me. Just like the great friend she was, she seemed to understand my reluctance, and she was with me for support.

Finally the two of us came to stand in front of Miss Jenkins's wheelchair. Just like the two previous times I'd seen her, she reached for my wrist. This time I saw it coming, but in spite of wanting to, I didn't pull my arm away. To my surprise, when she gripped me, her fingers were soft. They no longer felt like desperate talons the way they had before.

She stared at me for a long second, and her eyes widened as if she was trying to tell me something

Important. She only let go when doctor took a small whiteboard and slid it under her wrist. He put a felt-tip marker in her hand and wrapped her fingers around it. That's when Miss Jenkins started writing. It took a while, and her letters were like chicken scratches, but I could make them out.

You found my ring.

My own eyes were probably as big around as saucers, but I managed to nod. "Uncle Charlie and Ruth and Bubba Simmons had it."

I know.

"You do?" I exclaimed.

So sorry I couldn't say what I meant. Mind has been fuzzy.

The doctor who was handling her wheelchair put his hand on her shoulder. "You're doing great," he said. "Take your time."

Miss Jenkins nodded, but she kept trying to write. I watched the letters she struggled to form with her shaking hands. *Never meant your father stole.*

Something exploded inside me. "You never meant to say that my father took your gold!" I exclaimed, unable to keep myself from finishing her sentence.

She raised her eyes to me and nodded, and something like a smile flitted across her frozen features.

The doctor spoke. "When Miss Jenkins arrived for her therapy session this morning, she was very agitated. She has always worked hard to communicate with us, but frankly she had made little progress. Apparently this morning she had seen you and your friend with your uncle, and she felt that something was terribly wrong. We gave her the marker, and she tried harder than ever, didn't you, Miss Jenkins?"

Miss Jenkins blinked a nod. She might even have smiled again.

"For almost a year, Miss Jenkins has been unable to tell anyone what really happened when her money was stolen. This morning, however, she was so worried about you and your friend that she made a tremendous breakthrough in her recovery and found a way to communicate much more than she ever has since she had her stroke."

I looked down at Miss Jenkins. "So you were trying to say something different every other time I saw you?"

Couldn't say his name. She had tears in her eyes, and she added, *Sorry.*

I reached for her hand and gave it a squeeze. "Thank you for working so hard to say it today. You helped to save our lives."

The next hour or so passed in a big blur. A police car went back to Mrs. Middleton's trailer and brought both Grandma Em and Mrs. Middleton. They came running toward us and threw their arms around Bee and Skoogie, and then after a few seconds, Grandma Em grabbed me as well. Both of the old women were crying and darned near beside themselves with relief that we were safe.

It turned out that when Bee didn't show up for breakfast, Grandma Em had decided she was sleeping awful late. She finally checked Bee's bed and, finding her gone, walked down to the dock to see if Bee and I had taken an early swim. But the dock was deserted, and because it wasn't like Bee to leave the house without telling her, she started to get worried. She tried to call Uncle Charlie's house to see if Bee was with me there, but her phone was out of service because Uncle Charlie and Bubba had cut the line. When she tried to drive to Uncle Charlie's, the tractor and manure spreader blocked the drive.

Not knowing what else to do, Grandma Em walked to Uncle Charlie's house but found it locked and empty, because by that time Ruth and Charlie had gone down to Felony Bay for Uncle Charlie's press conference.

From there she walked to the barn, and when she didn't find either one of us there, she started to get really worried. Not knowing the property very well, Grandma Em started walking out the plantation drive, intending to head toward Mrs. Middleton's to ask to use her phone. On her way she saw One Arm Pond in the distance and the dirt track that led to it, and on the chance that Bee might be there, she walked in that direction. When she got near the pond and spotted the half-sunk canoe, she freaked out and decided she needed to call the police right away, because she was worried that something bad might have happened to us.

Grandma Em hurried down the road to Mrs. Middleton's trailer, where she found Mrs. Middleton also frantic because Skoogie hadn't returned from going to spy on what was going on with Bee and me. The two women jumped in Mrs. Middleton's pickup and drove far enough toward Charleston to get a cell signal. They called the police to report their grandchildren missing, then went back to the trailer to wait.

After Grandma Em and Mrs. Middleton calmed down, I also learned that the second phone call that helped save us really had come from Jimmy Simmons, who to my surprise had turned out to be a friend after all.

The police took statements from Bee, Skoogie, and me, and we told them about the broken canoe at One Arm Pond, and showed them where we had found Miss Jenkins's ring in the cabin. We also pointed out the fresh ashes in the fireplace. Finally Bee and I remembered one other thing, and we took them around the side of the cabin, where Bubba had tossed the straps into the bushes. The straps were still there.

"They used those straps to lower the crate down into the hole," Bee said. "I bet if you check the bottom of the crate, you'll find some of that material caught in the splinters."

After the police finished taking our statements, we watched Uncle Charlie being led toward the back of one of the Charleston police cars. Uncle Charlie never looked at me, and when the police put him in the car, he sat hunched forward and stared at the floor. He looked like a man who knew his life was ruined. Even though he was my uncle, after everything he'd done, I couldn't find it in my heart to feel sorry for him.

Ruth was also in handcuffs, and as I watched they led her to another police car. Unlike Uncle Charlie, who seemed to be feeling sorry just for himself, she was crying and looking totally shamefaced. I was betting that it wasn't going to take long for Ruth to start confessing everything that she and Uncle Charlie had done.

We had just finished watching Ruth get led away when another car came down the dirt track toward the old cabin, moving pretty fast. The car skidded to a stop, and a second later Custis hopped out.

"Abbey!" he said. "You okay?"

"What are you doing here?" I asked, happy to see him but also surprised.

"Mr. Barrett said that the hospital had called him and told him that there was a development with your dad and that he was going there, and that I should come out and make sure you were okay." He looked around at all the police cars and the satellite trucks that were just now putting everything away and getting set to leave. "What have I missed?"

I hadn't really listened to any of what he had just said. "The hospital called Mr. Barrett, and he told you to come here?"

He looked at me and shook his head. "That's what I just said."

"Did the hospital call you too?"

"I assume they just called the office, but Mr. Barrett took the call. He just told me to come here." Curtis shrugged.

"Why would he tell you that?"

Custis gave me a funny look. "What are you getting at, Abbey?"

I didn't answer him, because my mind was moving way too fast for me to speak. I had that funny feeling that you sometimes get when you're working on a jigsaw puzzle and you haven't found any pieces for a while, but then all of a sudden you see where a bunch of things fit.

I had been thinking that everything was going to be okay now, because we had been rescued, and Uncle Charlie, Ruth, and Bubba Simmons were in handcuffs. But all of a sudden I realized that wasn't true. There were three really important things I had forgotten. Who had put up the two million dollars to buy Felony Bay? And who had spoken from the shadows when Uncle Charlie, Ruth, and Bubba buried the treasure chest? And who had gotten the combination to Miss Jenkins's safe?

Whoever that person was, he was still out there, and if he knew what had happened here today, he was probably desperate. If he had stayed in the background during the robbery, just like he had last night, Miss Jenkins wouldn't know who he was either. Uncle Charlie, Ruth, and Bubba might tell the police about the mystery person, but could they prove it? It might just be the mystery person's word against theirs, and the mystery person might stay out of jail. That is, unless there might be one other person who could testify—at least he could, if he could ever manage to wake up.

It had to be one of two people, and one of them was standing right here beside me.

I felt panic welling up inside.

"We gotta go!" I said.

Custis screwed up his face and looked at me like he thought I was crazy, but I wasn't going to explain. I couldn't risk it yet.

I grabbed the arm of the policeman who had just taken our statements. "We need to get to the Medical University Hospital right away," I said. "It's a matter of life and death."

The policeman looked at me. "Is it related to all this other stuff?"

"Yessir. There's one other person who's been involved in this plot to steal Mrs. Jenkins's gold. I think he might be trying to kill my father."

He paused, then made his decision. "Let's go."

I looked over at Bee, but Grandma Em had her all wrapped up in a hug. There was no time to explain and get her free, so I nodded the policeman, who put Custis and me in the backseat of his car, told us to fasten our seatbelts, and then hit the siren and raced us all the way back to Charleston. On the way in, he talked on his radio, but the sound of the siren, the roaring of the engine, and the wind whipping past drowned out his voice completely.

He wheeled us around the entrance circle at the hospital, then jumped out of his car and came in with us. We went up the elevator, and I ran down to the corridor leading to Daddy's room and leaned on the buzzer for the nurse to let us in.

I had yelled into Custis's ear on our way to the hospital and told him what I was afraid of, and why. I could see from the expression on his face that he didn't like hearing what I was saying, but he also didn't argue with me.

It seemed to take forever for the nurse to come and buzz us in, and then she tried to hold up her hands and stop me when I bolted through the door and sprinted toward Daddy's room. As I got close, I could see that the door was open, and as I got closer, I saw two blue uniforms standing just inside the doorway.

They were looking into the room and didn't see me, and I burst past them and came to a halt. I had tears in my eyes, so I could barely see what was happening, but I saw Mr. Barrett standing beside the bed with his hands cuffed behind his back, and I saw a pillow on the floor, and I knew right away that I was too late.

I still had my knife in my sheath, and I went for it with one hand and started to launch myself toward Mr. Barrett. I was going to kill him if I could, because I knew he'd just smothered Daddy.

Just as my feet started to leave the ground, a huge blue arm circled my chest and arms and stopped me cold.

"Let me go!" I snarled.

"It's okay," a gentle voice said into my ear.

"It's not okay. He killed my father!"

"No, he didn't."

I froze.

"He didn't kill him," the policeman said. "He wanted to, but we caught him in time. Now I need for you to relax, because I'm going to take that knife out of your hands. Okay? And then I'm going to put you down. But first you have relax and promise to let me have the knife."

I nodded and let my arms go and relaxed my hand so the policeman could take my knife. I wiped the tears from my eyes, and when I did, I saw that Mr. Barrett was looking at me with an expression like a junkyard dog might get when it wanted to get off its chain and tear out my throat.

"You okay now?" the policeman asked.

I nodded.

He put me down very gently, and as he did, I heard Custis come into the room behind me. "Crawford, my God. Abbey said it was you. But I didn't believe it."

Mr. Barrett didn't say anything; he just turned his head and looked out the window.

"I almost forgot about him," I said to everyone in the room, "but then I remembered that there had been another person that night when they buried the crate. We couldn't see him, because he stayed in the shadows, and we couldn't hear his voice well enough to recognize it. But I knew it had to be somebody with enough money to buy Felony Bay, because Uncle Charlie and Bubba Simmons sure didn't have that much, and also somebody who had managed to get the combination to Miss Jenkins's safe. Only two people were supposed to know that combination, Miss Jenkins and Daddy, right? That's why everybody thought Daddy stole the money."

I was talking really fast. I knew I was running on at the mouth, but I couldn't help myself. "And then I thought even if I could solve everything else about Felony Bay, people would still think Daddy had been in on it unless I could figure out who stole the combination.

"My first idea was that maybe Esther Simmons got the combination somehow and gave it to Bubba, but that still didn't explain how they got the money to buy Felony Bay." I turned and looked at Custis. "Sorry to say that I suspected you, but I realized it had to be either you or Mr. Barrett, and when Mr. Barrett wanted to go to the hospital alone, and he sent you out to Felony Bay, I was pretty sure it had to be him. Mr. Barrett wanted to make sure the coast was clear so he could kill the only other person who could have tied him to the robbery."

Behind me a couple of the policemen started to clap. When I glanced back, they were smiling and nodding. The policeman who had driven us to the hospital laughed and said, "I think we've got us a twelve-year-old Sherlock Holmes."

Another one of the policemen grew serious and added, "If it hadn't been for you, this might have ended very differently. When we came in, Mr. Barrett here was just starting to put a pillow over your father's face."

I turned and looked at Mr. Barrett, but he wouldn't meet my eyes. "You think you're such a big-shot lawyer," I said. "Let's see if you can talk your way out of this one."

"Come on," one of the policemen said, reaching out

to take Mr. Barrett by the arm. "No reason for you to stay here. We got a nice cell for y'all down at police headquarters."

"Officer," I said. He stopped and looked in my direction.

I glanced at Daddy. His eyes were closed the way they always were, but deep in my bones I could feel something changing. I knew he was slowly coming awake. Maybe the doctors didn't know yet, but I did. It might not be today or tomorrow or even next week, but it was happening, just as surely as corn was growing in our fields. "My father can't speak to me yet, but I think I know what he would tell me to do if he could."

The policeman's eyebrows went up in question.

"This," I said, and with that I turned and kicked Mr. Barrett in the crotch as hard as I possibly could.

He let out a wonderful sound of surprise that changed into a groan of serious pain. Behind me, the policemen broke into laughter, and when Mr. Barrett tried to straighten up and come after me, the policeman who had him by the arm laughed. "How's it feel, Mister Big Shot?" he said as he dragged Mr. Barrett out of the room and down the hallway. "Taken down by a twelve-year-old girl."

Twenty-nine

I asked Custis if I could stay for a while and spend some time with Daddy, and he said he would ride back out to Felony Bay with the policeman and get his car and then drive me back to Reward when I was ready to go. I sat beside Daddy's bed, holding his hand, dozing off from my own exhaustion, and then, when I was awake again, trying to stuff down my impatience for him to wake up. Once of Daddy's doctors stopped by, and when I told him that I was sure Daddy was getting ready to wake up, he got a sad look on his face and told me that waking up from a coma isn't like waking up from a long nap. He said that *if* Daddy woke up—and there was no way to be sure that he would—the whole process might take days or even weeks.

I might have been discouraged if somebody had told me that earlier, but Bee and I had gotten away from Green Alice and we had beaten Uncle Charlie and Mr. Barrett at their dirty game. Right at that moment, I knew that there wasn't anything I couldn't do if I really put my mind to it. If I had to spend the rest of my summer visiting the hospital and talking to Daddy without him talking back to me, that would be okay. Because I knew for certain that things were getting better.

I didn't think about much else, like where I was going to live from then on, until later that afternoon when Custis came back to the hospital to take me out to Reward. Daddy was sleeping, just like always, but I told him I would be back tomorrow. On our way out, Custis told me that Grandma Em had arranged for someone to come with a horse trailer and pick up Timmy and Clem from Miss Walker's.

I felt terrible for a moment, because I realized that I had totally forgotten about the horses. "They were okay, weren't they?" I asked.

Custis laughed. "It apparently caused quite a stir when the head of school found a carriage horse blocking the way into her office."

That actually made me laugh. The Miss Walker's head of school was a nice lady, but she was sure a stickler for the rules. I loved picturing her trying to order Clem to get out of her way and him not paying her the slightest attention.

In the next instant all my humor disappeared, because it suddenly struck me that Custis was taking me back to an empty house. Uncle Charlie and Ruth were in jail, and I certainly didn't think they would be coming home soon. I thought about Rufus, who had been stuck in the house for hours. And then I also thought about the two of us living in Uncle Charlie's house all by ourselves, every night of the year, and it scared me.

I must have fallen so silent that Custis sensed it, because he turned to look at me. "Grandma Em called earlier to let me know that the police had given her your uncle's house keys, and she and Bee went up to the house to get Rufus."

I nodded. That made me feel better, but only a little bit. I was still feeling small and lonely, thinking about living in the house all alone.

"Grandma Em has already put a dog bed under the kitchen table for Rufus," Custis said.

I nodded.

"And she said they've already gone and moved your clothes up to the big house. You and Bee will be sharing your old room, if that's okay with you."

I looked at him, and suddenly I understood. It was more than I could ever have hoped for. I felt a huge smile burn through all my exhaustion and loneliness.

When we reached Reward, Custis drove me straight to the big house, where I found Bee throwing tennis balls for Rufus out in the yard. Bee was jumping up and down in excitement, because she had heard the news about Daddy and was so happy about me moving in with them. Rufus was jumping up and down, which is what he did most of the time, since Labrador retrievers are just born happy. The only time they are even happier than usual is when there is a bowl of food nearby.

We went in the back door and found Grandma Em in the kitchen, where the aromas told me that she was slow cooking baby back ribs that I knew she would finish on the grill later. A big pot of collards was simmering on the stove, and I saw that she had also made tomato pie and corn bread. There was so much food on the counter that it looked like she was having a party rather than cooking for just herself and Bee . . . and maybe me.

She turned around, saw me, and came over to give me a big hug. "We are so excited that you will be staying with us."

"Thank you," I said.

She straightened her arms and held me out at arm's length so she could look me in the eyes. "You know that you are going to stay right here in this house just as long as it takes. You are part of this family, and you will always be part of this family."

The next morning Bee and I woke up early, and after we went down to the barn and fed and watered the horses, we walked over to Felony Bay to watch the police remove the crate Uncle Charlie and Bubba Simmons had buried. They had brought a much bigger backhoe than the one Bubba Simmons had used, and they dug a much bigger hole, so they could get the crate out in one piece without doing any damage.

As the crate came out of the ground and the dirt dropped away, we could see a little bit of red fuzz on the bottom that must have come from the straps Uncle Charlie and Bubba used to lower it in place. That made me feel good, because Daddy always said a person could never, ever have too much proof when they were trying to win a case.

But for Bee and me, the huge surprise came when the backhoe operator got ready to fill in the hole. We were standing alone near the edge just watching, and both of us caught sight of it almost at the same time. Along one side of the hole it looked like the backhoe bucket had scraped some other object, and whatever it was had partly crumbled into the hole.

Bee and I could see that it wasn't dirt or rock, but more as if the backhoe had sheared off what looked like a couple rotten boards. They must have been so soft and crumbly that they had made no noise, and unless a person was standing right where we were, they were invisible. It wasn't the rotten boards but rather what had been behind them that made our eyes go wide.

Bee sucked in a deep breath. I knew she was about to shout something out to the backhoe operator, but I grabbed her arm.

She turned and looked at me like I was crazy, but I shook my head. A second later she totally got it and nodded.

We backed up, and both of us watched in silence as the backhoe quickly filled the hole. I marked the location exactly in my brain, and once the police left, I paced it off and wrote down the exact number of paces from the cabin and from a nearby pine tree.

Daddy would be exonerated. Uncle Charlie, Bubba Simmons, Ruth, and Mr. Barrett were going to jail, where they belonged. But there was one more job left to do. And I was finally going to do it, just the way Daddy would have wanted.

Thirty

It is early morning, mid-August. Seventh-grade classes at Miss Walker's begin tomorrow, and even though it's the hottest time of the year, for Bee and me summer is coming to an end. I am leaning against the fence watching Clem and Lem and Timmy and Bee's new pony, Buck, graze in the pasture. Mist is rising off the grass; the air is humid as a shower stall and already heavy with heat. The sky is the deep blue that comes just after sunrise as the color slowly comes into the world.

In a few minutes the sun will be over the live oaks, and the sky will be the same hard blue as a robin's egg.

This is the perfect time of day to wonder how it would be possible to live anywhere as good as Leadenwah Island.

When I look back, I can see Bee following slowly out the plantation drive. There is no longer even a trace of a limp when she moves, and the doctor has told her she can play on the middle school tennis team this fall. She is rubbing the sleep out of her eyes, but at least she is awake. Bee definitely likes to sleep more than I do, but I am trying to make her understand how great it is to be up before the rest of the world. This morning at least I have succeeded.

"Last day of summer vacation. What are we going to do?" she asks as she comes up to me.

I hold up my hand and pop up my fingers as I list off the ideas. "First we ride, then we swim, then we make eggs and bacon," I say, knowing Grandma Em still won't be in the kitchen when we finish our swim.

Bee nods. "What about eggs first?"

"Forget your stomach. We have to ride before it gets too hot."

Grandma Em says Bee is going through another growth spurt. I think it may be true, because I think she is even taller than she was a month ago. In any case, all Bee can think about other than sleeping is getting more food in her stomach. I'm just hoping that one of these days I go through a growth spurt, too.

Of course, that's not the only thing I'm hoping for. Daddy is still in his coma, but I haven't lost hope—well, at least I haven't lost hope too many times. The doctors have told me that if he does wake up—they don't understand that he *is* going to wake up—he's not going to just jump out of bed and be his old normal self. Doctors are smart people, but they're not right on everything.

In the barn we put some oats into two buckets, then walk into the pasture and catch our ponies. We saddle them fast and take a fairly short ride, not wanting to get them overheated in the August sun. On our way to the barn we take a detour out to the township road, where we grab the morning paper from the mailbox. Back in the barn we bathe both ponies, put their fly coats back on, and leave them in their stalls, where it will be cooler than out in the hot sun of the pasture.

"Last one in the water has to do the dishes," Bee says. She is closer to the barn door than me, and she takes off as fast as she can. I start about twenty yards behind, but even though Bee's legs are longer, I start to gain on her right away. My lungs are burning after the first few hundred yards, but neither one of us wants to clean up egg yuck from the dishes, so we keep running.

Rufus has been hunting in the soybeans across the drive from the barn, and when he hears us running, he gives a happy bark and comes racing after us.

All three of us are basically in a tie when we reach the dock. Bee and I tear off our jeans and shirts as fast as we can because we've got our suits on underneath, while Rufus barks and turns happy circles because he knows we're going swimming. We race down the dock, and I can feel a big splinter go into my right foot, but I don't care. I jump and manage to hit the water just a half second before Bee, but we both come up laughing. Rufus stands above us still on the dock, wagging his tail like crazy and finally jumping between us to make a huge splash.

Back in the kitchen of the big house a little while later, I crack the eggs into a bowl and stir them up and afterward toast some bread and then smear on butter. Bee cooks the bacon, which takes the longest time, and that gives me time to read the paper. Grandma Em says that Bee and I have become "news junkies" over the past month or two.

The reason is that Tom Blackford, the reporter at the *Post and Courier* I went to visit a couple months ago, has once again taken a big interest in everything that happened with Daddy and Uncle Charlie and Mr. Barrett and Miss Jenkins's gold. He has been out here a bunch of times to interview Bee and Grandma Em and me, as well as Mrs. Middleton and Skoogie. He has also gone to the jail and interviewed Uncle Charlie and Ruth, who have basically been blabbing pretty hard to try to get their jail sentences reduced when they come to trial, even though Mr. Barrett has refused to talk.

Over the past month and a half Tom Blackford has written a bunch of articles about what he now calls "The Mystery of Felony Bay." Obviously Bee and I knew a lot of those facts already, but there are some things both of us wondered about but had never been able to explain. First off, according to what Uncle Charlie and Ruth told Tom Blackford, Mr. Barrett was the one who put the whole plot together after he managed to get the combination to Miss Jenkins's safe. The whole question of how he'd gotten that combination really bothered me, because I didn't think Daddy would *ever* have told anyone, and I also knew he was way too careful to let it slip out in some careless mistake.

Mr. Barrett hasn't admitted a single thing so far, but Tom Blackford interviewed Martha, Daddy's legal secretary, and she said she was pretty sure she knew exactly how it happened. She told Tom Blackford that just a few weeks before the robbery and Daddy's "accident," Mr. Barrett had gone into Daddy's office one day with a very sad expression. Mr. Barrett had closed the office door, but Martha sat right outside the office, and she had overheard Mr. Barrett tell Daddy that he'd just found out he had cancer. He said he hoped it was treatable, but that just in case he got really sick, really fast, he and Daddy needed to share the passwords to their computers "just in case." That way, no matter what happened, either one of them would be able to take care of the other partner's clients.

When I read that in Tom Blackford's column, I knew right away that had to be *exactly* how Mr. Barrett got the combination. Daddy lost my mother to cancer, and when he heard that his law partner had the same terrible disease, he would have been too upset to even consider turning down Mr. Barrett's suggestion. Once he had the computer password, it would have been a piece of cake for Mr. Barrett to stay late one night and then go into Daddy's office after the last people had gone home for the night and snoop the combination off the computer. Daddy would have been so worried about Mr. Barrett's health, he would never have suspected that anything like that might happen.

Martha told Tom Blackford that she had wondered

about Mr. Barrett's cancer ever since she'd overheard that conversation, but that he'd never mentioned it again and pretty much acted as healthy as the day he'd been born. She said she'd tried to figure out if he was having cancer treatments like radiation or chemo that usually leave somebody feeling sick and very tired, but she was pretty sure he wasn't. She also said she'd kept her questions to herself because by that time Daddy was in a coma, and with Mr. Barrett running the firm, there wasn't really anybody else she could talk to.

Another thing I'd wondered about for a long time was just how Mr. Barrett came to be so friendly with Uncle Charlie and Bubba Simmons, because on the surface that just didn't seem to make any sense. Mr. Barrett was supposed to be smart and high class, which Uncle Charlie and Bubba Simmons certainly weren't. Tom Blackford found out that Mr. Barrett loved to gamble as much as those other two. which most people didn't know but which pretty much explains how those three knew each other. Tom Blackford also found out that Mr. Barrett was a lousy gambler—he owed big money to some other gamblers and was desperate to find a way to pay it back. Miss Jenkins's safe must have seemed like the perfect thing to him.

Another thing that Tom Blackford wrote about

was that Bubba's wife, Esther, who was Miss Jenkins's nurse, had no idea of the robbery plan. About the only thing she did wrong was to tell her jerk husband that the doctors were pretty sure Miss Jenkins wouldn't ever be able to move or speak again. Bubba mentioned that to Mr. Barrett and Uncle Charlie one night during a poker game, and their plan began to take shape. After all, even if she saw them steal her stuff, how was some paralyzed old lady ever going to testify against them?

According to Tom Blackford, Mr. Barrett cooked up the idea of "finding" the treasure at Felony Bay because he knew that Uncle Charlie had been a treasure hunter years earlier. Mr. Barrett also decided that Daddy was the logical choice to take the blame because he was supposedly the only one besides Miss Jenkins who knew the safe combination. If Mr. Barrett ever felt bad about framing and killing his partner, he never let on. Uncle Charlie had always resented Daddy for working hard and being smart, so he went along with it, too. Bubba just wanted the money and didn't care who got blamed. Tom Blackford also wrote that from the very beginning Ruth had seemed to feel worse about it than the others.

Custis says that Uncle Charlie and Ruth's blabbing strategy isn't going to keep them out of jail once the trial gets started. He says that it's an "open-and-shut case," and that Uncle Charlie and Ruth, along with Mr. Barrett and Bubba, are going to be "breaking rocks in the hot sun." Custis says Ruth probably won't go to jail for as long because when Bee and I testify at her trial, we'll both say that she seemed to feel bad about what was happening. However, Custis is pretty sure the other three will each get convicted of three counts of attempted murder—one count being Daddy and the others being Bee and me—which means they won't be out of jail for a good long time. That is just fine with me.

Custis says that another thing that's going to make it an "open-and-shut case" is that Miss Jenkins is going to be able to testify, because she's been getting better and better and can actually talk a decent bit now, and she's known the truth about who stole her gold the whole time. It turns out that Bubba had called Esther one day; he suckered her into thinking he had an emergency and that she had to leave Miss Jenkins's house to help him. While she was gone, Mr. Barrett and Uncle Charlie snuck in and cleaned out the safe.

They thought Miss Jenkins was asleep in her wheelchair, but she was actually wide-awake and saw them take everything. Because of her stroke all she'd ever been able to say was "Stole it." Everyone assumed she meant Daddy. They had no idea she meant Uncle Charlie and Mr. Barrett, but now that she's better, she'll get that across loud and clear in the trial.

Another thing Tom Blackford wrote that I hadn't known about: According to Uncle Charlie and Ruth, right after they finished cleaning out Miss Jenkins's safe, Mr. Barrett called my father and said he had a big problem and needed to have a private conversation. He asked if they could meet at Daddy's house rather than downtown in their offices. Thinking it was probably more bad news about Mr. Barrett's cancer, Daddy wouldn't have been suspicious. I was off at school, which meant the house was empty. They went into Daddy's library, and when Daddy's back was turned Mr. Barrett hit him over the head with a lead pipe. Then he tossed a bagful of Miss Jenkins's jewelry around the room, got the stepladder from the kitchen, put it up, and loosened some panels in the ceiling that Uncle Charlie had told him about. Custis says Mr. Barrett's going to claim that he never meant to kill Daddy, but I don't think the jury's going to buy it any more than they're going to believe he wasn't trying to smother Daddy the day the police caught him in the hospital.

What is both scary and amazing is that Mr. Barrett and Uncle Charlie and Bubba almost got away with everything. If Bee hadn't arrived when she had, and if we hadn't gone walking around the plantation and found the No Trespassing signs, I probably would have believed them when they announced finding the treasure. If that had happened, it's likely that no one would have ever found out the truth, and Felony Bay would have added one more mystery to its list.

"Bacon's done," Bee announces. "Stop daydreaming and make the eggs."

I force myself to shake off all my heavy thoughts, push back from the kitchen table, and stand. I pour most of the bacon grease out of the pan but keep just a little bit for making the eggs. "What about after? Swimming again?" I ask.

Bee nods. "And then let's go see what's happening on the cabin."

I smile. Exactly the choices I would have made.

We eat our eggs and bacon, and we're just finishing with the dishes when Grandma Em comes into the kitchen. "Good morning, girls," she says. Grandma Em says that after almost forty years of teaching and being a principal, the one luxury she insists on is the ability to sleep until eight o'clock in the morning. Bee and I are in big trouble whenever we make too much noise and wake her up early.

Now she looks over at the three rashers of bacon that have been left on a plate beside the stove. "Thank you, girls," she says with a smile. She sees that we are on our way out the door. "What do you two have up your sleeves on this last day of summer vacation?"

We tell her we're going to jump in the river and then head over to Felony Bay to check on the new house.

"Come get me after your swim, and I'll walk over there with you," she says.

Forty-five minutes later the three of us walk out the plantation drive and then go left on the dirt township road to where the old dirt track winds down to Felony Bay. The dirt track used to be pretty hard to find, but now it's starting to look like a regular road with well-worn tire tracks since the construction crews have started rebuilding the cabin.

As we start to see the sunlight glinting off the water of the bay, more memories come flooding back. I remember how Bee and I told Custis and Grandma Em what we had seen the day the police dug Uncle Charlie's crate out of the sand. Then, when Bee's dad came home from India and spent over a month here, we sat down with him and explained how Mrs. Middleton's family had lived in that Felony Bay cabin since the 1870s without ever paying rent, but how

Uncle Charlie had kicked her off by suddenly start-ing to charge rent she couldn't possibly afford. We also told him that Daddy found out what Uncle Charlie had done and that he had been just about to formally give the land back to Mrs. Middleton when Mr. Barrett hit him over the head and put him in a coma.

Bee's dad was all ears, because he already knew a whole lot about heirs' property and how a lot of African American people have gotten cheated out of valuable land over the years because they didn't have a legal title and didn't know that they could get one. But what he didn't know about were the stories about Felony Bay and the *Lovely Clarisse* and the rumors of buried Confederate gold. And he also didn't know what Bee and I had seen in the hole the day the police were dig-ging up the evidence, so we told him all of that, and then all of us kept our mouths shut tight.

Once Bee's dad got involved, it didn't take long for a judge to decide the Felony Bay land should never have been sold to Mr. Barrett and the others and that it still belonged to Daddy. After that, Bee's dad got together with Custis, who now has power of attorney for Daddy's stuff, and Custis totally backed Bee and me up, saying that it was absolutely clear Daddy intended to give the Felony Bay property over to Mrs. Middleton.

Bee's father said that since Daddy was still in a coma, it wouldn't be right to give his property away, even though he agreed it was the right thing to do. Instead, Bee's dad told Custis he wanted to buy the property from Daddy, which he did, and then he turned around and gave it to Mrs. Middleton along with all the legal papers so there would never be any confusion ever again about who owned it.

The whole thing cost Bee's dad a lot of money, but he said it gave him great pleasure to see another descendant of what he called the Greater Force Family get their due. Bee's dad was also the one who paid to have the cabin fixed, and now in few months Mrs. Middleton and Skoogie will move back into an old, but brand-new, house.

I also know that there were other reasons that Bee's dad bought Felony Bay. One night I overheard him talking to Grandma Em in the kitchen when they thought Bee and I were asleep, and I learned that the real reason he insisted on buying property that Daddy was actually going to give away was to make sure there would be money for me to go to college someday, just in case Daddy never wakes up. I almost walked into the kitchen and told him it wasn't necessary because Daddy *is* going to wake up; I know it even if nobody else does.

But then I thought about how absolutely amazing it was that a person whose ancestors had once been slaves owned by my family was doing something incredibly generous to make sure I was going to be okay. Daddy says there are some moments in life that are just too perfect to change, and I decided that was one of them. For once I managed to keep my big mouth shut and creep back up to bed.

As Bee and Grandma Em and I come around the last curve on our way down to Felony Bay, we hear a saw blade buzzing through wood and a hammer pounding nails. When the cabin finally comes into sight, the shingles on the new roof sparkle in the sun and the new windows gleam.

"I still remember the look on Mrs. Middleton's face," says Bee.

"Me too," I said, smiling as I think back to the day after the papers were signed and the property legally belonged to Mrs. Middleton.

Bee's dad hired a backhoe, and Bee and I showed him where to dig. All of us were there, along with Grandma Em, who had picked up Mrs. Middelton and Skoogie and brought them down. The backhoe operator dug down about six feet, and then Bee and I told him to stop. We got into the hole and used shovels, but we only had to dig down another foot or so before we hit the same rotten crate the police backhoe had grazed. We dug all around it and carefully brushed off the layer of sand that remained on top. The black-stenciled letters were very faint, but we could still make them out. They said PROPERTY OF THE CONFEDERATE STATES OF AMERICA.

When we tried to pry up the boards, they were so punky with age and rot that they pretty much crumbled. We tore them off, looked inside, and saw the neat stack of gold and silver bars, each one stamped with the letters CSA. It wasn't as large as the crate Uncle Charlie had buried, and there wasn't as much gold, but it was more than enough to change Mrs. Middleton's and Skoogie's lives hugely for the better.

We wave to the carpenters who are working on the cabin, then head along the path that runs along the river for several hundred yards and circles back to the big house. The day is hot and quiet, and the breeze at this time of year has pretty much died. It is cooler in the shade but just as humid, and this is also where the mosquitoes hang out. After just a few seconds they are buzzing around our heads and trying to land and get a good bite. Grandma Em picks up the pace and leads us along the path so quickly that Bee and I nearly have to trot to keep up.

In addition to everything else that happened this summer, Bee and I have become business partners. In the offices of the law firm that is now called Force & Pettigrew there is another much smaller sign behind the receptionist's desk. It says FORCE & FORCE INVESTIGATIONS, just in case anybody wants to hire two twelve-year-old detectives. It's kind of a joke, but truth be told, Bee and I would love it if somebody came along and hired us.

So far no one has, but for right now that's fine with me. After all the craziness we went through with Felony Bay, I've been very happy to while away the rest of the summer riding ponies with Bee, swimming in the Leadenwah River, and reading books in the shade of the big live oaks.

Of course the other thing I've done this summer is spend a lot of time thinking. There have been lots of times like right now when I find my mind drifting back to everything that happened in the past year and looking at it differently. Bee and I solved one part of the mystery of Felony Bay, but that was the easy part. For me the other part of the mystery doesn't involve treasure but the mystery of why people do the things they do.

For example, what made Uncle Charlie and Mr. Barrett and Bubba Simmons so greedy that they would stoop to robbery and murder? What made Ruth go along with it?

At the same time, what made Mrs. Middleton struggle out to the bus stop on her walker to help me the day Jimmy Simmons was choking me? And what made Skoogie risk his life with Green Alice? What made Miss Jenkins force herself to finally speak the words she'd wanted to speak for months?

I know part of the answer to all those questions involves willpower, character, and courage. But how does one person end up with so much strong willpower and character and courage when another person has only laziness and greed? I've been wondering about all these things a lot, and so far the answer seems to be that it isn't whether people have money or education, or whether they're born into a "good" family. Instead, for each of us our willpower, character, and courage end up being the result of the little decisions we make all by ourselves every single day. Just like grains of sand add up to make a beach, our choices add up to making us who we are.

I've also decided that who a person is deep down can be a moving target, and that means I have to keep an open mind about people. I've tried to do that, and over the past couple months I have even become friends with

Jimmy Simmons. His mother got him into that special school program that helps kids with dyslexia, and getting in seems to have made him realize that he isn't just a stupid kid. Now instead of being a miserable jerk and a bully, Jimmy's actually become sort of a nice kid, at least for a boy. So maybe it's more than just willpower and character and courage. Maybe it's also having somebody give you a break once in a while.

Also, as part of this willpower, character, and courage stuff, I constantly think about the fact that two hundred years ago my own family owned slaves, among them Bee's ancestors. I badly want to believe that even though my ancestors made some terrible choices by owning other human beings, I'm not doomed to follow in their footsteps and make the same kinds of bad choices. Jimmy Simmons is part of the reason I can believe that's true. He is already trying hard to become a much better person than his father ever thought of being.

I've come to believe there isn't any reason that Jimmy won't succeed. And all I have to do is look at Bee and her friendship with me to see that members of one generation don't have to make the same mistakes as people in an earlier generation, and even more, they can forgive the bad things done by a previous generation.

I figure I might never understand all the mysteries we discovered at Felony Bay, but I know one thing. It comes down to choices, and we have to make them every single day. Some people chose badly, others chose well. I need to keep making good choices, and I need to get smarter so I'll be able tell the difference between good ones and bad ones. It's clear that a lot of people, even adults, get pretty confused about which choices to make.

"Will you *stop* thinking already," Bee says with a laugh.

I turn to look at her and shake my head as if I'm clearing out all those heavy thoughts, but of course I'm not. They seem to stay with me no matter what else I'm doing. I look out past Bee at the river, where the sunlight turns the brown water the color of caramel. She is absolutely right. It's the last day of summer, and it's time to have fun.

"Race you to the dock," I say, knowing it's time for our third swim of the day. "The loser has to clean out the stalls tonight."

I start to sprint, but Bee already saw the challenge coming. She is racing along the path ahead of me, running fast for home.

Acknowledgments

A big part of my desire to write this book comes from having a fourteen-year-old daughter, who was twelve when I started writing *The Girl from Felony Bay*. Her pony at that time was also named Timmy. Another part of my desire stems from my love of the Lowcountry sea islands. They are places of haunting beauty, and while some have become resort developments, others remain much as they have been for the past several centuries, quiet and rural with tight-knit communities.

While Reward Plantation and Felony Bay are imaginary, I would like to express my appreciation to the Sinkler family, whose friendship has made it possible for me to spend time over the years at Rosebank Plantation, unquestionably the inspiration for Reward Plantation.

Furthermore, I would like to thank Lieutenant Steve Sierko of the Charleston Police Department for his patience and willingness to answer my numerous stupid questions about police procedure and all kinds of other things relating to police work.

I would be incredibly remiss if I did not thank Stephen Barbara, my packhorse agent, who carried me to HarperCollins Walden Pond Press and negotiated the sale with this wonderful book group. I refer to Stephen as a packhorse not because he is plodding in any sense of the word, but because of his refusal to be deterred by failure and his steady, unstinting hard work on this book and others. Am I getting heavy yet, Stephen?

Also, thanks to Jordan Brown, my tireless editor who refused to leave any question unanswered, any inconsistency uncorrected, and any plot opportunity unexplored. The book would never have become what it is without his insight and insistence on perfection. Thank you, Jordan!